D0769690

A Wedding

DATE

IN HOT SPRINGS, ARKANSAS

A Wedding
DATE
IN HOT SPRINGS, ARKANSAS

ANNALISA DAUGHETY

BARBOUR
PUBLISHING

© 2012 by Annalisa Daughety

Print ISBN 978-1-61626-740-7

eBook Editions:
Adobe Digital Edition (.epub) 978-1-62029-632-5
Kindle and MobiPocket Edition (.prc) 978-1-62029-631-8

All rights reserved. No part of this publication may be reproduced or transmitted for commercial purposes, except for brief quotations in printed reviews, without written permission of the publisher.

All scripture quotations, unless otherwise indicated, are taken from the HOLY BIBLE, NEW INTERNATIONAL VERSION®. NIV®. Copyright © 1973, 1978, 1984, 2011 by Biblica, Inc.™ Used by permission. All rights reserved worldwide.

Scripture quotations marked NLT are taken from the *Holy Bible*. New Living Translation copyright© 1996, 2004, 2007 by Tyndale House Foundation. Used by permission of Tyndale House Publishers, Inc. Carol Stream, Illinois 60188. All rights reserved.

This book is a work of fiction. Names, characters, places, and incidents are either products of the author's imagination or used fictitiously. Any similarity to actual people, organizations, and/or events is purely coincidental.

Cover design: Faceout Studio, www.faceoutstudio.com

Published by Barbour Publishing, Inc., P.O. Box 719, Uhrichsville, Ohio 44683, www.barbourbooks.com

Our mission is to publish and distribute inspirational products offering exceptional value and biblical encouragement to the masses.

 Member of the
Evangelical Christian
Publishers Association

Printed in the United States of America.

Dedication

To Kelly Shifflett. God didn't give me a sister,
but He gave me you as a friend—and for that I am grateful.
Thank you for cheering me on and for offering insight as
I wrote this book. We've shared so many adventures together
and I have no doubt there are more to come.

Acknowledgments

Writing a novel can be a daunting task. Sometimes I learn
many more life lessons than my characters do. This book
in particular was hard for me on many levels and I am thankful
for those who helped make it possible. Thanks to:

My heavenly Father. You continue to bless me even though I
fall short time and again. Thanks for giving me the opportunity
to write, and I pray my stories always glorify You.

Vicky Daughety. If not for you, I'm not sure this one
would've gotten finished! Thanks, Mom, for "curbside
meal service" and for being my first reader.

Jan Reynolds. For brainstorming and critiquing—and for always
being honest about what is working and what isn't. It takes a
village to write a book, and I'm glad you're part of mine!

Kristy Coleman. You gave me input on this book—
and a ton of encouragement and prayers as I was trying
to finish it. I appreciate that more than you know!

Vickie Fry. For the prayers, encouragement, and input.
I love knowing that no matter how crazy my questions
are, you will answer willingly and honestly.

Dax Torrey. You believe in me even when I don't believe in myself,
and that means the world. Thank you for lending your grammatical
expertise and the occasional character trait. Anyway. . .

Megan Reynolds. For checking on me even when I'm in scary
deadline mode, and for always making me laugh no matter how
stressed I am. Thanks, also, for "taking one for the team"
and going with me to Hot Springs for a spa day.

Always be joyful. Never stop praying.
Be thankful in all circumstances, for this is
God's will for you who belong to Christ Jesus.
1 THESSALONIANS 5:16–18 NLT

Chapter 1

To: Staff@MatthewsLaw.com
From: Sampson.Matthews@MatthewsLaw.com
Date: August 17, 4:45 p.m.
Subject: Mandatory Meeting

There will be a mandatory staff meeting on Monday at noon in the boardroom. I look forward to seeing everyone there.

Violet Matthews was usually the last to arrive to the office. But not today. Today was a special day. A life-changing day. She'd started counting down to noon as soon as her feet hit the floor that morning. She'd never looked forward to a Monday before.

Her iPhone rang as she pulled into an empty spot in the parking lot of her Little Rock office. "This is Violet," she said, turning off the engine.

"Don't ever get married. Whatever you do, no matter how cute he is or how tired you are of checking that 'single' box, don't do it.

Your life will never be the same," Reagan McClure declared.

"Chad out of town again?" Violet grinned. Her best friend offered the same advice at least once a month, usually whenever her husband of ten years was traveling on business.

Reagan sighed. "Not only is he out of town. He's in Vegas. *Vegas.* For a week. He's at some conference, and as luck would have it, the kids are getting over the stomach flu. I'm pretty sure Dante may have had my life in mind in some of his writings."

"That bad, huh?" Violet couldn't help but chuckle. "I don't recall the staying-home-with-four-sick-kids-while-husband-is-away part of the *Inferno*, but it's been a few years since I've read it." It did sound pretty awful, but she'd never say that to Reagan.

"Don't make fun. I'm seriously losing it here. I don't remember the last time I had on something that was clean, and earlier this morning I scared myself when I looked in the mirror. No wonder Chad wants to be in Vegas."

Violet shook her head. "Chad loves you and the kids. I feel certain that he didn't arrange this trip to purposefully get out of helping you." She'd known Chad McClure since their freshman year of college. He'd doted on Reagan since he'd first laid eyes on her all those years ago, and from what Violet could tell, not much had changed.

Reagan groaned. "Don't you know you're supposed to be on my side even when I'm being unreasonable? Don't take up for him."

"I *am* on your side. I just hate to hear you so upset. Isn't there someone you can call to come over and help out?"

"My parents are too far away to help, and you know how Chad's mom is. Anytime I ask her to do anything, she uses it as an opportunity to point out all my failings as a mother and a wife."

Chad's mom was a piece of work, that was for sure. Violet had heard some of her "helpful advice" over the years, and it was no wonder Reagan didn't want to call her. "I'll do better, I promise. Do you want me to come over and watch the kids tonight so you can take a hot bath or go for a run or something?"

Reagan sniffed. "You're so nice. But no. The last thing you need is to catch whatever awful virus they have. Thanks though."

"The offer stands if you change your mind." Violet climbed out of her SUV and slung her bag over her shoulder. "I'd better run. Today's a big meeting, and I have a ton to do beforehand."

"I totally forgot this was the big day. Call me later and give me the details, okay? Although I'll never understand why you'd even want a promotion, seeing as how you don't like your job at all."

It was the biggest source of contention between them. Reagan had always thought she was crazy for not following her dreams, but Violet had opted for a safer route. "Don't be silly. I'm thrilled. Besides, I'm kind of far along the path to change course now, don't you think?" She said good-bye and hurried toward the multi-story building.

"Nice dress," Kelsey Klein said, giving Violet the once over as she entered the lobby. "But you look more like a forties pinup girl than a lawyer." She glanced around the tastefully decorated lobby with its neutral colors and back at Violet's emerald-green dress. "If it weren't for you, I swear I'd drown in a sea of beige." Kelsey had begun working as the office manager and receptionist after she'd graduated from the University of Central Arkansas in May. Only Violet knew she was biding her time and getting some experience until she could find a marketing position somewhere. "Where did you find that dress anyway? I could never pull off that look, but you sure do."

Violet smoothed the full skirt of her latest vintage find. "A little shop in New Orleans. I was down there last month for a conference and managed to slip out for the afternoon and go to a vintage store Reagan told me about." She grinned. "You're right about one thing, though. It's forties style. My favorite." She gave a little twirl, and the skirt flowed around her. "Can't you just imagine all the wonderful places this dress has been?"

Kelsey laughed. "You were definitely meant for a different time." She raised her perfectly arched eyebrows that were just a shade darker than her blond hair. "Any idea what the big meeting is about today? When your dad asked me to schedule it in the boardroom, I tried to get him to tell me what was going on." She shrugged. "He was totally closemouthed though."

Sampson Matthews was definitely a man of few words, at least until you put him in a courtroom. "I'm not sure." Violet almost shared her suspicion about the meeting with Kelsey, but thought better of it. The girl was nice and all, but she could give the town crier a run for his money. "Any calls for me?"

Kelsey shook her head. "Not so far. Want me to put them to voice mail?"

"Please." She needed a few uninterrupted hours to go over the stack of paperwork on her desk.

"Oh, wait. There was one call for you. Your mom. Since you weren't here, I sent her to your dad."

"What did she want?"

"She mentioned something about your grandmother, but I'm not sure what she was talking about."

Violet froze. Her only living set of grandparents lived in Hot Springs, a little more than an hour away from Little Rock. Surely everything was okay or else they would've called Violet on her cell. Still, though. They were in their eighties and not as spry as they used to be. "Okay, thanks. I'll call her soon." She stepped into her office and closed the door.

She sank into the leather chair behind her desk and picked up the framed picture she kept on her desk. It had been taken the day she'd graduated from the University of Arkansas School of Law. Grandpa Matthews had still been alive then, and he beamed in the picture, thrilled that his oldest granddaughter had followed in his footsteps. She'd promised him on that day that she'd someday move back to Little Rock and work in the firm he had founded.

She carefully put the photo back on the desk. It was hard to believe it had been seven years since graduation. After two years of living and working in DC, she'd followed up on her promise to her grandfather and joined the family firm. The past five years she'd worked hard, rarely even taking a sick day—much less a vacation.

And all her hard work would soon pay off.

Violet grinned with anticipation. Noon couldn't come soon enough.

Jackson Stratford had lost track of what the blond across the table was talking about. He forced himself to smile and nod at what seemed to be appropriate intervals, but mostly he just couldn't believe he'd let his life get to this point.

Maybe his rule of never dating a girl over the age of twenty-three needed to be reevaluated.

"Are you even listening to me?" Whitney asked.

He nodded. "Of course. You were saying something about your last trip to the lake." He took a stab, pretty sure he'd heard the words *lake* and *boat* at some point during the past twenty minutes.

She flashed a smile and a dimple. "Yes." She tossed her hair. "So anyway. Megan had brought her dog with us, and it was not okay with being on a boat." She rolled her eyes. "And I was like, are you kidding me? Your stupid dog is going to get all boat sick, and I just had it cleaned." Whitney sighed. "Megan said it would be fine, but then the dog got sick. Needless to say, we're not speaking now."

"You and Megan or you and the dog?" Jackson asked, grinning.

Whitney giggled. "Megan, silly. Dogs don't speak."

Jackson took a sip of his Dr Pepper as Whitney rambled on. He deserved this. At least that's what his friend Jeff would say. Jackson's dating habits might be the only thing the two of them disagreed on. That and their running Braves versus Cardinals argument.

"Do you?" Whitney asked.

Jackson furrowed his brow. "Do I what?" This time he had no clue what she might be talking about.

"Want to drive to Dallas next weekend? There's a really cool music festival going on."

Outdoor music festivals used to be one of Jackson's favorite things. But last year at Little Rock's Riverfest, his date had thrown up on his shoes and then a drunk guy in the parking lot had dinged his new Range Rover, and his opinion of music festivals had begun to change. In fact, Jackson felt certain he wasn't up for that kind of fun any longer. "I believe I'll pass."

Whitney frowned. "Are you sure? The weather is supposed to be great, and there are some awesome bands playing." She grinned. "Maybe even some that you've heard of. You know, like, from the eighties."

"Very funny." Both times they'd gone out, Whitney had been appalled at the preset stations on his satellite radio. "For your information, music today is not nearly as good as it was in the seventies or eighties."

"You sound just like my uncle. He's always trying to get me to listen to some big-haired eighties band. The other day he asked me if I'd heard of Cinderella." She giggled. "I totally thought he meant the Disney princess."

Jackson groaned. He'd been a Cinderella fan back in the day. "Just out of curiosity, how old is your uncle?"

"Way old. Like in his forties." She widened her blue eyes.

And that would about do it for this friendship. Jackson's next cake would have thirty-six candles on it.

"Do you have any aunts?" he asked with a grin.

Chapter 2

Violet Matthews: SORRY YOU'RE HAVING A BAD DAY. WHEN CHAD GETS BACK, LET'S PLAN A GNO. (Text message sent August 20, 11:48 a.m.)

Reagan couldn't remember her last girls' night out. Probably before the twins were born, which meant at least ten months ago. A night out would be fun, but what she'd rather have was a nap. And a shower that lasted more than five minutes.

She responded to Violet's text and tossed her phone onto the coffee table that had two little tooth-shaped chunks out of the corner, compliments of her oldest child, Izzy. Now that she was five, she no longer chewed on the furniture, but she found other ways to wreak havoc. Like last week when she finger painted a family portrait on the bathroom wall.

"Mommy, my tummy is grumpy." Ava Grace peeked her blond head around the corner. "And Scarlett is crying." She clutched her ever-present pink bunny. "But not Simon, he's sleeping." At three, Ava Grace was her mommy's eyes and ears. She watched her younger siblings like a hawk, always happy to report what they were up to. Reagan suspected that someday they'd call her a tattletale, but for now she was happy to have her daughter's reports.

Reagan frowned at the baby monitor sitting on the table. She hadn't heard any cries. Had it stopped working? "Okay, sweet girl." She picked up Ava Grace. No fever, so that was a good sign. "Do you want to eat a bite? Maybe some toast or crackers?" Izzy had been well enough to go back to school today, but the other three were still feeling puny.

Ava Grace nodded, her blond curls bouncing. "Goldfish."

Reagan put Ava Grace in her booster chair and poured some Goldfish on a paper plate. "Here you go, sweetie." She put the plate on the table in front of her daughter. "Do you want a drink?"

"Yes."

Reagan grabbed the Dora the Explorer sippy cup from the fridge and put it on the table. "Here's your drink. I'm going to run up and check on the twins."

Ava Grace nodded, her mouth already full of Goldfish.

Reagan picked up the baby monitor and held it to her ear. Silence. Great. Something was wrong with the monitor. Just one more thing to add to the list.

She hurried up the stairs to the nursery. She'd complained when they first moved into the house that the master bedroom was on the bottom floor and all the rest of the bedrooms were upstairs. But Chad had been sure it wouldn't matter much, and the house had been the right price.

Four kids later and Reagan was certain whoever had come up with the layout was somewhere laughing about the poor mothers having to go up and down stairs a million times a day to their kids' rooms.

She peeked into the nursery. Even though she'd hoped to redo it after moving Ava Grace into her own room, it was still the same pink it had been since Izzy was a baby.

Poor Simon. The lone boy in the family deserved a room filled with baseballs and boats. But she'd been too busy with Izzy and Ava Grace, and then she'd spent the last month of her pregnancy on bed rest for high blood pressure.

She'd hoped Chad would take some time off work to take care of it or at least hire someone to handle it. But no.

Violet had been the one to get Simon's crib bedding, and she'd chosen an adorable blue-and-green frog-themed set. It might clash terribly in the bubble-gum room, but Reagan loved it.

She reached down and smoothed her son's wispy hair. He didn't stir. If only she could sleep like that.

She crossed to Scarlett's crib and picked her up before she started crying again. Scarlett was a beautiful baby, with rosy cheeks and bright blue eyes. "Let's go downstairs and let your brother sleep." Reagan snuggled the baby to her chest and inhaled the sweet smell of her daughter. These would be her last babies, and she knew how fast they grew. They'd be little people before she knew it. It seemed like only yesterday they'd brought Izzy home from the hospital, and now she was in kindergarten.

Where had the time gone?

She nestled Scarlett against her and carefully maneuvered the stairs. It was her constant fear—that she'd trip while holding one of the kids.

"Are you finished with your Goldfish?" she asked Ava Grace once she reached the kitchen.

"Uh-huh." Ava Grace grinned. "All done."

"Good girl. Do you want to watch Dora for a few minutes?" She'd hoped to never be the kind of mom who encouraged TV, but some days it was a lifesaver.

She settled Ava Grace in the living room. "Just one show, okay?"

"Okay."

The phone buzzed against the coffee table. "Hello."

"Hey, babe." Chad's voice sounded muffled. "Just wanted to see how everyone was doing today."

"Izzy was well enough to go to school. She took the bus this morning, and Katie's mom is going to bring her home this afternoon so I don't have to get the other three out." It would be an absolute nightmare to load three sick children in the van.

"That's nice."

The distinct sound of water in the background caught Reagan's attention. "Where are you?"

"I'm at the hotel."

"*Where* at the hotel?"

Silence on the other end confirmed her suspicions. "Chad Michael McClure. Are you at the pool? Tell me that you are not at the pool in Vegas while I am at home with your sick children. And a busted baby monitor." May as well let him know that he'd be going out to buy a new one as soon as he got home.

"Don't middle name me like I'm one of the kids. My flight was delayed for a few hours, and I've already checked out of the room. What else am I supposed to do?"

She couldn't even form words.

"Babe. Come on. Don't be like this. I've worked long hours for the past month. If I get the chance to relax at the pool for a few hours before my flight, you should be happy for me."

"Yeah." She fought to keep her voice pleasant in front of the kids. "I've barely had a shower in four days. I haven't been out of the house except for Wednesday when I had to take the kids to the doctor. By myself. Do you have any idea how difficult it is to take four sick children to the doctor?"

"I'll make it up to you. I promise."

She'd heard that before.

The other line beeped, and she held it out to check the caller ID. "I've got to go. Izzy's school is on the other line." She hit the button. "Hello?"

"Mrs. McClure? I hate to call you so close to the end of the day, but we're going to need you to come pick up Izzy. I guess she isn't over that virus after all."

Reagan took a deep breath. "I'll be there as soon as I can."

She glanced down at her old T-shirt and maternity yoga pants. They'd never actually seen a yoga class, but they sure were comfortable. It would have to do. No way did she have time to change clothes *and* load three kids into the van.

All while her husband sat at a pool in Vegas and basked in the sunshine.

Her life certainly hadn't turned out the way she'd planned.

Violet paused outside of the boardroom and smoothed the skirt of her dress. She pasted on a smile and opened the heavy doors.

"Good of you to make it, Violet." Mom tapped her watch. "I was beginning to think you wouldn't be here."

Violet looked up in surprise. She'd had no idea her mother would be at the meeting. The totally unprecedented nature of her attendance confirmed her suspicions of the meeting's topic. "I'm not even late. It's not noon yet." She gave her mother a quick hug.

Julia Matthews waved a manicured hand around the board-room. "But almost everyone else is here. It doesn't look good, dear, for the boss's daughter to be so lax about things."

I will not roll my eyes. I will remain calm. Violet had been coaching herself around her mother for so many years, it was second nature. "Sorry, Mom."

"Hey, y'all," Amber Matthews said, walking into the room. "Sorry I'm late, Mom." Violet's younger sister gave their mother a quick peck on the cheek.

"Oh, that's okay, honey. We know how busy you are with school."

Typical. Mom reamed her out for not being prompt enough but let Amber slide. Her sister was in her final year of graduate school and was dangerously close to becoming what Violet thought of as a professional student. She wouldn't be at all surprised if Amber announced she was going for a doctorate next. Their parents might be proud, but Violet suspected it was all a ploy to avoid getting a real job. "Glad to see you, Amber."

Amber smiled prettily. "You, too." Her eyes lit up. "Oh, there's Landry. He looks so handsome. I picked that suit out myself."

Violet followed her sister's gaze to Landry Baxter, Amber's boyfriend of three years. Violet and Landry had been friends in law school, and she'd been pleased when he'd joined the firm. She'd introduced him to Amber at the company Christmas party, and the rest was history.

She nodded at her sister and hurried to take an empty seat.

"Any idea what this is about?" Ryan Harpeth asked from across the table, a worried look on his face. He'd just started with the firm and had done his undergraduate work at Harding University, just like Violet.

She shook her head. "I don't think it's anything to worry about." She grinned. "So you can relax."

"I haven't been here long enough to know if these meetings are common or not," he explained. "But Kelsey was making a big deal about it this morning when I came in, asking if I'd heard anything."

Violet laughed. "She just likes to stay on top of things." More likely she'd wanted an excuse to talk to Ryan.

"Thanks for coming, everyone." Sampson Matthews always liked to make a grand entrance. Today was no different. He strode into the room and took his place at the head of the table. "I won't keep you long, but there is a bit of business to discuss."

Violet had always admired her father's ability to command attention. It was part of what made him such a great lawyer. He thrived on cases that went to trial. Violet had always preferred to settle out of court. She'd never been comfortable in her role, never felt as in command as her father always appeared. But she'd worked hard nonetheless and had a lot of success during her years with the firm.

"Everyone here knows the history of this firm. My daddy founded it right out of law school, and it was an honor to come and work for him once I completed my own law degree." He shot a smile in Violet's direction. "And I'm thrilled that a third generation of the Matthews family is part of the firm today."

Violet sat up straight. This was it.

"Legacy and history are important to us here at Matthews Law. So when it came time to add another partner, I didn't take the decision lightly."

Violet grinned.

"That is why it is with great honor that I announce Landry Baxter as the newest partner in the firm."

Applause rang out all over the room. Violet forced her hands to clap, but it was like banging two concrete blocks together. She couldn't believe her dad had chosen Landry over her.

"Thanks, everyone." Landry stood up, a huge grin on his face. "Of course, I'm thrilled to begin my new role here and am honored that Mr. Matthews is placing such confidence in me."

Another round of applause. Violet caught sight of Amber's gleeful face. She should've known her sister wouldn't be here for her. How could she have been so off the mark?

Once her father adjourned the meeting, Violet peeled herself off the chair and started toward the door. Maybe she could get out of here without having to speak to anyone, have Kelsey take messages for the rest of the day, and sneak out early.

"Violet," Mom called, waving her over. "Be at the house at six sharp tonight, okay? We're having a little celebration."

A celebration for Landry. Of course. "Oh, I don't know."

"Do you want Landry to think you aren't happy for him?" Mom raised an eyebrow. "You know how much he means to your sister."

Violet sighed. "Fine. I'll see you at six." She hurried out the door and to her office, wondering why the day had blown up in her face.

Chapter 3

Violet Matthews: You are not going to believe what just happened. Dad made Landry partner instead of me. I'm sure Mom and Amber put him up to it. I need chocolate. (Text message sent August 20, 2:46 p.m.)

Reagan McClure: No way. That stinks. If it makes you feel any better, my husband is sunning himself at a Vegas pool and Izzy is throwing up again. Trade lives? (Text message sent August 20, 3:52 p.m.)

Reagan put the final load of laundry in the washing machine and started the cycle. Few things satisfied her more than emptying the hamper. And with four small children, it was a rare occurrence.

"Anybody home?" Chad poked his head into the laundry room.

She nodded. "I'm always home. Unless I'm picking someone up, dropping someone off, or at the grocery store." If he hadn't had a sunburned nose, she probably could've kept her cool.

"Still mad?" He tossed a pile of clothes into the hamper she'd just emptied.

Reagan stared at her husband. He'd known her for fifteen years, since their freshman year of college. He should know her better. Shouldn't he? "I had to load the kids up and go pick up Izzy after I talked to you. She still has a touch of the stomach flu. The baby monitor isn't working. Ava Grace pulled Simon across the nursery by his leg, so someday when he doesn't walk right, it will be because I had to go to the bathroom and leave them alone for a second." She ticked off the highlights of her day. "And you hung out at a pool. Tell me what sounds fair about that?"

At least he had the decency to look sheepish. "Sorry you've had a tough time. But I'm here now." Chad grinned. "Didn't you miss me a little?" He raised his eyebrows up and down.

She shrugged. No reason to further emphasize how poorly she'd handled her stint as a single parent. "Did you miss *me*?"

"Of course. I wish you'd gone with me."

Reagan crossed her arms and leaned against the washing machine. "Easy for you to say, considering we both know that wasn't possible." She wouldn't be going anywhere anytime soon, or at least as long as the twins were still nursing.

"I can't win." Chad raked a hand through his blond hair. "There's no pleasing you these days." He jerked his chin toward the doorway. "Are the kids asleep?"

"Naps for all." *Except me.* There were precious few minutes to tackle the never-ending list of chores that needed to be done. Whoever had come up with the adage of sleeping when the baby slept must not have had other children to look after. Or a husband whose idea of helping out meant throwing his clothes in the hamper instead of on the floor.

Chad tugged on his tie. "I think a nap sounds like a great idea. Wake me before dinner, okay?"

She watched him go. There'd been a time not that long ago when he'd have suggested she join him, especially if the kids were napping. But not anymore.

Reagan glanced down at her stained shirt that couldn't hide the post-pregnancy belly that hadn't seemed to shrink as much as it did with the last one. Twins were harder on the body than she'd expected. Couple that with no makeup and hair that hadn't been properly washed and dried in what seemed like forever and it was no wonder Chad was content to nap alone.

She blinked back the hot tears that threatened to spill down her cheeks.

How had things gotten to this point? And more importantly, was there any way to keep them from getting worse?

Jackson poured himself a second cup of coffee and sat back down at his desk to look at the specs for a building he thought might be perfect for one of his projects. He'd been wooing a large appliance company for the better part of six months, trying to get them to open their new warehouse just outside of Little Rock. It would be a huge coup for the Arkansas Economic Development Commission to land the company, but Jackson was concerned. During their last meeting, he'd sensed some hesitation from the project manager. But maybe finding this building would satisfy the man. It more than fit their specifications.

His assistant's voice crackled over the phone's intercom. "Mr.

Stratford, there's someone here to see you."

He picked up the receiver. "I didn't know I had anyone scheduled."

"He says his name is Ricky Bobby, but that can't be right," Sheila whispered. "I think that's the name of a character from a Will Ferrell movie."

Jackson burst out laughing. "Send him in. I'll explain later." He and Jeff had used the same running joke for years. Always a different movie character name whenever they made restaurant reservations or just to mess with unsuspecting receptionists.

"Check you out," Jeff Galloway said from the doorway. "Cute assistant, big fancy office. Not that anyone would've expected anything different."

Jackson grinned. "Sheila's married with two kids, so don't get any ideas. And this office will do for now, but I'm hoping for bigger and better things down the road." He motioned toward a leather seat that sat opposite his desk. "Sit down and tell me what brings you here." Jeff and Jackson had been friends since they were assigned to the same little league team in the sixth grade. Even so, Jeff had never made an office visit.

"I've got news." Jeff leaned back in the chair. "Big news that I think you're gonna like."

Uh-oh. If Jeff's wife had another fix-up in mind for him, he'd be hard pressed to get out of it. A few years ago she'd insisted he go out with one of her coworkers, and the night had been a disaster. "Should I be nervous? Is Lauren in a matchmaking mood again?"

Jeff burst out laughing. "Are you kidding? After the way things went with you and Marie, I'm pretty sure she'll never let you get within ten feet of another of her friends."

"Marie. That was her name. I couldn't remember. She's a sixth-grade science teacher."

Jeff shook his head. "No. She's a first-grade music teacher. No wonder things didn't go well if that's as much attention as you paid her."

"We were a total mismatch to begin with. She was not impressed by me at all. Made no effort to hide it." He sighed. "Didn't help any when a girl I'd just gone out with ended up being our waitress."

"The way Marie told it, you were so busy ogling the waitress that you didn't even realize she'd left the table and called a cab."

"Pretty much sums it up." Jackson shrugged. He'd told Lauren he wasn't interested, but she'd insisted. "Left me with two plates of food to eat though." He grinned. "So what's the big news?"

"I'm here in an official capacity as a member of the Brookwood Christian School's board to let you know that you are going to be named our Alumnus of the Year at this year's centennial homecoming celebration."

Jackson shook his head. "Don't mess with me."

"I'm not. It was unanimous. Your family has such a legacy with the school, and your financial contributions mean a lot." He shrugged. "Plus you've volunteered a lot of time over the years, too."

A slow grin spread across Jackson's face. "My dad received that award when I was in junior high. The plaque hung on the wall in his office until last year." Walter Stratford's untimely death had been a shock to all, but especially to Jackson. "Now Mom has it hanging in the living room. She says it was one of his proudest achievements."

Jeff frowned. "How's your mom doing?"

"Still adjusting. We all are, I guess."

"That's to be expected." Jeff tapped his fingers against the arm of the chair. "I should get going. I just wanted to give you the news in person." He stood. "I'll e-mail you more information. The event is in mid-January, so it's still a few months off. There'll be a big dinner and silent auction on the Friday night before the homecoming basketball game on Saturday. We'd like for you to give the address that night. Talk about whatever you'd like." He turned to go, then turned back to face Jackson. "I do have one message for you from Lauren."

Jackson groaned.

Jeff laughed and held up his hands. "She wants you to call her. And if you don't, she will track you down." He grinned. "And she's the queen of tracking people down. If you don't believe me, ask her kindergarten best friend who she just found on Facebook. The poor girl lives somewhere in Wyoming and barely even remembers living in Arkansas when she was five."

Jackson told his friend good-bye and settled back at his desk. Alumnus of the Year. It didn't seem right that he was even old enough to receive such an award.

He did some quick math. He'd been fourteen when his dad received the award, and his dad had been. . .thirty-five. That couldn't be right. Could it?

He was thirty-five.

The same age his dad had been when he'd received the honor. Yet his dad had seemed so. . .settled. So grown up. He'd had a wife and two kids.

Jackson couldn't help but compare.

His dad had looked out at a table full of loved ones cheering for him when he'd given his speech.

Who would Jackson have?

The answer wasn't a pretty one.

Chapter 4

Amber Matthews: Vi, please don't be late for Landry's party. And also, don't wear anything green. Landry and I are both wearing green, and I don't want anyone else to wear it because it will spoil the pictures. Thanks. (Text message sent August 20, 4:59 p.m.)

Violet pulled into her parents' driveway and turned off the engine. At least the day couldn't get worse.

An older model Buick pulled in behind her. Mom hadn't mentioned her grandparents would be at the party.

Violet climbed out of her SUV and smoothed her skirt. She'd run home after work to let her dog go outside and to change into something besides her new green dress. She had a feeling if she'd been wearing blue today when Amber had seen her, it would've been blue that had been prohibited tonight. It was too much trouble to fight her sister though.

"Hey, Grandma." Violet hugged her grandmother as soon as the elderly woman got out of the car.

Rose Wallingford smiled at her oldest grandchild. "I'm so glad to see you, Violet. I wasn't sure if you'd be here or not."

"If Mom had told me you were coming, I would've been a lot happier about being here."

Grandma laughed and patted Violet's arm. "Oh, honey. Julia told me that Sampson made Landry partner in the firm." She leaned closer to Violet. "Might be the best thing that ever happened to you," she whispered. "I have an idea we need to discuss."

Before Violet could find out what her grandmother was talking about, a sullen teenage girl climbed out of the backseat. Her Goth style startled Violet. What was this girl doing with Grandma?

"Violet, I'd like you to meet Shadow Simmons. You might remember her grandmother, Betty Kemp from next door," Grandma said.

Violet watched as Betty climbed out of the passenger side. "Nice to meet you, Shadow." She could see the teenager was pretty underneath the dark hair, dark eyeliner, and black clothes. "Hi, Mrs. Kemp," she said as the older woman came to stand next to Grandma.

"Hello, dear." Mrs. Kemp smiled. "I guess you've met my girl." She put an arm around Shadow, but the girl shrugged her away. "She's living with me and Oliver for the school year. It's so nice to have a young person in the house again."

Violet vaguely remembered that the Kemps' only daughter had been killed in an accident a few years ago. Shadow must be her daughter. "I'm sure it is." She smiled at Shadow. "How do you like living in Hot Springs?"

Shadow stared at her with dark-rimmed eyes. "You've been

there. It's boring. My dad sent me to live with them so he can focus on his new family." She frowned.

Mrs. Kemp didn't miss a beat. "That's why we're here tonight. To break up the boring week."

Grandma smiled at Violet. "Your grandfather couldn't make it tonight, so I was glad for the company." She motioned toward the house. "We'd better get inside. Julia and Amber will be wondering what's keeping us."

Violet followed them up the path. She couldn't wait to see Amber's face when an angry Goth teenager walked in to Landry's celebratory dinner.

It more than made up for not being able to wear her new dress.

And then some.

Jackson stood outside of Main Street Bakery and waited for Lauren. He'd called her soon after Jeff left, and she'd asked him to meet her here on the way home from work.

"There you are, the second most handsome man to ever grace the halls of Brookwood Christian." Lauren grinned. "Actually, scratch that and make it the third. Bennett started kindergarten last week." She gave Jackson a hug. "Can you believe my baby is old enough to be in school?"

Jackson shook his head. "I sure can't. It seems like just yesterday we were there, doesn't it?" Jackson had known Lauren even longer than he'd known Jeff. She'd been in his class from the very start, way back when he'd worn Garanimals and carried a *Dukes of Hazzard* lunch box. Aside from his dad, Bo Duke had been his hero. Every now and then he still had the urge to slide into a car through the open window.

"Have you ever been here?" she asked, motioning toward the bakery. "It's one of our favorites. Jeff loves their buttercream frosting, and the kids think no dinner out is complete without dessert from this place."

Jackson held the door open for her, and the sweet scent of fresh-baked goods invaded his senses. "Nope. I've seen it on my way home but never stopped."

"Well you're in for a treat."

They ordered cupcakes and coffee, and Lauren led him to a table in the corner. "So how have you been?" she asked once they were seated.

He shrugged. "Okay. Busy with work. You know the drill."

"I do." She took a bite of her chocolate cupcake.

Jackson eyed her suspiciously. "What's this meeting all about anyway?"

"Can't I just get together with an old friend without raising an alarm?" she asked.

He narrowed his eyes. "No. Your husband comes to my office today to give me good news, news I'm sure you know about. For all I know, you're the one who nominated me. And he tells me I need to get in touch with you or you'll relentlessly track me down like you did to some poor girl in Wyoming." He grinned. "Who was it anyway? That weird girl who ate glue and accidentally got locked in the janitor's closet?"

Lauren laughed. "That was Suzy Jenkins. And for your

information, I didn't nominate you. Mrs. Chastain did."

"The librarian? I thought she hated me." Freshman year he'd put a fake mouse in one of the card catalogue drawers. Mrs. Chastain had made him sweep the library every afternoon for three weeks to make up for it.

"Guess not. Or maybe she's got a nice granddaughter she wants to fix you up with." Lauren grinned mischievously.

Jackson groaned. "Why don't you have your friend Marie have a talk with her. That'll nip it in the bud."

"I'm impressed that you remember her name."

He didn't have the heart to tell her Jeff had reminded him of it earlier at the office. "What do you think I am? Some kind of Neanderthal?"

She cocked her head. "Well. . ."

Jackson rolled his eyes. "Seriously. What's the deal here?"

"You won't like this much. But hear me out."

He already didn't like the sound of things. "What?"

"I talked to Kathleen the other night. She and I decided one of us had to have this talk with you." Lauren grinned. "And I lost."

"Great. What kind of scheme have you two cooked up this time?" Lauren and his sister had been inseparable growing up. Even though Kathleen lived in Memphis now, they still saw each other often.

"It's about the award. More specifically the dinner."

"If you're worried I'll say something off-color in my speech, don't worry. I'll be on my best behavior. Wouldn't want to let Mrs. Chastain down, after all."

She frowned. "That's not it. We're more worried about who

you're going to bring."

He crossed his arms and leaned back in his chair. "I won't embarrass the family, if that's what you're worried about."

"Jackson, you're a grown man. You'll be thirty-six in a few months."

"Easy now. Don't put me in the ground before it's my time." His joke fell flat.

Lauren took a sip of her coffee. "The last time you double-dated with me and Jeff, do you remember what happened?"

He might've known she'd bring it up. "Do we have to rehash this?"

"Yes." She raised an eyebrow and gave him a stern look. "That girl, bless her heart, was sweet. And very pretty. But let me just say that it's hard to take someone seriously as a real prospect for you when it turns out that I was her babysitter when I was sixteen."

It had been a nightmare. "She was only ten years younger."

Lauren shook her head. "It's not even about age. If you were going out with someone ten years younger than you who was a good match for you—who liked the things you do and could carry on an actual conversation—I'd be all for it." She shrugged. "But for some reason you choose to go out with girls you know there's no future with."

She had a point, but he wasn't going to give her the satisfaction. His lunch date with Whitney had really hit home with him today. "What exactly do you want me to do?"

"Think about the future. As far as I know, you've never been serious about anyone. You deserve more than that, Jackson. Jeff thinks so, too, but he'd never be so blunt as to tell you." She grinned. "He's lucky to have me, huh?"

Jackson chuckled. "I guess."

"So you promise? No bubble-headed girls at the awards banquet. You've got several months to find someone suitable. Someone you can be proud of to have at your table." She smiled. "Someone who cares about you for who you are, not the car you drive or how much money you make."

He'd never thought of himself as the kind of guy who had bad luck with women. In fact, he'd rather enjoyed himself over the years. He dated whenever he wanted, never got serious, and walked away unscathed. Not a bad way to live. "Fine. I promise to bring a suitable *woman* to the dinner. I'll leave the—what did you call them?" He grinned. "The bubble-headed girls behind for one night."

She sighed. "One night is a start."

It would have to be. Because while he might be able to admit that he was a little behind the curve on the "happily ever after" life that so many of his friends had found, that his dad had possessed when he was thirty-five, Jackson wasn't convinced it was the life for him.

Chapter 5

Reagan McClure: CHAD MADE IT HOME WITH A NICE
SUNBURN FROM THE POOL. NOW HE'S NAPPING WHILE
I COOK. WHAT IS WRONG WITH THIS PICTURE? (Text
message sent August 20, 5:28 p.m.)

Violet Matthews: SORRY. HANG IN THERE. I HAVE A GREAT
STORY TO TELL YOU LATER THAT INCLUDES A TEENAGE
GOTH, AMBER, AND SOME STINKY CHEESE. YOU'LL LOVE IT.
(Text message sent August 20, 7:02 p.m.)

Violet took a seat at the table between Grandma and Shadow.
"Looks good, doesn't it?" she asked. From the fresh flowers in
the center to the fancy china, it looked like Martha Stewart herself
had planned the party.

"It sure does." Grandma placed her napkin in her lap. "It isn't
every day I have such a fancy dinner." She took a sip of sweet tea.
"Your grandpa and I hardly ever sit at the dining table anymore."
She grinned. "Most of the time we eat on TV trays and watch

Wheel of Fortune. I guess we've turned uncouth in our old age."

Violet laughed. "I don't know about that."

"Are those. . .lobster?" Shadow asked in a disgusted tone when Amber placed a heaping platter in the center of the table. "Because I don't eat that."

Betty frowned at her granddaughter. "No need to broadcast it, dear." She lowered her voice to a still-audible whisper. "I don't either. We'll drive through McDonald's on our way back to Hot Springs."

"What's with the weird food they have?" Shadow whispered back. "Haven't they heard of normal stuff like chicken or pizza?"

Violet fought back a smile. Shadow had started out trying to be a good sport until Amber had insisted everyone taste the cheese she'd gotten at a gourmet food store. It stunk to high heaven. Amber had looked positively murderous when Shadow had declared it tasted like feet. "I promise you that I didn't grow up eating stinky cheese and lobster on a regular basis," Violet explained. "I'm guessing my sister planned the menu."

"Yes she did." Mom walked into the dining room in time to hear the end of Violet's statement. "And she's done an excellent job."

Once everyone was seated and Dad had offered thanks, Landry stood up. "Thanks so much for coming tonight to celebrate the second best day of my life."

Second best? If he said meeting Amber was the best, she might just gag.

Amber jumped up and grabbed his arm, a giant grin on her face. Her green sundress exactly matched his polo shirt.

"In fact, we have a little announcement to make," Landry said.

Amber thrust her left hand out and revealed a huge diamond. "We're engaged!" she squealed.

Everyone around the table offered their congratulations, but Violet froze. She'd always assumed that as the oldest she'd be the first to marry. Of course she'd also assumed Dad would make her partner in the firm. Lesson learned: don't assume, even if it seems logical.

Grandma nudged her.

All eyes were on Violet, waiting for her response. She blushed. "Wonderful news!" She mustered up all the enthusiasm she possibly could. "I'm so happy for you both."

Amber smiled, appeased. "Thanks." She and Landry sat back down. "The wedding will be in December. I know it's quick, but we hate to spend another day apart. Right before Christmas will be perfect."

Of course. Violet had always hoped to have her own wedding around Christmas. Amber had always said she wanted a traditional June wedding. "Really?"

Amber's blue eyes flashed. "Really."

Violet turned her attention to the lobster. She really was happy for her sister. But seeing Amber's happiness and security with Landry only reminded Violet of what was missing in her own life.

Reagan turned on the sound machine in the nursery, and soothing sounds of the ocean filled the room. Scarlett must be the lightest sleeper in the world. Couple that with the world's loudest older sisters living down the hall, and the machine was a lifesaver.

"Everybody down?" Chad asked as she walked into the living room.

She nodded. "Yes. Thank goodness."

"Rough few days, huh?" Chad propped his feet up on the coffee table and flipped the channel to ESPN.

Reagan set the laundry basket on the couch. "Can you fold these towels while I go get the rest of the laundry out of the dryer?"

Chad didn't respond.

"Please?"

Nothing.

"I'm going to be out of town next week, and I'll need you to keep the kids."

Chad peeled his eyes away from *SportsCenter*. "Huh?"

She frowned. "Fold. The. Laundry." She enunciated every word and pointed to the basket. "Please."

He made a face but picked up a towel. "By the way," he said as she started toward the laundry room. "I fixed the baby monitor."

She stopped. "You did?" She smiled. "I'm surprised you remembered I'd mentioned it wasn't working."

He grinned. "It wasn't working because it was unplugged. Before you freak out about something being broken, maybe you should check to make sure it's plugged in."

Rookie mothering mistake. She should've thought to check that before complaining to Chad. He'd never let her live it down. "I'll bet Ava Grace is responsible. No matter how many times I tell her to stay away from outlets, she doesn't always listen."

"Great. One of our children is going to get electrocuted

someday because they don't listen to you."

Reagan's eyes filled with tears. Stupid hormones. Why couldn't she just get angry without also being emotional? "Well I'm sorry you think they're so unsafe at home with a mother like me. Would you rather put them all in daycare? Because I'd be happy to go back to work."

He regarded her for a long moment. "You know that isn't what I meant."

"Sounded like it to me."

Chad sighed. "Come on, Reagan. Don't fight with me. I'm tired, you're tired. We'll just say stuff we can't take back."

At least they'd be talking. It had been months since the two of them had engaged in a conversation about anything other than the kids. "Just fold the laundry. I need to get the rest of the clothes out of the dryer and fix Izzy's lunch box for tomorrow. Hopefully today was the end of the virus." She watched as Chad haphazardly folded a towel. He didn't even make the corners match up. "I'll do that tomorrow." She took the basket from the couch. "Just forget it."

He shrugged. "Suit yourself." He clicked the OFF button on the remote. "I'm going to bed."

"Can you take Izzy to school in the morning?"

He stood up and groaned. "You know that puts me to the office later than I like." Chad worked as an HR manager for Baptist Health, one of the largest employers in the state.

"I hate to put her on the bus. Besides, I know she'd love the extra time with you on the way to school."

He shook his head. "Tomorrow is not a good day. It's my first day without an assistant, and my day is going to be crazy."

"What happened to Barbara?" The older woman had worked closely with Chad since he started the position.

"She retired. I told you that."

Reagan shook her head. "I'd remember that. I would've taken the kids to say good-bye. She's been so nice to us." When Barbara found out Reagan was carrying twins, she'd brought several days' worth of frozen casseroles and made Reagan promise to use them on days when she was too exhausted to think about cooking. They'd been gone before she was halfway through her second trimester.

"I'll give you her home e-mail address. I'm sure she'd love to hear from you." He motioned toward their bedroom. "I'm headed to bed now." Chad disappeared into the bedroom before she had the chance to ask any more questions.

She tried to ignore the pang of uncertainty. It wasn't like him to forget to tell her something like that. And she didn't like the way he'd gone to bed in the middle of their conversation.

Her buzzing phone put a stop to her pity party.

"You are not going to believe this," Violet said.

Reagan cradled the phone against her ear and carried the basket into the laundry room. "What happened?"

"They're engaged. *Engaged.* Kill. Me. Now."

Reagan couldn't help but laugh. "I didn't realize it was so serious. I guess Landry being made partner makes more sense now though, huh?"

"True. But I was totally shocked. I wonder what it would be like to have the kind of sister you're close to, the kind who actually shares personal information with you instead of springing it publicly."

"As an only child, I can't answer that question." Even so, Reagan hoped her girls grew up to be best friends, not just tolerate one another the way Violet and Amber did. "Maybe this will be good for Amber. Surely she'll grow up a little now that she's going to be someone's wife." Reagan had met Amber when she was just an annoying junior-high kid who used to sleep on the floor of the dorm room when she came for visits. Through the years, Reagan had watched her grow into a spoiled twenty-something who always managed to get her way.

"Let's hope so. Amber and I got along for the first twelve years of her life. Sometimes I wonder if we'll ever get back there."

"At least she has good taste. Your bridesmaid dress should be pretty."

Violet let out a laugh. "Oh, I didn't make the cut to be a bridesmaid. She actually said she felt like bridesmaids over thirty were kind of pathetic, so she'd rather I just serve the cake."

"Well that's just nuts. You'd make a beautiful bridesmaid regardless of your age. And everyone knows serving cake is the worst job. You can't enjoy the reception."

"Well, I might not be able to fully enjoy the reception, but I know one thing. I'm *not* going to that wedding alone."

Reagan grinned. "Does this mean you're finally ready to date again? I was beginning to think Zach had ruined you forever."

"Not to mention my best friend warning me against marriage all the time," Violet teased.

She deserved that. "Sorry. Want me to sugarcoat married life? Because I'd be glad to."

"Don't be silly. I know you don't mean it."

Reagan didn't have the heart to tell her that sometimes she did. Sometimes being married with four kids seemed like the hardest job she could imagine. All the fairy tales and romantic comedies in the world couldn't prepare a girl for that. "So what's the plan? Join the church's singles group? Online dating?"

"I'm starting right out with the big guns," Violet said. "After I left my parents' house, I stopped at Main Street Bakery for a double chocolate cupcake. Up at the cash register, there was a stack of business cards for a matchmaker."

"A matchmaker? Seriously?"

"There's a money-back guarantee. My love life will be in someone else's hands. It's a great plan."

"I guess."

"Come on. What could be more perfect? I'll meet with them once, and then they'll do the work for me. They'll weed out the losers and find someone who meets my specifications. It's a no-brainer."

Reagan wasn't sure, but she'd muster up as much support as possible. "Sounds great." Despite her complaints about Chad these days, they'd had a lot of happy years together. She couldn't imagine having to date again.

Although it would be nice to have a date with her husband every now and then.

Dear Mama,

Is it weird to write to someone without an Earthly address? Maybe. Nana gave me this journal though, and I don't really know what to do with it. She also gave me your journal from when you were sixteen. I think she's just trying to keep me happy, but I don't know if that's possible. I miss my friends and my old room. But I'm not too sad to be away from Stephanie. She's always trying to act like she's my mom, but she isn't. It makes me so mad when she does that. Daddy tries to stay out of it, but I'll bet he's kind of relieved I'm not there now.

Nana is trying to introduce me to people here, but so far I haven't met anyone too interesting. We went to a party the other night and this girl named Amber got really upset because I spit out some kind of fancy cheese she'd bought. It tasted like dirty feet to me though! I don't think Amber will be inviting me and Nana to any more of her dinner parties.

Oh, and now that I'm in Arkansas, me and Axel broke up. Nana found his picture in the trash and asked me why I threw away a picture of Ozzy Osbourne. Ha ha. I'm surprised she even knows who that is.

Now she's trying to get me to dye my hair back to my normal color, but I don't know.

I love you and miss you.
Shadow

Chapter 6

To: Violet.Matthews@MatthewsLaw.com
From: rosewallingford@myinternet.com
Date: August 27, 10:33 a.m.
Subject: My idea

I didn't get the chance to tell you my idea last week
because of the wedding ruckus. I thought you might
like to know that the shop owner next to the Kemps'
antique store is moving to be near her grandkids down
in Louisiana. The place is adorable and would make a
perfect bakery. I don't want to interfere with your life, but
sometimes you have to take a leap of faith. Think about it
and then call me.
Love,
Grandma (Grandpa says hi, too)

Violet sat in the restaurant parking lot and stared at her
grandmother's e-mail. She had too much on her mind right

now to even consider opening a bakery. Besides, meeting her perfect match for lunch was enough of a leap of faith for now.

She'd been pleasantly surprised when Mimi Maxwell from Mimi's Matches had called her Friday to let her know that she'd found someone who met nearly all of Violet's specifications. Apparently he'd interviewed on the same day Violet had. Mimi assured her this was a good sign because it meant they were both at the same place on the journey to love.

Violet had fought back a sarcastic remark. She would be a good sport about this and believe matchmaking could work. Or at least work well enough that she wouldn't be dateless for Amber's wedding.

She climbed out of her SUV and grabbed her purse. If the late August heat was any indication, they were in for a typical Arkansas fall—hot, humid, and a few more weekends at the lake before the weather actually turned cool.

Violet took a deep breath. What kind of man had Mimi found for her? At least there were background checks done on the prospects so she wouldn't have to worry about meeting some criminal who'd steal her identity and credit cards.

She squared her shoulders and walked into Zaza, a popular eatery in the Heights area of Little Rock. She'd been here a couple of times and had always been impressed.

"I'm meeting someone here," Violet told the hostess. "Under the name Mimi Maxwell." Mimi had refused to give the name of her date. *"We don't want you Googling each other and jumping to any conclusions. Best to go in with an open mind."* Violet had laughed because that was the first thing she would've done if armed with a name. Even more than diamonds, Google was a single girl's best friend.

The hostess ran her finger down the list. "The other party is already seated. Follow me." She motioned toward the dining area.

Violet's heart raced. First dates made her nervous. But blind dates made her feel stupid. She hated walking into a situation without knowing what to expect.

She scanned the room, hoping to spot him before he spotted her. Her eyes landed on a handsome man at a table for two. He was engrossed in his phone, furiously texting.

"Here you go," the hostess said.

The man looked up from his phone and cast steely blue eyes on Violet.

Familiar blue eyes.

It couldn't be.

"Violet Matthews." He stood up, a grin on his handsome face. "You have got to be kidding me."

Jackson Stratford had been the bane of her existence her senior year of college. Handsome and charming, yes. But also conceited and spoiled and totally unreliable. And also the reason she'd graduated a semester late. "You." She shook her head. "No way that you are my perfect match."

"Well it's nice to see you, too." His blue eyes twinkled. "I mean, it's only been what? More than a decade?" He grinned and nodded toward her chair. "Have a seat."

Violet took in his expensive suit and stylish haircut. He was better looking than when they'd been in college. He'd filled out some over the years. She vaguely remembered that he'd been a couple of years older than the rest of their classmates. Something about a gap year in Europe before college. It still sounded as pretentious now as it had back then. "Eleven years. I guess I haven't seen you since that presentation we did for our Business Ethics class." Actually she hadn't seen him since they'd been called into their professor's office right after their disaster of a presentation, but surely he remembered that.

He frowned.

For a split second Violet wondered how she looked to him. She'd changed since college, too. Found her own sense of style and finally learned that her fair complexion wasn't suited for a suntan. And learned to embrace her sometimes wild hair. "So you're living in Little Rock now?"

Jackson nodded. "I've been here for a year. I work in economic development. I spent the past several years living on the Gulf coast."

Too bad he hadn't stayed there. Then she might've met a real match today. "That's nice."

The waitress stopped by their table. "Can I get y'all something to drink?"

"Sweet tea, please." Jackson grinned at the waitress.

Violet shook her head. "Nothing for me. I won't be staying."

The waitress raised her eyebrows but didn't say anything.

"Can't we let bygones be bygones?" Jackson asked once the waitress was gone. "You're here, it's lunchtime. You may as well stay and eat. Just two old friends catching up."

They hadn't exactly been friends, but she hated to point it out. "I don't think so. This wouldn't be a good idea."

Jackson shrugged. "Suit yourself." He picked up his iPhone and swiped the screen.

It certainly hadn't taken him long to lose interest. "Have a good lunch." She clutched her bag and stood.

He looked up and locked his blue eyes on her. "I'm sorry I wasn't what you were looking for, Violet. I didn't know what to expect from a matchmaking service, but it certainly wasn't you." He sighed. "But it was nice to see you again, regardless. I wish you the best, and I really am sorry for any trouble I caused you in college."

She paused. He sounded almost. . .sincere. That couldn't be right. Still though, now she felt bad. It wasn't like her to be rude. "It was nice to see you, too." She smiled. "The truth of the matter is that I'm really just looking for a date to my sister's wedding. Not a real relationship. So this would be a waste of your time." There. That should do it. Now she could have an excuse for leaving other than not wanting to spend time with him.

"Really?"

She nodded. "Yeah. So there's no point in staying here and having lunch with you like a real date. I expected to just meet some nice stranger and hit it off enough to take him to the wedding. But I'd never do that to you." She raked her fingers through her hair. "You deserve to find someone who is looking for the same thing you are."

The jubilant grin on his face set off warning bells.

And the smolder in his eyes told her to run.

But she didn't.

Jackson wasn't easily surprised. His years in business had taught him to expect the unexpected. But when Violet Matthews sashayed into Zaza, he could've been knocked over with a feather.

Those piercing green eyes and that dark red hair were the same he remembered from college. But she'd definitely blossomed in the years since he'd last seen her.

And in a good way.

She wasn't one of those petite girls who looked like the wind might carry them away or one of those super-skinny girls who never ate in front of anyone. Her simple yellow dress showed off the kind of curves women would kill for and men dreamed about.

"I think you should sit back down." His eyes grazed her slightly upturned nose and full lips. She'd been pretty in college. But now she was a knockout. He couldn't wait to walk into his awards banquet with her on his arm.

"Didn't you hear me?" she asked. "I said I wasn't really looking for a match. Just a date. Not a relationship."

He couldn't hide his smile. "Oh, I heard you. And I think you're going to want to hear what I have to say."

She tentatively perched on the chair. "I'm not eating."

"Suit yourself."

The waitress placed a glass of tea in front of him. "Are you ready to order?"

"Bring us a Petit Jean Ham and Pineapple Pizza. And a water for the lady." He fought back a grin as Violet scowled.

The waitress hurried off.

"I thought you might at least want a slice of pizza and some water while you hear me out." He grinned. "It's the least I can do."

"I could've ordered for myself." She ran a hand through her wavy hair. "You haven't changed much since college."

"I beg to differ. But we can discuss that later. Right now there's something I'd like to propose." He took a sip of his tea. "Bet you never thought I'd be proposing to you."

Violet narrowed her eyes.

"Fine. You don't like my jokes." He shrugged. "I can live with that."

"What do you have in mind, exactly?" she asked.

He leaned back in his chair and regarded her for a long moment. If he put this out there, he'd have to stick with it. All in. "I visited Mimi's Matches for much the same reason as you. I'm receiving an award at a banquet in a few months and am delivering the keynote speech. I'd like someone with me who isn't a bubblehead." He raised an eyebrow. "What do you do for a living?"

"A bubblehead?" She seemed offended. "I'm a lawyer."

"Perfect."

She glared. "What are you saying, exactly?"

"I'm saying, let's forget Mimi and avoid any other awkward encounters with well-meaning people who might be looking for something more than what either of us is interested in finding. Let's pose as each other's significant other. We have a history— albeit a rocky one. It would be easy for people to believe that we reconnected and are in a relationship." He let his idea sink in. It was the ideal situation. All he had to do was get her to agree.

And from the look on her face, that might be tough.

Chapter 7

Violet Matthews: APPARENTLY MY PERFECT MATCH IS
JACKSON STRATFORD. REMEMBER HIM? I'M JUST GLAD
MIMI HAS A MONEY-BACK GUARANTEE. (Text message sent
August 27, 2:02 p.m.)

Reagan McClure: FROM COLLEGE? SERIOUSLY? MAYBE MIMI
CAN FIND YOU SOMEONE WHO DIDN'T CAUSE YOU TO MISS
GRADUATION. . . . (Text message sent August 27, 2:17 p.m.)

R eagan stopped the van at a red light and flipped on her blinker.
They weren't even out of the neighborhood yet and all three
kids were screaming. "Ava Grace, let's sing 'Jesus Loves Me' for the
twins."

"I don't want to sing. I want my Bah." She let out a wail, and
the babies joined in.

Reagan took a deep breath. How had they managed to leave
the pink stuffed bunny at home? For three years that bunny had
gone everywhere Ava Grace did. Yet somehow they'd loaded up

without it today. "Bah is probably taking a nap at home. When we get back, he'll be nice and rested and ready to play."

Ava Grace continued to sob.

Sometimes leaving the house just wasn't worth it. "Can you be a big girl and sing for Simon and Scarlett?"

"No. I need Bah." Ava Grace's wails grew louder.

Reagan turned on the radio. There was no reasoning with Ava Grace right now. Maybe the twins would be lulled to sleep. "We're just going to drive through the pharmacy and then to school to get Izzy, and then we'll be right back home to Bah."

She'd asked Chad to pick up the prescription yesterday, but he'd forgotten. Even though loading up the kids was hard, sometimes it ended up being easier than trying to get Chad to handle an errand. Inevitably he forgot or got the wrong brand of whatever item was needed.

Once she'd picked up the prescription, she headed toward Izzy's school. They were actually running ahead of schedule. She glanced in the backseat. The twins had fallen asleep, and Ava Grace's wails had been replaced by pitiful whines and sniffles. Reagan would take that over loud cries any day.

She flipped on her turn signal. What she needed right now was Starbucks. They were out of creamer at home, and the thought of coffee with plain milk hadn't been appealing.

Reagan turned into the Starbucks entrance and glanced at the patrons sitting outside on the patio without a care in the world. One young woman had her head tilted up toward the sunshine. A man walked to her table and handed her a drink, and she laughed at something he said.

Reagan looked in the rearview mirror. No one behind her. She tapped the brakes and peered closer at the scene unfolding on the Starbucks patio. The woman tossed her dark, glossy hair and took a sip of her drink. The man finally took his seat so Reagan could see his face.

Chad.

Her husband was enjoying an afternoon coffee with a gorgeous woman. A woman Reagan had never seen before, except maybe in a Pantene ad.

A horn honked behind her.

Reagan pressed the gas pedal and drove past the drive-through. She didn't want coffee any longer.

She just wanted to get out of there.

Her eyes filled with tears as she pulled onto the main road.

Fifteen years, ten of those as husband and wife.

Four kids.

Did that mean nothing to him? Did she mean nothing to him?

Reagan wasn't sure she wanted to know the answer.

Violet closed her office door and sat down at her desk. What a disaster of a day. She picked up her phone and punched in a number. "Mimi?" she asked.

"Yes."

"This is Violet Matthews. You had me meet a Jackson Stratford today at Zaza." Her mind still reeled not only from the surprise of seeing Jackson, but also from his preposterous idea.

"How did it go? Did you two hit it off immediately?" Mimi trilled.

Hardly. "That's the thing. Jackson and I actually know each other from college. We aren't exactly compatible."

Mimi giggled. "I beg to differ, dear. You both fit the bill almost perfectly for what the other is looking for. I rarely make a match like that."

"Maybe on paper. But not in real life. In real life we'd kill each other." Violet drummed her fingers on her desk. "Please tell me you can find someone else for me. And fast."

The sound of fingers clacking away on a keyboard came through the line. "I'm looking at all of your available matches right now."

"And?" Violet held her breath.

Mimi giggled again. "And there's exactly one. Jackson Stratford."

Violet let out a loud groan. "This is ridiculous. There's got to be more than one man in your whole database who is a match for me."

Mimi clucked her tongue. "You forget, dear, that you also have to be a match for him. And only one person in my database fits that bill for you. Jackson Stratford."

"Stop saying his name." Violet pushed a strand of hair out of her face. The situation bordered on insane. "Surely there is another option."

"I offer a money-back guarantee. If you aren't satisfied with your encounter with. . .*him*, then I'll be happy to refund your money."

"Then what am I supposed to do?"

"I can't help you there, dear. There are other services out there, but I can't speak to their success rate. I can only tell you that according to the questionnaire you two filled out, as well as what I saw in your personal interviews, the two of you are—in my professional opinion—very well suited for one another."

"But why, exactly?" She couldn't imagine what she and Jackson had in common. He was probably a cat person who hated the outdoors and only ate takeout. He probably hated to travel and only listened to classical music. No way was he her match. No way.

Mimi sighed. "I encourage my clients to find that out for themselves."

Violet had had enough. "No thanks. I'll come by your office later in the week for my refund." She hung up the phone.

So much for that.

Her intercom buzzed. "Violet?" Dad's voice boomed through the office. "Can you come in here please?"

"Sure." She smoothed her yellow dress and hurried down the hallway. She smiled widely as she walked into the ornate corner office.

"Have a seat." He motioned toward the leather couch.

Violet sat down and waited for him to talk.

Dad paced in front of his desk.

"Is everything okay?"

Dad stopped pacing and looked at her. "We need to talk about the amount of pro bono work you do."

It was a fight they had about once a year. "You know that's important to me."

He leaned against his desk. "I know. And I'm proud of the work you do. It's just that over the past year, that has been the bulk of your workload."

"And you want me to find a better balance."

Dad nodded. "Sometimes we don't always get to do what we want to do. Sometimes we have to think of the good of the firm."

Violet hadn't done what she wanted to do in years. She'd dabbled in art in college and taken some creative writing classes. But her liberal arts degree wasn't too helpful in landing a job, so she'd chosen law school out of desperation. "I know. It's just that those are the only cases I enjoy."

Dad frowned. "Violet, you're not always going to enjoy every minute of your day. It isn't possible."

"I disagree. I think there are a lot of people who enjoy every minute of their days. You do, don't you?"

He shrugged. "I'm a different kind of person. I wanted to be a lawyer since I was a little boy and your granddaddy would let me come with him to the office."

She'd never felt that way. Not once. She'd wanted to be partner because it seemed like the kind of accomplishment she could be proud of, that her parents could be proud of. But not because it was fulfilling some kind of lifelong passion. "I want to be the kind of person who is happy with every minute. We're only given so many minutes to live."

Her eyes filled with tears as she realized what she had to do.

Jackson couldn't concentrate on work. He'd like to think it was just a bad case of spring fever, but he had an idea it was because of his redheaded lunch date. Or nondate, as she'd been quick to point out.

His cell phone buzzed against his desk.

Kathleen.

"Hey, sis. What's going on?" She was his only sibling, and despite past differences, they were great friends now.

"Oh, you know. Trying to find my Superwoman cape, but I keep losing it."

He chuckled. "How are Andy and the kids? Everyone well?"

"Andy is busy with work. Olivia and Tyler are both playing soccer this year. You'll have to come to a game."

Jackson nodded. He loved his niece and nephew dearly. "I'll be there. Send me a schedule." The drive from Little Rock to Memphis wasn't a bad one, and he tried to visit at least monthly.

"They'll be thrilled. And you know Andy and I would love to see you any time."

"Thanks."

Kathleen cleared her throat. "Have you seen Mom lately?"

"Sunday at church. Why? Is something wrong?" Since their dad's death last year, Kathleen and Jackson had been monitoring their mother closely.

"Not exactly." She sighed. "She called yesterday and seemed awfully chipper. After we talked for a few minutes, she told me she was having dinner with a man from her Sunday school class."

"What?" Jackson hadn't expected this news. "That's crazy."

"Not really, if you'll just keep an open mind. Daddy's been gone for a year. I kind of expected it to happen eventually."

"It's too soon." Jackson raked his fingers through his hair. "Way too soon."

"I had a feeling you might have that reaction, so that's why I wanted to give you a heads up." Kathleen had always been the calm one. "Don't overreact though. She's only fifty-six. Not exactly over the hill, you know? It's perfectly normal for her to want to date."

Jackson wanted his sister to be as outraged as he was. Clearly that wasn't happening. "I still say it's too soon. And what does Mom know about dating these days? Things have changed since she and Dad got together."

Kathleen laughed. "Mom is a smart woman. She'll figure it out. Does she text you as much as she does me? She loves her new iPhone so much that she wants an iPad for her birthday."

Jackson hadn't even gotten an iPad yet. "She texts sometimes. And I know she's a smart woman. That's why I'm surprised she's starting to date."

"Do you expect her to stop living? Relationships are an important part of life." Kathleen paused. "Speaking of. . . Did Lauren talk to you yet?"

He groaned. "Yes. She made her point—your point—very clear."

"We're just worried about you. Life can be more fun if it's shared."

"I've gotten along just fine over the years."

She laughed. "Let me rephrase. Meaningful relationships make life worth living. You're getting too old to keep playing games."

He loved his sister, but between the bombshell about Mom's newfound dating life and the analysis of his own love life, he'd heard enough. "I'd better go. Thanks for the info. E-mail me the kids' ball schedule."

Jackson hung up the phone and tried to concentrate on work.

But Violet's yellow dress and pretty face kept flashing through his mind.

Chapter 8

Violet Matthews: I JUST QUIT MY JOB. (Text message sent August 27, 4:22 p.m.)

Reagan McClure: I THINK CHAD IS HAVING AN AFFAIR. (Text message sent August 27, 4:24 p.m.)

"You win." Violet clutched the phone to her ear as she boxed up her personal belongings from her office.

"Actually just the opposite. I lose. Big time." Reagan's hiccup gave away her recent crying jag.

Violet crammed some framed pictures into a box. "Tell me what happened." She listened as Reagan described seeing Chad and a woman having coffee.

"It's no wonder. I'm just a big old blob. I'm always covered in pee and poop and vomit. And I'm cranky. Not exactly the kind of woman a man wants to come home to."

Violet stopped what she was doing and sat down in her chair. "First of all, you aren't a blob. You look great considering you had twins just a few months ago. And who can blame you for being cranky? You haven't had a good night's sleep in forever. Let Chad get up with the kids all night and I'll bet he is a little cranky, too."

Reagan snorted. "Like that will happen."

"Seriously. Don't sell yourself short."

"Do you see those Hollywood actresses on the cover of *People*? Four or five days after they give birth, they're back in their size twos and strutting on a red carpet without a care in the world."

Violet let out a chuckle. "Come on, Reagan. First of all, I'm sure Photoshop is hard at work on some of those pictures. And second of all, I'd definitely put you on my list of hot mommies that I know."

"Shut up. I am *not* in that category at all."

"It's probably like ninety-percent attitude. Cut yourself some slack. It isn't exactly like you've had time to focus much on yourself during the past several months."

"True. And now Chad is off cavorting with some woman at Starbucks."

"Seeing him at Starbucks with a woman isn't exactly proof of an affair. Chad is in HR. He interviews people all the time and not always in the office. You know that."

"An interview? You think that's what it was?" Reagan asked.

"Until you know otherwise, that's what I'd guess. Try not to jump to conclusions, okay? I know things haven't been perfect lately, but try to keep calm."

"Calm." Reagan let out a laugh. "My life hasn't been calm in ages. I mean, I managed okay with just two kids. There were two of us and two of them. I wanted to wait to try for a third. I told

Chad I really wanted Izzy and Ava Grace to be a little older. But he wanted a boy so badly, and then when we found out we were having twins. . .well, I guess that's the last time I was calm." She sighed. "I love them all dearly. I'm so blessed to be their mama. And I know this part flies by so fast that I'll look back and wish I had it back."

"Still though. You're overwhelmed. Have you thought about calling your mom and seeing if she can stay with you for a couple weeks? Maybe if you have an extra pair of hands for a little while it will help you get a handle on everything."

"She and Daddy just got settled in their new place in Branson. He's finally feeling better, but I know he depends on her a lot. I hate to even ask because I know she'll come over right away. It would be different if Daddy would come, too, but I know he'd rather be at his own house." Reagan's dad had a variety of health problems, and her mother served as his primary caregiver.

Violet emptied her top drawer. "Isn't there someone who could look in on him for a little bit so she could come stay with you? And I know you don't want to consider this, but Chad's mother isn't too far away. Can you put up with her if it means preserving your sanity?"

Reagan didn't say anything for a long moment. "Maybe." She let out a huge sigh. "But I'm still not sure what I saw today. They were talking and laughing. It definitely didn't seem interview appropriate."

"So ask him. Tell him you thought you saw him there and see how he reacts. Just don't jump to the worst conclusion possible until you have some facts. Okay?" Violet hated the situation Reagan was in, but sometimes looks could be deceiving. Lots of interviews probably took place every day at Starbucks. Of course lots of affairs probably started there, too, but she'd keep that to herself.

"You're right. I'll ask him. Now what's this about you quitting?"

It was Violet's turn to sigh. "I resigned. Is that the craziest thing you've ever heard? First I learn that Jackson Stratford is the only man in the state of Arkansas that I'm a match for, and then I up and quit my job without even having a plan in place." Her dad had tried to talk her into staying put until the end of the year to give her plenty of time to find a new firm, but she'd asked for an immediate release.

"I can't even process all of that. The job first though. What happened?"

Violet filled her in on the conversation she'd had with Dad. "I normally take a ton of time in making big decisions like that. I pray about them, and I think about them. But in that moment in his office, I knew there was only one thing I could do. And that meant quitting."

"What will you do now?"

Violet finished filling the box. "I have no idea." She sighed. "I *could* interview for another firm, one that's more focused on pro bono work." She hated to tell Reagan about the other possibility.

"This is an important decision for you. You haven't been happy with your job in years. Ever, maybe. You could reevaluate."

"And what? Start a new career?"

Reagan sighed. "I'm just saying. Once upon a time in a land far, far away, I had a career that I loved. Adored. I was happy at work. Fulfilled." Reagan had worked as a graphic designer and had dabbled in photography. She'd given it up when Izzy was born, and she and Chad had agreed she'd stay home until the kids were all in school.

"I know. And you were good at it."

"So find what you're good at. Find your passion. I've been telling you for years that you should rethink your career."

It was the truth. Violet's favorite thing about being a lawyer when she'd gotten out of law school had been living in DC. Not her career. And when she'd moved back to Arkansas to join the family firm, she'd always thought she'd find the joy, but the only time she'd come close was doing the pro bono cases where she felt like she was actually making a difference. "Well. . .there is one thing I'm considering." She paused. "But it's totally crazy."

"Sometimes the best ideas are, don't you think?"

"Grandma e-mailed me this morning to let me know the shop next to Mrs. Kemp's is available."

"I'd forgotten about Mrs. Kemp's shop. What's it called?"

"Aunt Teak's." Violet smiled. "There's a shop right next door that used to be a sandwich place. Grandma thinks I should consider finally opening my own cupcake place."

Reagan let out a squeal. "Oh, Violet! You've always wanted to do that. And I have to say, every time we have a birthday party everyone always wants to know what bakery I use." She laughed. "Of course, now I'll have to start paying you."

Violet giggled. "Let's not get ahead of ourselves. This would be a gigantic decision. I mean, moving to a new city is a huge deal, even one as nearby as Hot Springs. Not to mention launching a store."

"I could design your logo. And website. And come in and do some pictures." Reagan's voice grew more animated than Violet had heard in a long time.

"I'll keep you posted on my decision. I need to go home and really think things through and look at my finances. I might go to Hot Springs soon though, just to look at the space." She couldn't believe she was saying this out loud.

"Well I, for one, am totally supportive. Even though it would mean you'd be an hour away."

Violet smiled. She could always count on her friend for support. It was just one of the many blessings in her life. "Thanks. If you want to pray for me to make a good decision here, I'd appreciate it."

"And if you want to pray that Chad and I can get on the right track, I would, too."

"Done." Violet hung up and picked up her box. She wanted to leave before Dad came to see her. He'd been pretty upset.

She hated disappointing her parents. But maybe it was time to start living out her own dreams.

Dear Mama,

Did you really like working at Aunt Teak's? Because I'm totally bored being around all that old stuff all the time. Nana says you liked it, but so far I haven't found anything in your journal to back her story up.

I'm trying to talk them into letting me get an after-school job somewhere a little cooler than an antique store, but so far I'm not having much luck. Nana's friend from across the street told me that her granddaughter might be opening a bakery next to Aunt Teak's. I haven't told Nana yet, but if that happens, I'm going to get a job there.

I met a cute boy at church on Sunday. His name is Chase, and he plays tennis. He invited me to play sometime, so I've been practicing by playing Wii tennis with Granddaddy. I don't think it's going to help much, but we're having a good time.

I miss you.
Love,
Shadow

Reagan put the last of the dirty dishes in the dishwasher and closed the door. Maybe they should start using paper goods. It would be bad for the environment, but it might save her sanity.

She glanced at the clock. Almost nine. This was getting ridiculous. She'd tried all day to put the scene from Starbucks out of her mind. Of course Violet was right. It was probably an interview. But each time she'd texted Chad after she got home, he hadn't mentioned it. Only said it was a hectic day and he'd be home late.

So once again she'd been alone to feed, bathe, and put the kids to bed.

"The door was unlocked," Chad said.

Reagan jumped at the sound of his voice. "I didn't hear your car."

"I was driving my super stealthy silent car tonight." He grinned. "But seriously, you should lock the door. Do I need to put that on your list?" He opened the fridge and took out a Coke.

She stopped wiping the counter and glared at him. He'd made fun of her list for months now. "I have a lot on my mind. You try getting out of the house with four kids and see if you can remember everything without looking at the list." She'd written all the necessities on a Post-it and stuck it next to the back door. One trip to church with no diapers in the diaper bag had been one too many.

"Easy there. I was only being helpful."

"You sure are in a chipper mood for someone who just worked a twelve-hour day." Did his Starbucks outing have something to do with it? "What's going on?"

"I wanted to wait until it was a done deal to tell you the news." Chad grinned.

"Please tell me you inherited a million dollars and we're hiring a nanny. And a housekeeper."

He rolled his eyes. "I'm being serious."

"So am I." She crossed her arms and leaned against the counter.

"I officially hired a new assistant today. And she won't be like Barbara and just answer the phones and make appointments. I've restructured things so the new position will actually handle some of the things I used to handle." He looked positively gleeful.

A sinking feeling washed over Reagan. "I meant to tell you that I think we saw you at Starbucks today."

Chad nodded. "You probably did. I wish you'd called. You could've stopped and met Reese. You'll love her."

Reese. Even the name made her blood run cold. Coupled with that perfect hair and nice figure and it was enough to make Reagan want to cry. "Reese, huh? How old is this Reese person?"

He frowned. "It's kind of illegal for me to ask that in an interview. But based on the years she graduated from high school, college, and graduate school, I'd say she's about twenty-six."

Of course she was. "Is she from here?"

Chad took a sip of Coke. "She's from a small town in northeast Arkansas. Went to college in Fayetteville and got her MBA from Vanderbilt."

Fancy. "Well that's just great."

He furrowed his brow. "What's wrong? I thought you'd be pleased that I'm going to be able to transfer some of my responsibilities. It should mean more free time and less late nights."

Right. Until he figured out how much more fun it was to stay late at the office with some hot twenty-six-year-old than it was to come home and wrestle four kids through dinner, baths, and bedtime. "So what does her husband do?"

Chad finished his Coke and tossed the can into the garbage. "She's not married. I know that because she mentioned today that she didn't know anyone here. She just moved from Nashville."

"Why exactly was your meeting at Starbucks? Why not at the office?"

He shook his head. "I do a lot of interviews out of the office. You know that. She had another appointment on that side of town, so it just made more sense for me to meet her there."

Reagan rolled her eyes.

"What is your problem?"

She knew that nothing she could say would make him understand. Anything negative about Reese and her shiny hair and perfect body would only make Reagan look stupid and insecure in comparison. And right now she had nothing to compete with but an extra fifteen pounds of baby weight and a belly that would never be totally flat again. "I don't have a problem. Let's just go to bed."

"You go on." He motioned toward the living room. "I'm going to catch up with the DVR."

Reagan closed the bedroom door behind her and went into their bathroom. She stood in front of the mirror and took a long look. Her ill-fitting clothes made her look even lumpier than she felt. Her blond hair hung limply around her makeup-free face. She leaned closer to the mirror. Dark circles beneath her blue eyes told the story of the past months.

And now Chad would be going to work every day and spending time with some single twenty-six-year-old.

She could let the news knock her down. She could let her insecurity squash the last embers of fire from her marriage. But she wouldn't go out without a fight. And if that meant taking some time to focus on the way she felt about herself, then that's what she'd do.

So starting tomorrow Operation Hot Mommy would begin.

And Reagan was ready.

Chapter 9

Kathleen Morgan: MARK YOUR CALENDAR. WE'RE COMING
TO THE LAKE HOUSE IN TWO WEEKS FOR ONE LAST BIT OF
SUMMER. (Text message sent September 4, 2:43 p.m.)

Jackson Stratford: SOUNDS GREAT. CAN YOU BELIEVE
I HAVEN'T BEEN THERE YET THIS YEAR? P.S. MOM
INTRODUCED ME TO HER DINNER DATE SUNDAY AT
CHURCH. I'M NOT OKAY WITH THIS. (Text message sent
September 4, 3:16 p.m.)

Jackson pulled his Range Rover in front of a small bungalow-
style house. Thanks to Google and White Pages, he'd tracked
down Violet's address. Did this make him some kind of stalker?

He shrugged off the feeling of uncertainty and hurried up the
path that led to the front door. He squared his shoulders, feeling a
bit like he might be headed into a war zone.

One more shot.

After being unable to get Violet off his mind over the weekend, he'd decided to give it another try. She really would make the perfect date to his event, and besides that, she was the kind of woman who would show Kathleen and Lauren that he could date someone they'd approve of. He knocked on the door.

A dog barked inside.

After a few seconds, the door swung open and Violet stood on the other side. Her red hair was twisted into a messy bun, and she wore an apron emblazoned with bright flowers. Her eyes widened at the sight of him. "What do you want?" she asked with a frown. "No, a better question would be how did you find me?"

Jackson grinned. "Southern hospitality must be a thing of the past."

"I'm very hospitable to invited guests." She glanced down at her apron. "Clearly I wasn't expecting company."

"This will only take a second."

She sighed. "Fine. Come on in."

He stepped into her house and inhaled. The sweet scent of vanilla permeated the air. "Smells good in here." It reminded him of summers spent at his grandparents' house.

A tiny smile played across her face. "Cupcakes. I'm baking." She motioned for him to follow her. "You can talk while I finish icing."

He stepped into her kitchen. Red appliances stood out against the white walls. It suited her. Bright and cheery. "Looks like you spend a lot of time in here." He sat down on a red barstool that looked like it belonged in a fifties diner.

"I bake when I'm upset. Or happy. Or confused." She smiled and picked up a tube of icing.

He watched as she expertly iced a cupcake. It smelled heavenly. "So which is it today?"

She glanced up and locked her green eyes on his. "Which is what?"

"Upset, happy, or confused?"

Violet sighed. "D. All of the above." She held up a cupcake. "Want one?"

"Do you even have to ask?" He grinned.

She put a cupcake on a small red plate and placed it in front of him. "Something to drink? Water? Milk?" She motioned toward a red coffeemaker. "Coffee?"

"Milk, please." He touched his tongue to the chocolate icing. "This is so good. You should open a bakery."

She laughed. "Here you go." She put a glass of cold milk next to his plate. "Enjoy."

Jackson bit into the cupcake. It was moist but not undercooked. Perfection. "Seriously. This is better than I had last week at some fancy shop in the River Market." Little Rock's River Market district was a hodgepodge of shops, restaurants, and nightclubs along the Arkansas River.

"Thank you. My grandma and I worked together on the recipe. It's many years in the making." She returned to her icing.

"So I was serious earlier. What's got you upset, happy, and confused?" He knew he was prying, but he sensed a melancholy air about her that hadn't been present at lunch the other day.

She shook her head. "Just some big decisions to make."

"I know you don't like me much, but I'm good at decisions." He smiled. "I'm very practical."

Violet rolled her eyes. "I'm sure you are. But I think this is a decision I have to make alone."

"Fine. Just trying to help." He popped the last of the cupcake into his mouth.

She regarded him for a long moment. "I quit my job last week. Aren't you glad I didn't agree to your stupid plan now? You wouldn't be able to pass me off as a lawyer anymore."

Jackson took a drink of milk. "So you'll find another job. Law firms are a dime a dozen."

Violet didn't say anything. She turned her attention back to her baking. Finally she looked up at him. "I don't know if I'll go back to a firm."

"So start your own practice." It's what he would do if he were in her position. Jackson had always wanted to be his own boss. He'd given thought to opening his own small business but had never settled on what kind. Plus he enjoyed his work in economic development. There was something very satisfying about bringing in new industries and businesses. Sometimes one industry could breathe new life into a stagnant town.

Violet pulled a fresh pan of cupcakes from the oven. "Why are you here again?"

The words from anyone else would've offended him. But not her. She had every reason to be suspicious of him, every reason to dislike him. He'd earned it after the way he'd treated her in college. "I came to discuss our lunch meeting last week. But that can wait."

"Good. Because I don't see that there's anything to discuss. It was a fluke."

A fluke his foot. It was the answer to what they were both

looking for. No strings. No complications. A believable solution. But she'd have to come to that conclusion on her own. "If you say so." He picked up his plate and carried it to the sink. "Want me to wash this?"

She shook her head. "Just put it there. I'll get to it later."

"So why did you resign anyway?" His curiosity got the better of him.

Violet stopped icing the cupcake she was working on. "Did you ever think maybe you were going down the wrong path? And you were going downhill and the only way to stop was to jump?"

Oddly, he understood. "Yes."

"That's kind of what happened." She gave him a tiny grin. "So I jumped."

Violet couldn't believe she was spilling her guts to Jackson, of all people. She'd sequestered herself to her house for the better part of the past week, only leaving to get groceries and go to church on Sunday. The rest of the time she'd baked and prayed and cried and paced. And ignored the barrage of calls from her mother. "When I was in college, I always admired those people who knew what they wanted to be when they grew up." She perched on one of the bar stools and dipped her finger into the icing for a taste.

"You seemed to turn out okay," Jackson said.

She shrugged. "I wasn't one of those people. What I was going to be depended on which day of the week you asked me. An author, an artist, a dancer, an archaeologist." She sighed. "I had a lot of interests. And I wished I were one of those who'd always known their path."

"Sometimes it's more fun to figure it out as you go."

She shook her head. "Not if you're me. My younger sister can get away with that. But everyone has always expected more from me. So when I graduated with the broadest liberal arts degree possible and wasn't really qualified to do anything but pour coffee. . ." She trailed off.

"You went to law school," Jackson finished for her. He grabbed another cupcake.

Violet nodded. "Yep. How nuts is that?" She held up a hand. "No. Don't answer that."

He grinned. "There are crazier things to do than become a lawyer."

"My grandfather started the firm when my dad was a baby. They were so pleased when I became the third generation to work there. But I hated it. Every single day I hated it."

"What prompted you to finally own up to that?"

She shrugged. "Have you ever taken a long look at your life and not been happy with what you saw?"

Jackson's blue eyes met hers. "I sure have. More than once."

"A few weeks ago my dad made someone else partner. At first I was really hurt. Outraged even. But then I realized it wasn't even something I wanted in the first place. Just something I thought I *should* want."

"So what do you want to do now?"

She lifted up a cupcake. "Something I'm passionate about. Something I love. And something that will pay the bills."

He grinned. "I'll be a customer."

Violet filled him in on the possible bakery in Hot Springs. "Moving and opening my own business just seems like such a leap of faith."

"But given the alternative—joining another firm and continuing to do something you have no desire to do—how can you not take it?"

"It isn't that simple."

"It never is."

She regarded him for a long moment. It was the closest to a civil conversation she'd ever had with Jackson. He must be up to something. "So that's my story. And the reason for my baking marathon."

"And now you're headed to Hot Springs for a few days to check out the place?" he asked.

"Just for a day." She pointed out the kitchen window where a boxer-mix dog lay in the sun. "That dog in the yard is Arnie. I put him outside before I opened the door for you, otherwise we would have had to endure a barking fit." She grinned. "He's old and nearly deaf, but he's still pretty protective of me. I can't take him with me because Grandma is allergic. So that means I'll need to make a quick trip."

Jackson pulled his keys out of his pocket and removed one from his key ring. "Here." He handed the key to her.

She furrowed her brow. "What's this?"

"The key to my lake house. Right on Lake Hamilton." He grinned. "It's the most peaceful place you could ever hope for. And dog friendly. My sister's family never visits without their dog, Max."

Violet stared openmouthed. "Oh, I couldn't. Really." She thrust the key back at him.

"Come on. It's empty. I haven't used it all summer. And you could spend a few days there making your decision." He grinned. "Maybe this would make up for you graduating a semester late?"

She rolled her eyes.

"Okay. Maybe not. But consider it this way—you'll have a home base while you get things figured out. You can take your time and make your decision. No need to rush back." He shrugged. "Just trying to help."

Violet thought for a minute. She didn't want to be in his debt. At all. He'd been a charmer in college, and she knew he hadn't changed. There was always something in it for him. "What do you get out of this arrangement?"

An indignant expression flashed across his handsome face. "Give me a little credit, okay? I'm not such a bad guy."

That was debatable. But she was sort of desperate. If she was going to move to Hot Springs and open a business, she needed to get the ball rolling as quickly as possible. "Okay. Well, thanks." She smiled. "Really. Thanks."

Jackson wrote down the address and security code on the back of a piece of junk mail. "And here's my phone number in case you have any questions about anything." He pushed the paper across the counter to her. "Stay as long as you need." He grinned and picked up another cupcake. "One more for the road."

Violet followed him to the front door, not sure what to think.

Jackson waved and headed to his car.

She watched him climb inside and drive away.

What had she just gotten herself into?

Chapter 10

Violet Matthews: I AM AT JACKSON STRATFORD'S LAKE HOUSE IN HOT SPRINGS. CAN YOU SAY "PLACE I NEVER EXPECTED TO BE"? (Text message sent September 6, 10:23 a.m.)

Reagan McClure: WELL I'M AT A GYM. ME. A GYM. WHO HAVE WE TURNED INTO? AND I'M GOING TO NEED SOME DETAILS ON YOUR LAKE ADVENTURE. . . . PLEASE TELL ME JACKSON ISN'T THERE. (Text message sent September 6, 11:16 a.m.)

Reagan glanced around her. She couldn't remember feeling more like an outsider. These women were fit, tan, and looked about twenty-two. And the men were either beefy or elderly. But the reviews she'd read online had been good ones, plus they had a daycare area for kids. Ava Grace hadn't been super happy about it until she'd spotted a Disney princess dollhouse.

The three college-aged girls watching the children had oohed and ahhed over the twins. Even though Reagan wasn't used to leaving the kids with anyone, knowing she'd be right across the hall made her feel better. Besides, after a week of trying to force herself to exercise while the kids napped, she was ready to admit she needed professional help.

A gym employee waved her over. "Would you like your personal training consultation now? It comes with your membership."

Reagan peered at the perky girl's name tag. "Thanks, Heather. What all does that entail?"

"Oh, you know. Weighing, measuring, determining your BMI. . .you know, just stuff like that."

"BMI?"

"Body mass index." Heather smiled. "We also do a complete nutritional evaluation where we help you to make better choices when it comes to food."

Reagan shook her head. "I think I'll wait on that. I'm just interested in starting slowly."

Heather nodded. "Okay, great." She pointed to a set of double glass doors. "That's the weight and exercise room. Ellipticals, treadmills, exercise bikes, and all the strength-training equipment you need is in there. Look for James. He'll have on a blue shirt just like mine. He can give assistance on any of the equipment." She handed Reagan a sheet of paper. "This is our class schedule. We offer pretty much everything. Aerobics, Zumba, yoga— you name it." She grinned. "There's also a pool for swimming and water aerobics."

Reagan felt so overwhelmed. This was much more complicated than she'd expected. Right now she mostly wanted to curl up on the couch with a Sam's Club-sized tub of cheese balls and watch mindless TV.

"Ma'am?" Heather asked. "Are you okay?"

Reagan looked up numbly. This had been a mistake. She turned to go, clutching her schedule. She'd get the kids and leave. She could cancel her membership over the phone. No one would ever have to know. She hadn't even told Chad what she was doing in case she failed.

"Overwhelming, isn't it?" A woman in a navy sweat suit asked as she filled her water bottle with water from the fountain.

Reagan nodded. "Very."

"I'm Maggie. I've been a member for about six months." She patted her stomach. "Lost ten pounds."

"That's great." Reagan smiled and introduced herself. "I haven't exercised in years. But after I had my twins, I've had a hard time getting rid of the extra weight."

"Twins!" Maggie exclaimed. "How old?"

"Nine months."

"Girl, you look great." Maggie smiled broadly. "You have any more kids?"

Reagan told her about Ava Grace and Izzy. "I never expected to have four. And can you believe my husband thinks we should try for one more? Says then he'll have enough for a basketball team."

Maggie clucked her tongue. "Why don't you wait and make that decision after you've had a few full nights of sleep?"

Reagan laughed. "Is it that obvious?"

"Honey, I've been there. Not enough hands, not enough hours in the day to get it all done. Little people depending on you for everything, and you start to feel like a nonperson. A husband who comes home from work late and tired and has no idea that your job is a job, too."

That summed it up exactly. "It's like you live at my house." She smiled. "But I love them dearly. I wouldn't trade it for anything."

"But you don't know who you are anymore. It's hard to tell if you're coming or going."

Reagan nodded.

"Well I think you've done a good thing by joining here. A little time for you." Maggie smiled. "Want me to show you the ropes?"

"Please. I don't have much time before we need to get home for naps and then go pick Izzy up from school."

Ten minutes later, Reagan had decided the treadmill was where she should start. "Thanks for your help."

"No problem." Maggie smiled. "I usually take the Tuesday and Thursday morning Zumba class. You should give it a try sometime."

Reagan shook her head. "I'll stick to walking for now. But you never know." She stepped on the machine and hit the START button. She should've thought to bring her earbuds so she could listen to music. Maybe next time.

Next time.

She was really doing this.

Maggie was right. She'd desperately needed to do something for herself.

So she ignored the guilt over all the things she could be doing for her kids, her husband, or her house, and she walked. It might be a slow pace, but it was something.

Operation Hot Mommy had begun.

Violet stood on the deck of Jackson's lake house and took in the view. The spectacular view.

She'd always hoped to have a house like this, right on the water with a sunny garden area and a hammock in the backyard. Not to mention the to-die-for kitchen.

She enjoyed one more second of sunshine before hurrying toward her car. Arnie was sound asleep on his bed in the family room, and Violet was confident he'd sleep most of the afternoon. Now that he'd lost most of his hearing, he could sleep through just about anything, including the sound of boats zooming past the dock at the edge of the yard as lake lovers took advantage of the last few hot days before fall set in.

Violet got in her car and drove toward downtown Hot Springs. Ever since she was a little girl, she'd loved visiting the town. Hot Springs was steeped in history, and people had been coming to bathe in the natural hot springs for hundreds of years.

Traffic along the main drag between the historic Arlington Hotel and Bathhouse Row was terrible. Violet slowed for a group of pedestrians and finally found a parking spot not too far from Aunt Teak's.

"There you are," Grandma called. "I was beginning to think you were going to stand me up."

"Not a chance." Violet grinned and pushed a strand of red hair from her face. "It took me a little while to get to the lake house and then back here."

Grandma gave her a quick hug. "Is Arnie okay?"

"He's hanging in there. The vet says he's doing well considering his age, but I don't know." The dog would be fifteen later in the year, and Violet knew the time he had left was short. "He's my longest successful relationship, you know."

Grandma joined in her laughter. "He's a good dog, dear. I'm just sorry you couldn't stay at my house for a few days because of my allergies." She smiled. "But if I ever were going to let a dog inside the house, it would be him."

Violet linked arms with her grandmother, and they walked toward Aunt Teak's. "Is Mrs. Kemp planning on staying in business?"

"Oh yes. She and Oliver adore the shop. Me, I like retirement. But they seem really happy." Grandma had taught kindergarten for thirty years before retiring.

Violet paused to look at the exterior of the building. "It's really beautiful." The first story of the Victorian-style building was a glass storefront, but the upper floor revealed large bay windows and turrets.

"I think you could have a wonderful little business here," Grandma said. "No pressure though. The Realtor left a key with Betty. You can look around and decide if this is something you want to pursue." She held the door open to the antique store.

"Good afternoon, Violet." Mrs. Kemp smiled from behind the counter. "It's been a long time since you've been in. There are some new items that you might like to see."

Violet adored things with a history. Her love of vintage clothes was only the beginning. "Every time anyone comes in my house, they want to know about the typewriter." She'd purchased a green Optima Super model typewriter from the store a couple of years ago. "I love thinking about the stories and letters that machine must have typed back in the fifties."

Mrs. Kemp nodded. "I'm sure it looks wonderful in your home. Rose showed me some pictures she took the last time she was there of some books you'd gotten at an estate sale."

"I love hardback copies of classic books," Violet explained. "I think they look so pretty on the shelf, not to mention how they smell."

"You like the way old books smell?" Shadow asked.

Violet hadn't noticed her sitting in the corner on a plush footstool. "I sure do."

The teenager made a face. Gone was the all-black attire and inky hair, and in its place was a tennis dress and light brown locks.

"I like your hair," Violet said.

Shadow absently touched her ponytail. "I'm not sure about the color, but it will do for now." She stood up and picked up a tennis racket. "I'm walking to the courts. I'll be back soon."

Mrs. Kemp nodded. "Don't be late. We'll leave here promptly at five to go home. Your granddaddy wants to go eat barbecue tonight at McClard's."

Shadow shrugged and walked out.

"Teenagers." Mrs. Kemp sighed. "That girl is her mama made over."

"How's she adjusting?" Grandma asked.

"She won't talk to us, so I don't know. She's struggling trying to fit into a new school. But she met a boy at church last week,

ANNALISA DAUGHETY

so maybe that's a step in the right direction." She grinned at Violet. "I saw a picture of her last boyfriend, and he had so many piercings sticking out of his nose and lip, I'll bet he has a hard time going through airport security."

"Well, at least she's moved on," Grandma said.

Mrs. Kemp nodded. "I just wish I knew how to reach her. These past years have been tough. First Jenny's accident and then Stuart remarrying. I guess it's no wonder Shadow is having a tough time finding her place in the world."

Violet understood something about that. She hadn't experienced the tragedies Shadow had, but she'd never felt like she was on completely solid ground either. "Maybe I could talk to her sometime," she offered. "Take her out to eat or shopping or something."

Mrs. Kemp's face lit up. "That'd be wonderful. You are only a couple of years younger than her mom would've been. She and Stuart married so young—right out of high school. Shadow came along a couple of years later. I always said she and her mama grew up together."

Violet froze. It was hard to comprehend that she could be nearly old enough to have a sixteen-year-old. And here she'd not even started on a family. "I have no idea if she would open up to me. I'm good with small kids, when just giving them a stick of gum or a lollipop makes you automatically cool." She grinned. "But I'm pretty sure a teenager might think I'm kind of lame."

"You're no such thing." Grandma patted her on the arm. "*I* happen to think you're very cool if it's any consolation."

Violet giggled. "Thanks, Grandma. You're pretty cool yourself."

"Are you ready to go next door?" Mrs. Kemp asked. She fished around in a drawer beneath the cash register. "Here's the key."

Violet took it. Would this turn out to be a blessing or a waste of time? Only one way to find out. "I'm ready."

"I'm going to let you go over first," Grandma said. "See what you think without me butting in." She smiled. "But then I'll come over and give you my opinion."

Violet laughed as she walked out into the September humidity. It was a nice spot for a shop. She could see Bathhouse Row from where she stood. Tourists from all over would pass by and might be unable to resist a cupcake. She unlocked the door to the empty building and stepped inside.

The sparsely decorated space had a lot of potential. Violet could already imagine how it would look with a fresh coat of paint and maybe a mix-and-match set of tables and chairs. Reagan could help her with the design.

She ran her hand along the counter and peered into the glass case that likely had once housed sandwiches and salads. But it would look even better with her cupcakes inside.

She sat down in a lone wooden chair in the corner and the wobbly leg explained why it had been left behind. Could she do this?

It would be a lot of work. A business plan, marketing, financing. She knew a little about those things but not a ton.

And baking for real customers scared her. She'd loved to bake in law school. Her favorite part of study groups had been baking goodies to get her group through the long nights. Making cupcakes and cakes for friends' birthdays and special occasions was one of her favorite hobbies.

But could she pour herself into a business venture without knowing what the outcome would be? It all seemed so scary.

Lord, am I crazy? No. Don't answer that. Just help me make the right decision. Please show me the path to take and give me the courage to take it. Amen.

She opened her eyes as Grandma walked inside.

"Well? It's perfect, isn't it?"

Violet nodded. "More than I ever could've imagined."

Grandma walked around the space. "So much potential. Don't you love the high ceilings? And that bead board wall? A little paint on that and it would look so pretty."

"It is my style, that's for sure." Violet stood up. "Let's go look at the kitchen."

She followed her grandmother into the good-sized kitchen and could immediately picture herself there. Baking. Icing. Creating new recipes.

Happy.

"Change has never been easy for me," she said.

Grandma nodded. "It isn't easy for anyone. And if they say it is, they're pulling your leg."

"What if I fail?" Violet whispered.

Grandma put an arm around Violet's shoulders. "I can tell you this. You'll never succeed if you don't try. And to me, that would be the real failure."

Violet considered the advice. "I'm going to sleep on it."

"I'll be praying."

Violet hugged her grandmother. "Me, too."

Dear Mama,

Well, I'm in trouble with Nana. As usual. I texted her to let her know I'd be back to the store a little later than I was supposed to be, but instead of waiting there for me, she drove her big old Buick to the tennis courts. It was so mortifying. Chase thinks I'm a total baby now because my grandmother came and made me get in the car so we could go home.

I have my driver's license. I don't understand why they treat me like a baby. Granddaddy told me that I'd have to prove to them that I was responsible enough to borrow the car and that so far I hadn't because I kept missing curfews and not doing chores. That's really only happened twice, and I said I was sorry. They make a big deal about nothing. Daddy didn't care about stuff like that. I wish I could just go back to Texas, except that I'm an outsider there, too, now that the new baby is here.

Did you ever feel like you didn't belong anywhere? That's how I've felt ever since you've been gone. I'm living up to my name and turning into a shadow that no one even notices or listens to.

What if I never fit in anywhere and have to live in some hut in the woods like Thoreau? (See, I was paying attention in lit class last year despite what Mr. Baker said on my report card. . . .)

Ily,
Shadow

Chapter 11

Mom: THIS NONSENSE HAS GONE ON LONG ENOUGH, VIOLET. IT'S BAD ENOUGH THAT I HAD TO HEAR ABOUT YOUR RESIGNATION FROM YOUR FATHER, BUT NOW MY OWN MOTHER INFORMS ME THAT YOU'RE IN HOT SPRINGS. AND YOU WON'T ANSWER YOUR PHONE. EVER. WHAT IS GOING ON? (Text message sent September 7, 5:02 p.m.)

Violet Matthews: I LOVE YOU, MOM. I'LL FILL YOU IN SOON. DON'T WORRY. (Text message sent September 7, 6:11 p.m.)

Violet sank into the comfy deck chair and leaned her head back. She'd called the Realtor this morning, and the man had graciously offered to give her one more day to consider things.

Grandma and Grandpa had tried to get her to go to dinner with them, but she'd declined. It was best that she stay focused. She'd made endless pro and con lists throughout the day and still came up uncertain.

She took a sip of water and stared out at Lake Hamilton. It was so beautiful here. A definite pro. She loved the outdoors, and moving to Hot Springs would give her endless opportunities to hike, fish, and water ski.

But would she really be happy here?

The distant sound of a doorbell interrupted her thoughts. Surely Mom hadn't found out where she was staying and driven over. She'd made it clear through her barrage of texts and voice mails that Violet was crazy for resigning and was clearly just going through some kind of "my little sister is getting married instead of me" brand of crisis.

As if.

Violet hurried through the house and banged her knee on an end table.

The bell rang twice in succession, followed by a series of knocks.

"Just a minute." She rubbed her knee. She just wanted peace and quiet. She peeked through the peephole and jumped back.

Jackson Stratford.

She glanced in the mirror above the offending end table. Her hair had air dried that morning, and it curled around her face like a lion's mane. Big hair might be her special talent. She hadn't bothered with makeup either.

The doorbell rang again. "Violet?" he called.

It irritated her that she looked so disheveled. Not because she wanted to impress Jackson, but because she hated to give him the satisfaction of seeing her less than perfect. She needed to be on her toes to deal with him, and looking all bare-faced and wild-haired put her at a disadvantage.

A girl needed her confidence to face someone like him.

Oh well. Violet opened the door. "Yes?" She crossed her arms.

He grinned. "Sorry about showing up like this. I called the house a couple of times, but you must not have heard the ring."

"Oh I heard it. I just didn't think it was my place to answer it." She'd had a suspicion it might be him calling to check in on her, but hadn't wanted to speak to him. Which, come to think of it, was probably a little rude considering he was letting her stay for free. "Sorry about that."

"Can I come in?"

She managed a smile. "It's your house. It's not like I could say no, could I?"

He chuckled and walked inside. "Well, I know I promised you peace and quiet."

"I've definitely had that." She narrowed her eyes. "Until now anyway."

Jackson didn't even have the decency to look sorry. Instead he grinned. "Come on now, you were probably ready for some conversation."

She ignored his comment. "It's an amazing space." She motioned to where Arnie slept on his bed in a corner. "Arnie sure thinks so."

Jackson nodded. "I see." He pointed at a closed door. "The vacuum is in there in case you want to make sure there's no dog hair left behind." He grinned. "If I were going into politics, that'd be a program of mine. No dog hair left behind."

"Ha-ha." His jokes were as corny as ever. "I'll have you know that Arnie doesn't shed like some dogs." She bent down to give

Arnie a pat on the head. "But I'd be happy to vacuum before we leave just the same."

"Thanks. I hate the thought of dog hair on the floor." He smiled. "The way I'm always vacuuming and sweeping drives my sister crazy every time her family visits. She always accuses me of being OCD about stuff like that. It's why I'd never have an inside dog."

"Never?" She couldn't imagine life without a dog in the house.

He shook his head. "Nope. Way too much trouble. Plus they'd dig up the yard."

"And provide unconditional love and companionship. Or is that something you don't know anything about?" She couldn't help it. He was crazy.

Jackson held up his hands. "Whoa there. I'm just telling you my position on inside animals. Don't get defensive."

"I'm sorry. I'm just offended on Arnie's behalf. He's a great dog. I can guarantee that your life would be more complete with a dog like him in it."

"Yeah. Completely full of dog hair." He snickered.

She glared. "You're impossible."

"I could say the same thing about you."

Violet sighed. The last thing she wanted was an argument. "Listen, if there's a problem with me and Arnie staying tonight, we can pack up. No big deal." There was surely a pet friendly hotel nearby. Or she could just drive home and come back tomorrow if she needed to.

"Don't be silly. I'm just giving you a hard time." He plopped down on the leather couch. "Besides, I need to talk to you."

She eyed him suspiciously. What was he up to? "What about?"

He pulled a folded piece of paper from his pocket. "This." He tossed it on the coffee table.

She scooped it up and unfolded it, quickly scanning the scrawled words. "A dating contract? You're crazy if you think I would ever agree to this." She couldn't believe he still thought she would agree to be his faux girlfriend. She thrust the contract back at him.

"It's more than fair." He smiled. "Besides, it's already September. Isn't the wedding in three months? Do you really think if you open a business and move, you're going to have time to find a suitable date?"

Violet scowled. Amber had texted her this morning to see if she wanted her invitation to be for "Violet Matthews and guest" or not. "First of all, I haven't made up my mind about moving. And second of all, what makes you think you're so suitable?"

He laughed. "Man, you really don't like me." He raked his fingers through his hair. "Don't you think we could let bygones be bygones, at least until January? I mean. . .we're in the same age bracket, both intelligent, reasonably attractive, and neither looking for a real relationship. What more do we need?"

"Reasonably attractive?" She couldn't decide how offended to be.

He gave her a sideways glance. "You fishing for a compliment?"

She didn't respond. How bad would the next few months of her life be if she agreed to this? She wasn't sure they'd make it through without killing one another. "Not at all. I assume you were talking about yourself when you said *reasonably* attractive."

Jackson grinned. "Come on. It will be one less thing you have to do. And frankly, one less thing that I have to do. My sister and friends are on my case. If I could just get them to back off for a few months, I could breathe easy."

"And then what?"

"We stage a breakup. Nothing that makes either of us look bad though. Maybe we don't see eye to eye on something important." He motioned at Arnie. "Like what to do with your inside dog."

She thought for a moment. "Fine. Let me see the contract." She held her hand out.

"It's pretty straightforward," Jackson began. "Four months. Thirty dates."

"That's too many."

He sighed. "Twenty-five dates and three weekend trips."

She widened her eyes. "Trips? Seriously?"

Jackson nodded. "We want to make this believable, right? One trip to Fayetteville for a Razorback football game. One trip to Memphis to see my sister." He grinned. "The other can be your choice."

She shook her head. "Twenty-five dates and a football game in Little Rock instead. Then one trip to your sister's."

"Tough negotiator."

"I'm a lawyer." She tapped the paper. "And what is this about professional events?"

"My office Christmas party in early December. And I'll attend one event of your choice."

She met his gaze. "Fine. What else?"

"Holidays. Specifically Christmas and Thanksgiving. We'll do Thanksgiving with my family. Christmas with yours."

She shook her head. "Yes to Thanksgiving. No to Christmas. It would be too soon for me to take a guy home for Christmas."

He stood up and grabbed a pen from the end table. "Fine." He took the paper from her and scribbled a note in the margin. "Now for the fun one."

She raised an eyebrow. "What's that?"

"Time to negotiate our physical relationship." He grinned.

Violet's face flamed. If Jackson Stratford thought they were going to have any kind of physical relationship, he was dead wrong. "There is nothing to negotiate."

His blue eyes danced. "That's where you're wrong."

Jackson couldn't believe she'd gone for it. He'd fully expected his plan to be rejected again. But she'd at least semi-agreed. "No couple who dates for four months isn't going to at least hold hands and kiss a little. We aren't Quakers."

She crossed her arms. "Not a chance."

Jackson sighed and walked over to where she stood. "Come on, Violet. Hear me out. I'm not proposing we make out like teenagers every chance we get. This would be very dignified and would only make our relationship more believable."

Violet shook her head. "No way."

"Five kisses. One at each of our big events and three just for fun." He grinned at the scowl on her pretty face. She was so much fun to mess with.

She rolled her eyes. "I don't kiss for sport."

"Fine. Three. One at each event and one that can be our first kiss story. You know. . .to keep it legit."

Violet's green eyes flashed. "You are incorrigible."

"Do people really use that word in sentences?"

"I just did, so I guess so. Why? Do I need to get you a dictionary? I know you're used to dealing with bubble heads, so maybe I'm too advanced for you." She smiled. "I'll try and dumb it down from now on."

"You exasperate me." He winked. "See what I did there? Maybe I don't need that dictionary after all."

She glared. "Do you have no concept of personal space?"

Jackson hadn't realized it, but he'd been moving closer and closer to her. He took a long look at her full lips. He could just kiss her now. Take her by surprise. Of course she'd probably hit him and toss him out. "Guess not." He smiled and took a step back. "Seriously though. I'm not just being some typical guy, trying to take advantage of you. I'm just saying, if we're going to pull off a faux relationship, we're going to have to make it look real. That means holding my hand and hugging me sometimes. I know it repulses you, but surely you can handle it." He didn't want to mention that he was kind of looking forward to knowing if her lips were as soft as they looked.

"So this relationship would have everything but—"

"But feelings." He cut her off. "No strings. No commitment after January. We'll just mutually part ways and continue along our separate paths." He grinned. "But we agree not to tell anyone. At all. No one."

She frowned. "So I'm supposed to let my best friend think this is real?"

"Only way it works is for us to keep it between the two of us. Oh, and I'll need you to change your Facebook relationship status."

She groaned and sank onto the couch. "I can't believe I'm considering this."

Jackson sat down next to her. "There's nothing to lose. You and I are a terrible match, and we both know it. For one, I'd never have an inside dog." His eyes landed on a pile of notebook paper she'd scribbled on and an empty Dr Pepper bottle. "And I'm much neater than you are."

"There are plenty of things I don't like about you, too. Don't think I've forgotten what happened in college. And I don't care if it was eleven years ago. You made a fool out of me. Not only did I graduate a semester late thanks to the incomplete we got on that project, but Clay Wells broke up with me because of you."

Jackson had hoped she'd forgotten that. "I was a jerk and I know it." He put a hand on her arm. "And if it helps, you dodged a bullet with Clay. I heard he lives somewhere out West and is a rodeo clown."

She raised her eyebrows.

"I'm not making it up." He chose not to mention that Clay was also a doctor by day. "I'm not the guy I used to be. I've learned a lot of lessons since then. Just give me a chance." He grinned and hoped his charm still worked. "I'll be the best fake boyfriend you could ever hope to have." He stuck a hand out. "Do we have a deal?"

Violet hesitated, the uncertainty flickering in her eyes. "Add moving to the list."

"What?" he asked.

She tapped the paper in his hand. "I think my fake boyfriend will be glad to help me move all my stuff from Little Rock to Hot Springs. Especially the heavy stuff."

He was pretty sure he saw the hint of a smile in her eyes, but couldn't be positive. "Fine. So, deal?"

Violet took a breath. Finally, she extended her hand. "Deal."

Jackson took her hand and shook it firmly. This might go down as the greatest idea he'd ever had.

He ignored the niggling thought that it could also be a disaster.

Violet would help him get Lauren, Jeff, and Kathleen off his back. And maybe she'd help take his mind off his mom's newfound dating life.

Only time would tell.

Chapter 12

Reagan McClure: Just listened to your voice mail—
or was that someone pretending to be you? Moving.
Dinner with Jackson. What happened to the Violet
I know??? (Text message sent September 9, 2:23 p.m.)

Violet Matthews: I needed to talk it out with you,
but couldn't get you on the phone. Sorry for the
frantic message. I decided to go for it with the
bakery! And I found an awesome house for rent.
Dinner with Jackson was a fluke. I think. (Text
message sent September 9, 2:39 p.m.)

R eagan used to be the kind of person who never missed her
Sunday afternoon nap. But it had been a long time since she'd
had that luxury. "Good lesson at church this morning, don't you
think?" she asked Chad once the kids were down.

"Sure was." He grinned. "Do you remember when I wanted to
be a preacher?"

She nodded. "You would've been great."

Chad sat down on the couch and patted the seat next to him. "Want to watch a movie or something?"

She knew if she sat down, she'd never get up until one of the kids woke. After two trips to the gym, she was so sore she could barely move. "I need to start on the laundry, and it would be great if you could stay here with the kids for an hour or so while I run to the grocery store."

Chad groaned. "Why don't you stay here now and go to the store later in the week?"

She put her hands on her hips. "Have you ever gone to the store with three kids? They take up most of the room in the cart, not to mention the inevitable meltdown Ava Grace has in the cereal aisle."

"My mom would be glad to help out." He raised an eyebrow. "You could call her to watch the kids while you go to the store."

They had the same argument at least twice a week. "Or you could just stay with them for a little while today and let me go get the errands done. Then we won't have to worry about it for at least another week."

Chad clicked on the TV. "Fine."

She grabbed her list and her purse and headed out the door. There had been a time when Sunday afternoons were for the two of them. Back when Izzy was a baby, they'd put her down for a nap and then lay on the couch and talk. No TV or anything. She couldn't remember the last time she and Chad had only focused on each other.

As she backed out of the driveway, the phone buzzed against the console. She glanced at the caller ID and hit the SPEAKER button. "I guess congratulations are in order," she said.

"You think I'm crazy, don't you?" Violet's voice filled the van. "Do you think it's a mistake?"

Reagan laughed. "Not about the bakery. Maybe about dinner last night with Jackson Stratford." The guy had done such a number on Violet back in college. Not only had his halfhearted effort on their project caused real problems for her in class, but he'd also insinuated that there was something going on between the two of them. Violet's boyfriend at the time had totally bought it and dumped her. It had been a terrible summer for Violet as she made up the class and dealt with a broken heart. "I'm not sure I trust him."

"It was just dinner," Violet said. "I think maybe he's trying to make up for some of the dumb stuff he did. Besides. . .people can change, right?"

Reagan didn't like the direction this conversation was headed. Was Violet seriously interested in the guy? "I know that matchmaker said y'all should give things a shot, but she wasn't there for you back when your world exploded and your heart was broken. I was. I'm just not sure it's a smart move, that's all."

Violet didn't say anything for a long moment. "But how about the bakery? Do you think that's a good idea?"

"That one I'm totally behind. In fact, I'm very proud of you for going after your dream. It's been a long time coming. And my offer to help with the logo and some of the design work stands." She flipped on her blinker at the red light next to Sam's Club. "Of course, you might have to house me and four kids for a few days while we work on things."

Violet laughed. "Y'all are welcome to stay. Grandma would be happy to help with the kids. And Mrs. Kemp's granddaughter probably would, too. She's going to work in the bakery once it opens. I talked to her about it today after church. I think she's super excited, but she's too cool to show it."

"The Goth girl? Are you sure that's going to be good for business?"

"Oh, she's not Goth anymore. Now she's all sporty. Wears tennis skirts and ponytails. She even lightened her hair some."

Reagan pulled into a parking space and turned off the van. "That's quite a change, huh?"

"I can't quite figure it out. She seems kind of lost. Drifting. I mean, my mom and I have certainly had our differences, but I can't imagine having grown up without her."

Reagan's eyes filled with unexpected tears. The thought of her kids growing up without her guidance filled her with sadness. There were so many things she hoped to teach them someday. So many milestones she looked forward to sharing with them. "That's tough. What about her dad?"

"Remarried, new baby. I get the impression that he doesn't know what to do with her, and the stepmother tries too hard to be her friend and not an actual parent."

Reagan hurried into the store. She figured she had thirty minutes before one of the kids woke up and Chad called to tell her to come home. "Maybe it's good that she'll be working with you. Sounds like she could use a good role model."

Violet laughed. "I wouldn't call myself that, but I did tell Mrs.

Kemp I'd spend some time with Shadow—take her shopping, that kind of thing."

"Sounds like a great plan. So what's the deal with the bakery?"

"I can't wait for you to see the place. It's perfect. I'm working on a business plan right now, just trying to figure out what all needs to happen between now and an opening. I want to move on things as quickly as possible."

"It does my heart good to hear how excited you are. I know how frustrated you've been, career-wise."

"This might fail. It might be the worst decision ever. But I would always wonder what might've happened. You know? I've recently spent a lot of time praying and thinking about this, and I really feel like this is the best plan for me."

"I'm so glad. And I'm excited about helping. I think it will do me some good to feel useful."

"You are already useful and you know it. Your husband and kids would be lost without you."

"You're sweet to say so, but I don't always feel that way." She put a package of paper towels in the cart. "But the gym is going well."

"What does Chad think about it?"

Reagan didn't say anything. She hated to admit that she hadn't told him yet. "He doesn't exactly know."

"You need to tell him. Secrets aren't good."

"I don't know how successful this will be. I'm so sore today, it's hard to walk. This morning I thought I was going to cry just trying to get Scarlett out of her car seat."

"I'm pretty sure Chad will be thrilled that you're doing something for yourself."

Reagan let out a bitter laugh. "Chad is at home right now on the couch. I'm at the grocery store. If he were too concerned, wouldn't he have offered to do the shopping?"

"No. You know that you have certain brands and certain ways you do things. Remember when we lived together and I bought the wrong kind of toothpaste? You'd have thought I'd committed a federal crime."

"I'm not that bad. I just know what I like."

Violet sighed loudly. "But wouldn't it be easier to let him help you rather than feeling like you have to do it all yourself? Couldn't you deal with a different brand of toilet paper or toothpaste if it meant your husband pitched in?"

Reagan didn't answer for a long moment. "Are you trying to say I'm a control freak?"

"Maybe a little. You've tried to be Superwoman for so long that I'm sure Chad doesn't think he could measure up to your expectations. Didn't you tell me that you got mad at him over coffee creamer a few weeks ago?"

Reagan winced. She'd forgotten about that. "He got the wrong kind. I like a certain flavor."

"Don't you think you could deal with the wrong flavor if it meant you didn't have to go to the store?"

"You don't understand. We've been married for ten years. He should *know* what kind of coffee creamer I like. That's the reason I get so upset. Because these things aren't rocket science. I'll bet you know my favorite coffee creamer flavor, don't you?"

"Hazelnut."

Reagan nodded. "Yep. How do you think it makes me feel that

my husband can't even pay enough attention to me to get that small detail correct? I've been drinking my coffee the same for years. He just doesn't notice."

"I'm sorry. I wish you'd talk to him and y'all would figure out a way to work on things. Maybe a marriage seminar or something."

That would be the day. "I don't think we'd be able to find the time for something like that. I just have to hope that when the twins get a little older, things will get easier." It was what Reagan had to cling to these days. Because she couldn't deal with the alternative.

Dear Mama,

I'm trying out for the tennis team. Can you believe it? I've been working with Chase and think I might really enjoy it. He says he's going to play in college. Maybe I will, too.

And a woman named Violet is opening a bakery next door to Aunt Teak's. Nana says I can work there after school if I want to. I talked to Violet about it. She's kind of a funny person. Nana calls her quirky. She's always wearing these dresses that look like they should be in black-and-white movies. She even has a bunch of old books and a typewriter at her house. I think it's kind of weird that she likes all that old stuff.

I wish you were here. Violet told me that she remembered you from when you were teenagers and she'd come visit her grandmother. She said that one summer y'all worked together at Aunt Teak's. I guess I like her a little more now that I know she knew you when you were my age.

Love,
Shadow

Violet put the last of her belongings into a box and taped it shut. She'd passed being tired hours ago and was headed full into the land of exhaustion. But it was worth it. During the past few days, she'd moved from disbelief over her decision through panic and had finally arrived at excitement.

She was opening her own bakery. Her own bakery!

It had been her dream since law school, maybe earlier. Some of her fondest memories as a child included standing up on the bar-stool next to Grandma, stirring the batter or learning to make homemade icing.

Cupcakes made people happy. And making people happy gave Violet a sense of accomplishment. She liked to feel that she'd brightened someone's day.

The doorbell rang, and she jumped up to get it.

"I think you should reconsider. It isn't too late." Mom barged in as soon as Violet opened the door. "You don't know what you're doing. You've never operated a business. There's much more to it than just baking some cakes and wearing a cute apron."

Violet sighed. "I'm sorry I didn't include you in my decision, Mom. But this is just something I have to do. If it fails miserably, I can go back to a law firm."

Mom paced the living room. "But you belong in the family firm. I know you're disappointed that Landry was made partner. But there's no need for a knee-jerk reaction like this."

Violet picked up a box and added it to the stack in the corner. She'd found the perfect house to rent in Hot Springs with plenty of room for her stuff and a great yard for Arnie. The papers were signed, and Jackson had promised to be there with a truck first thing Saturday morning. She had to admit, having a fake boyfriend during a move was quite convenient—even if it was Jackson. "That's the thing. This isn't a knee-jerk reaction. And it honestly has nothing to do with Landry."

Mom opened her mouth to speak, but Violet cut her off.

"Or Amber. This isn't about not being made partner or my sister getting married. This is about me taking control of my life and doing something that I've always dreamed of. Did the timing of those things help push me? Sure. But this isn't something I just thought of—it's something I've wanted for a long time."

"Honey, I just want what's best for you. And I can't see that taking such a big financial risk is what's best."

So that's what it was about. Money. "I've always been a saver. You know that. I have money saved up, and I'm already in the process of obtaining a small business loan. I'll be okay. People start businesses every day."

"And they fail every day, too."

Violet blew out a breath. "Can't you just be supportive? One time. Support my dreams."

"Not when your dream has the potential to end in disaster. Not to mention—how are you ever going to meet anyone suitable if you're always holed up in a bakery? And you'll be wearing awful clothes and all covered in flour. Not exactly the most attractive way for a single girl to be."

It was time to drop her bomb. "For your information, I'm seeing someone." Violet wished she had a camera to capture the shocked expression on her mother's face. "He works for the state in economic development. In fact, he's helping me with my business plan *and* coordinating my move." Sweet satisfaction.

"And you didn't tell me?" Mom raised her eyebrows. "How could you leave something like that out? Is he your plus one at the wedding? Amber told me you'd requested two spots at the rehearsal dinner and reception, but I figured you were just hoping to have a date by then."

Violet had been on the fence all week over her arrangement with Jackson. But in that moment, she knew she'd made the right decision by agreeing to his contract. "That's right, Mom. He'll be with me at the wedding."

And then she'd go play supportive girlfriend at his speech. And the week after his speech, they'd go their separate ways. What a beautiful plan.

Chapter 13

Jackson Stratford: Dinner Friday night? I know you're anxious to mark some of those contracted dates off the list. . . . (Text message sent September 13, 1:12 p.m.)

Violet Matthews: Did you really just ask me out via text? Just FYI, if this weren't a ruse, I'd say no. Friday's fine. Pick me up at 7. (Text message sent September 13, 1:17 p.m.)

Jackson walked past a For Rent sign on the way to Violet's front porch. He hadn't seen her all week, but they'd texted a few times. Mostly details about tomorrow's move. He knocked on the door and waited.

The door swung open. "Come on in." Violet ushered him inside.

The living room was littered with boxes and plastic totes. "I don't know if I could sleep in a house this chaotic." He grinned. "And you have so much stuff."

She made a face. "I'm sure you'd manage, Mr. OCD. I'm sorry that my chaos and clutter offends you so much." She grinned and motioned toward Arnie, who slept on a rug in between two stacks of boxes. "My super shedding dog doesn't seem to mind."

Jackson couldn't help but laugh. "Poke fun all you want."

Violet grabbed her purse and cell phone from the coffee table. "I won't make you stay in this mess any longer than necessary. Let's go."

"I've never seen you in jeans before," he said as they walked out the door. "What gives?" Not that he was complaining.

She grinned. "Well I didn't want to show you up by being the better dressed portion of a *reasonably* attractive couple."

He chuckled. "Are you always going to remember every dumb thing I say?" He opened the passenger door of the Range Rover, and she climbed inside.

"Probably. At least until the week after your speech." She grinned. "Then I won't care."

Jackson got in the car and glanced over at her. "So I was thinking. . ."

"First time for everything," she said with a laugh, cutting him off.

He pulled out of the driveway and headed down the street. "Very funny." He cleared his throat. "As I was saying. I was thinking that we should fast-track the whole 'getting to know each other' portion of things."

"And how do you propose we do that?"

"I'll text you a question. You answer it. You text me a question. I'll answer it." He grinned. "That way we can be a believable couple in a shorter amount of time."

Violet sighed. "Okay."

"I'll have you know that texting isn't my favorite form of communication, so I'm kind of making a concession here."

"How gallant of you."

Jackson merged onto the interstate. "Where do you want to eat?"

"Someplace where I can get vegetables. That isn't crowded. Or too expensive. How about Cracker Barrel?" She looked over at him. "And it just occurred to me that we haven't discussed money."

"Money?"

"This relationship is not real. I don't expect you to pay for dinners and things."

Jackson hadn't even thought about it. "It's four months. I'd go on at least twenty-five dates over the course of four months. So I'd be paying that money anyway." He shrugged.

"You'd go on twenty-five dates in four months? Where do you find these girls?"

"Jealous?" He grinned.

She laughed. "Hardly. I'm just mystified."

"For your information, I meet them everywhere. Starbucks. The gym. Work." He shrugged. "Church."

"You go to church?" From the incredulous tone to her voice, he may as well have said he met women on the moon.

Jackson was beginning to get irritated. "Yes. I go to church. In fact, I even teach the Wednesday night men's Bible class."

Violet sputtered. "Wonders never cease."

"There's a lot about me that you don't know. If you'd just throw out any preconceived notions you formed about me all those years ago, you might find that I'm actually a pretty nice guy."

Violet fell silent. Finally she cleared her throat. "I'm sorry. I didn't mean anything by that. It's just that I remember you as being something of a wild man back in college."

"I've done things I'm not proud of. But that was a long time ago." He gave her a sideways glance. "I've changed a lot." He frowned. "But you haven't."

He drove in silence the rest of the way to the restaurant.

Maybe this had been a bad idea after all. Violet might never see him as anything more than the guy he'd been in college. And even he could admit that guy hadn't been the greatest.

But didn't everyone deserve a second chance?

Violet was pretty sure she'd hurt his feelings. She'd just been so shocked at the thought of him teaching a Bible class that she'd not been able to control her mouth. "I really didn't mean to offend you," she said as he pulled into a space at Cracker Barrel. "I was just surprised."

Jackson turned off the ignition and turned to face her. "I'm not proud of the guy I was back then. I know I wasn't exactly walking on the straight and narrow. But I've done a lot of growing up since then." He gave her a tentative smile. "At least I own up to my mistakes."

She sighed. "Do you think I'm too judgmental?"

"I think maybe you just don't trust me." He took the keys from the ignition. "Yet." He shrugged. "And that's fine. There's plenty of time for that, and besides, in order for our plan to work, you don't have to trust me. You don't even have to like me."

"I just have to pretend that I do," she said softly.

Jackson nodded. "That's right. Let's see how good of an actress you are."

She laughed. "I was the lead in a play when I was in fifth grade. That's the extent of my acting experience until now."

Jackson opened the door for her and helped her out. He reached over and took her hand as they walked toward the restaurant.

She tensed.

"Easy there. I'm not going to bite. Just practicing." He dropped her hand at the door and held the door open. "After you."

Violet brushed past him, and her heart beat faster. Holding hands meant he'd be pushing for their fake first kiss soon. It had been so long since she'd kissed a guy. What if she'd forgotten how? Stupid Zach had really done a number on her.

"You okay?" Jackson asked once he'd put their names on the waiting list for a table.

She nodded. "Just thinking."

"Moving is overwhelming, huh? And starting a new business on top of it."

Violet smiled. "I'm overwhelmed, but in such a wonderful way. I've dreamed of doing this for such a long time. Now that I've made the decision, everything is just falling into place."

"God's plans are always better than we expect."

She looked into his blue eyes. Sincere blue eyes. "Aren't they though?"

Jackson smiled. "Once I finished my master's at Auburn I had the same kind of thing happen. I'd prayed and prayed that I'd find the job that was right for me. And then the job in Mobile came open, and it was perfection. Trusting that God would lead me in the right direction was hard, but once I opened myself up to things besides just what I wanted or what I thought was best, I ended up getting the perfect offer."

"I didn't know you had your master's."

He nodded. "Yep. I think that was really the time in my life when I grew the most. I wasn't at a Christian school any longer and wasn't surrounded by Christians. It was very difficult at first to make good choices, but eventually I found my own faith. There were some dark days, but ultimately I think it was the time when my Christian walk started—apart from what my parents believed or my friends believed. I searched and questioned and developed my own relationship with the Lord."

Violet was impressed by his candor. Maybe she'd underestimated him. "That's an amazing story. And I know what you mean. It's easy to make good choices when you're surrounded by people who come from the same kind of background as you. I lived in DC for a little while after law school. I loved the city, but I was faced with things I'd never been faced with before. I'm glad, though, because ultimately it made me stronger."

"Skywalker, your table is now available."

Jackson took her hand. "That's us."

"Skywalker?" she hissed. "Seriously?"

He grinned. "It's a thing I do sometimes. Call me Luke in front of the hostess." He squeezed her hand and led her to the hostess stand.

She burst out laughing. Jackson might not be the uptight guy she had him pegged to be.

Come to think of it, he might have some layers to him that she hadn't expected.

Dear Mama,

Chase and I broke up. And right after I spent all my money on a fancy tennis racquet. The store won't take it back either.

Nana says I can sell it on eBay or something, but I'll never get my money back. And I made a C on my history quiz.

So I'm having kind of a terrible week. Daddy called to see if I'd come to Texas for Thanksgiving. To tell the truth, I don't really want to. Stephanie will try to be my BFF and take me shopping and stuff. But she doesn't understand me at all. She keeps sending me these e-mails that say she wants to be my friend and be involved in my life and wants me to come back to Texas and be a good big sister.

But I don't want to. It makes my heart hurt to be there because I don't understand how Daddy could forget about you. I haven't forgotten. So why did he?

Oh, and I met a guy in the library the other day. His name is Thomas, and he is on the Quiz Bowl team. He has the cutest glasses. I think he is going to ask me out.

I miss you,
Shadow

Chapter 14

Jackson Stratford: Hope unpacking is going well. What's your favorite band? (Text message sent September 18, 10:34 a.m.)

Violet Matthews: Thanks for helping unload. Unpacking is a pain. Be glad you aren't here for the CHAOS. Ha. And U2. Or Bon Jovi. The old-school stuff from the late '80s. You? (Text message sent September 18, 10:39 a.m.)

Jackson Stratford: Remember that less is best. Want me to come throw some of that stuff out for you? I'm going with something more classic: The Beatles. (Text message sent September 18, 10:42 a.m.)

Violet opened the back door and let Arnie run into the fenced-in yard. This place was perfect. Not too far from the shop, but in a rural area. She couldn't believe it had been for rent, and the

Realtor had told her if she liked it, there was a chance the owners might want to sell.

She adored everything about the place, especially the big yard and big kitchen—two of her must-haves. And while three bedrooms seemed like a lot for one person, she planned to turn one into an office and have a guest room set up so Reagan could come visit.

The Lord had certainly blessed her.

She glanced around the sunny kitchen. It would be easy to get overwhelmed by all the things that needed to be done. Not only did she have a house to put in some kind of order, but she also had to make a lot of decisions about the business. Starting with a catchy name.

Her phone buzzed.

Jackson.

She picked up on the third ring. "The Beatles? Really?"

He laughed. "I'm a classy guy. I appreciate the finer things in life, which includes really good music."

"I guess." She took the tape off of a box labeled KITCHEN UTENSILS and began to unpack. "So what's going on? You trying to break the contract already?"

"Not a chance. Actually, I was calling to see what you have planned for Saturday."

"I guess I'll be unpacking and organizing. Why?" She peeked out the window to check on Arnie. The sweet dog was wriggling in the grass.

"It's the Legends Balloon Rally. I thought we might go to some of the festivities."

Violet wrinkled her nose. "I don't know. I'm a little overwhelmed here, trying to get settled and starting to work at the shop. I'm planning on painting the inside pretty soon."

"That's exactly the reason we need to go to the festival. You'll need a break by then. We'll eat, listen to some music, and watch the hot air balloons. It'll be awesome."

She sighed. "I just have so much to do."

"Tell you what. I'll stay at the lake house on Saturday night so I can help you paint on Sunday afternoon."

Violet thought for a moment. "Can we count painting as one of the contracted dates?"

He chuckled. "You never stop negotiating, do you?"

"Nope."

Jackson let out a heavy sigh. "Okay, fine. Saturday night and Sunday will each count toward the twenty-five *if* we grab dinner on Sunday. We'll be rid of each other before you know it."

She opened another box. "Sounds like a plan. What time will you be here on Saturday?"

"How about late afternoon? That'll give us time to go to the festival first, and then we'll have dinner. Maybe five?"

"See you then." Violet hung up and put the phone back on the counter. She'd never been to a hot air balloon festival before, but had always heard about it. Inevitably, they would run into her grandparents. It had been forever since she'd introduced a guy to anyone in her family. Not since Zach.

Reagan shimmied across the floor trying to keep up with the beat of the music. Maggie had finally talked her into a Zumba class, and Reagan had figured if a woman Maggie's age could handle it, so could she.

She'd been wrong.

Her whole body hurt, and she was pretty sure things were jiggling that weren't supposed to jiggle. She avoided the full wall mirror at all costs so she wouldn't see how stupid she looked.

"You're doing great," Maggie called. "Isn't it fun?"

Reagan gasped for breath and nodded. "It's different, that's for sure."

The music ended. "Water break," the instructor called.

Reagan collapsed on the floor. "The last time I huffed and puffed this much, I was in labor with the twins."

Maggie laughed. "How is everything going now that you've had a few weeks of exercise? Is your head clearer?"

Reagan leaned back and stared at the ceiling. "I think so. I feel better and seem to have more energy."

"What's your hubby say?" Maggie asked.

Reagan sat up. "I haven't told him." She wanted to wait until she'd been a member of the gym for a month. By then she'd know if she was going to stick with it or not.

"Secrets are never good, but I guess this one is going to end up being a pleasant surprise."

"I hope so. I've lost five pounds so far, but you can't really tell." Reagan had been thrilled when she'd seen the scales. Her clothes were starting to fit better, but she still wasn't back to her old size. "It isn't really about the weight, though. I know Chad loves me no matter what."

"You know how men are," Maggie said. "They're visual creatures. I'm sure he appreciates the extra effort."

Reagan sighed. She still felt pretty invisible at home and tried hard to forget that cute, tiny Reese was at Chad's office every day. "I guess."

"Girl, what you need is a romantic date night. Get some of the spark back." Maggie smiled. "Me and my husband took a class at our church several years ago, and the guy who taught it was a marriage counselor. He said date nights were important."

"It's been a long time. But with four kids, it isn't that easy to get a capable sitter." She and Chad hadn't been out just the two of them since before the twins were born. How was that possible?

Maggie smiled. "Do you think sometimes God puts people in your path for a reason?"

"Yes."

"Did I ever mention to you now that I'm retired I work as a nanny? Right now I'm working for a family with two kids, a boy and a girl. They're three and four."

Reagan's eyes widened. She'd just assumed Maggie was retired and had never thought to ask if she had a job. "I didn't know that. Do you enjoy it?"

"I love it. I used to be an elementary school art teacher— got my early childhood degree from the U of A. But I think I might enjoy this more. I didn't get to stay home with my own kids when they were little. The kids I keep are so sweet. Tuesdays and Thursdays are the days their mama works from home, which is how I find time to come here." She grinned.

Reagan had often thought about going back to work part-time and hiring someone to come to the house to keep the kids. But she'd never broached the subject with Chad. He'd always been so traditional that she knew he'd balk at the idea. His mom had stayed home with him and his sisters, and he'd always wanted the same thing for his own kids. "That sounds really nice. I'll bet you're wonderful." How lovely it must be for the family Maggie worked for, especially the mom.

"We're starting again." Maggie stood up. "Come on. Ten more minutes."

Reagan slowly got to her feet and focused on the instructor. Even if she felt stupid waving her arms and shaking her hips, she had to admit it was kind of fun.

Thirty minutes later, she'd loaded the kids in the van and headed toward the house. There'd be enough time for the kids to get a nap and her to get a shower before they loaded up again to get Izzy from school. "Ava Grace, you sit with Simon while I get Scarlett inside." She unhooked Ava Grace's car seat. "Can you sing to him for a minute?" She got Scarlett out of her car seat.

"Hi, baby Simon," Ava Grace said, leaning close to her brother's face.

He cooed.

Reagan grinned as Ava Grace sang "Twinkle, Twinkle, Little Star" to Simon. There might be nothing sweeter than her babies loving on each other.

"Down you go." She put Scarlett in the Pack 'n Play in the living room. "Mama will be right back." Now that the twins were crawling, it made it much more difficult to maneuver. She refused to think of how it would be when they started to walk. Mass chaos came to mind.

As soon as she got Ava Grace and Simon out of the car, her phone rang.

"Hey, babe." She was pleased that Chad had called during the day. That happened less and less often.

"Everyone okay?" he asked.

"I'm about to put the kids down for a nap and jump in the shower." She put Simon in the playpen with Scarlett and turned on the TV for Ava Grace. "Watch Dora for a minute while I talk to Daddy," she whispered.

"Can you look at the calendar for next weekend?"

She walked into the kitchen to the magnetic calendar she kept on the fridge. "Next weekend." She ran her finger along the calendar. It was hard to believe it was almost October. Time sure went by fast. "Ava Grace has been invited to a birthday party for Collin from her Sunday school class. And it's the deadline to sign Izzy up for gymnastics." She peeked through the opening over the counter and checked on the kids. "Why?" She couldn't help but hope he was going to suggest something fun. Maybe he missed their time alone as much as she did.

"I have to go to Miami for a conference. I just wanted to make sure I wouldn't be missing anything big before Reese books my flight."

Reese. Booking a flight to Miami for *her* husband. The uneasy feeling rose through her body. "You won't be missing anything big. Just life with your wife and kids. That's all. Nothing big." She couldn't keep the bitterness out of her voice.

Chad groaned. "Reagan, you know I'd rather stay home. My boss asked me to go in his place."

She fought the urge to ask if Reese was going. That was a conversation she wanted to have in person. "I think I'll take the kids to Hot Springs if you're going to be out of town. We'll visit Violet and check out her new place."

"Are you up for a road trip with all the kids by yourself?"

The fact that he doubted her abilities angered her. Didn't he realize that she took care of the kids by herself most of the time? "I'm pretty used to handling the kids by myself. We'll manage fine." Her eyes filled with tears. Any stress her Zumba class had gotten rid of had come back and brought friends. "I've got to go." She clicked off the phone and leaned against the counter. What if the wedge between them kept growing? Where would that leave them?

There was a cry from the living room. Time to focus on the kids.

And not on her crumbling marriage.

Chapter 15

Daddy: I'M PROUD OF YOU, VIOLET. I'M LOOKING
FORWARD TO THE OPENING OF THE BAKERY. LET ME KNOW
IF THERE'S ANYTHING I CAN DO TO HELP. I LOVE YOU.
DAD. (Text message sent September 22, 8:34 a.m.)

Violet Matthews: THANKS! THAT MEANS A LOT. I'M
WORKING ON NAILING DOWN THE DATE FOR THE GRAND
OPENING. I HOPE YOU AND MOM WILL ATTEND. (Text
message sent September 22, 8:41 a.m.)

Jackson sat on the back deck of his lake house. It was still hard to
think of it as *his* place. His dad had always planned on leaving it
to him, but Jackson had always imagined that would be way down
the road.

After Dad died last year, Mom had wanted him to go ahead and
take ownership. She'd said it was what his dad would've wanted.

It was weird. In the months after Dad's death, lots of people
had speculated what he would've said or would've done or would've

wanted. But Jackson couldn't help but wonder how they could be so sure.

Thinking about his dad filled him with a sadness he hadn't known existed. The death had been so sudden and had come without warning. It had really made Jackson take stock of his life though. Was he the kind of man his dad would've been proud of? He tried to be, but knew he probably failed sometimes.

He pushed the thoughts from his mind and turned his attention to the evening's plans. He'd cooked up a surprise for Violet. Whether she'd like it or not was anyone's guess. She certainly didn't cut him any slack.

Jackson went into the airy kitchen and took stock of the refrigerator's contents. He still needed to get a few items, but for the most part he was ready.

He smiled to himself as he pulled the picnic basket from a shelf in the pantry. This had the potential to be a wonderful night.

His cell phone rang, and he picked it up from the counter.

Jeff.

"Long time no talk."

Jeff chuckled. "The beginning of the school year is busy for kindergartners and their parents. Did you know that?"

"Can't say that I did. What makes it so busy? Don't they just color and stuff?"

Jeff let out a whistle. "No way. Bennett's got homework. It's crazy the way things have changed since we were kids. He's already starting to read."

"I don't know about all of that," Jackson said. "Seems like there should be more time for a kid to just be a kid." He hoped to have kids of his own someday and wanted to make sure his offspring knew the same simple pleasures of childhood that he'd known.

"Bennett's adjusting pretty well though. He seems to like his classmates and teacher a lot, and we're getting ready for his first soccer game. It should be a hoot if it's anything like T-ball was over the summer." The fatherly pride in Jeff's voice was evident. "But that's not why I called."

"What's going on?"

Jeff sighed. "Lauren's been after me to check in on you and see how things are going. So. . .how are things going?"

Jackson laughed. "I'm surprised she hasn't called me herself. I'm happy to report that I have a date tonight. With a woman who knows who Luke Skywalker is and likes the big-haired version of Bon Jovi—not the sleeker, more modern version."

"Got it. I'll relay to Lauren that you're finally dating someone she'd consider age appropriate." He chuckled. "She'll be thrilled."

"In fact, how about the four of us get together sometime soon? I'd love for y'all to meet her." Jackson would have to run it by Violet, but as long as it meant she got to check a date off their list, she'd probably be on board.

"Does this mystery woman have a name? If I don't give a full report, my wife will mercilessly dis my investigative skills."

Jackson grinned. "Violet. Her name's Violet. She's a lawyer but is getting ready to open her own business." He liked saying it. It was a new experience to be proud of someone he was seeing. Even if his relationship with Violet was fake, he was still proud to be associated with a woman like her.

"Impressive. I'm sure Lauren will be impressed, too."

"Well I aim to please."

Jeff laughed. "And we'd love to get together. Just let us know when and where."

"Will do." Jackson hung up and turned his attention back to the refrigerator. He might not be a gourmet cook, but he thought he could win some points for effort.

And considering the way Violet viewed him, he could use all the extra points he could get.

Violet took one last look in the mirror. She'd fought hard to straighten her hair and was pleased with the outcome. Even her mother would approve—she always commented when Violet's hair was less than straight. After thirty-three years of critique, Violet figured she should be immune to it, but that day hadn't come yet.

She stepped into one of her favorite dresses. It wasn't exactly orange, more like tangerine. She loved the lace detail on the bodice and the way it made her waist look tiny. There was a time when Violet would've been afraid it clashed with her red hair, but she got so many compliments when she wore it, she'd decided it was definitely one of her "good" colors, no matter what the woman at Color Me Beautiful had said when Mom had taken her to get her colors done in high school.

The doorbell rang. Jackson was right on time.

She opened the door. "Come in," she said with a smile.

"Wow." Jackson walked inside and looked around. "It's looking good." He ran a hand over the typewriter she had displayed on an antique secretary table she'd found at an estate sale. "And this is very cool."

Violet grinned. "I guess you didn't see that during the move because I had it boxed up. I adore old things." She did a curtsey. "In fact, this dress is vintage. I found it in a little shop in Atlanta last summer."

"It's nice." He returned her grin. "Are you ready? I have some fun stuff planned."

She raised her eyebrows. "You do? More than just going to the festival?"

"Yes."

She waited for him to elaborate, but he didn't. "I'm ready." She knelt down to give Arnie a pat. "Bye, sweet boy."

"Why do you talk to him if he's deaf?" Jackson asked as they walked outside.

"Are you serious?"

He nodded.

She sighed. "Partly habit. I've been talking to him for nearly fifteen years. But also because I don't want him to think I'm upset with him."

"Upset with him?"

Violet shrugged. "I can't imagine how it must be for him to not hear anything now and not understand why. Sometimes I worry that he thinks I'm mad at him or something." She waited while Jackson opened the passenger door.

"I'm sure he doesn't think that," Jackson said once he was behind the wheel. "But I'm sorry it upsets you so much."

His words seemed sincere. "Thanks."

Jackson headed toward town. "How are you settling in? Have you gotten much done at the shop?"

"The house is coming together fine. And I've got the paint picked out for the shop—a nice, cheery yellow. My friend Reagan is going to design the logo." She glanced over at him. "You might remember her from college. Reagan Thompson. She married Chad McClure, so she's Reagan McClure now."

He was silent for a moment. "Blond girl? And Chad was one of those studious types who was in the choir?"

She laughed. "Yes all the way around. Reagan was in the choir, too. In fact, they say they fell in love during the fall choral tour our freshman year. Honestly, I think it was more like they fell in love as soon as they laid eyes on each other."

"Love at first sight, huh? Do you believe in that?" he asked. "I didn't peg you as the hopeless romantic type."

She grinned. "I believe in it for everyone but myself. And I'm *not* the hopeless romantic type. How about you?"

He quirked his mouth into a smile. "You'd be surprised. I think I probably am a bit of a softy. And I definitely am more romantic than most guys. I love the idea of that old-school, traditional romance. Picnics, sharing popcorn at a movie, dancing in the rain." He glanced over at her. "Stuff like that."

She couldn't hide her surprise. "I never would've guessed." She wondered why someone with that kind of outlook was still single, but didn't want to pry.

"Speaking of picnics. . .I've prepared one for us." He grinned. "Hope that's okay."

Violet couldn't believe it. She'd never expected Jackson to go out of his way to do something nice for her. "You didn't have to do that."

"I just thought it would be nicer than having dinner at a restaurant. We can see the hot air balloons. I thought we'd picnic up near the mountain tower. I know the perfect spot."

"Did you ever go up in the tower?" she asked. The Hot Springs Mountain Tower sat atop Hot Springs Mountain inside the national park boundaries. From the top of the tower, visitors could see nearly one hundred and fifty miles of beautiful scenery. It was a favorite during the fall when the colors were at their peak.

He nodded. "My family did a few times when I was a kid. We used to spend a lot of time here at the lake house." He grinned. "And my sister and I loved going to Magic Springs." The amusement park was a favorite vacation spot for families.

"I did, too." She laughed. "My cousin and I used to bug our parents to let us stay in Hot Springs at our grandparents' house just so we could go ride the rides. The log ride was my favorite, until it got to the top."

"Right before the free fall down into the water?"

She nodded. "Yes. I loved the slow pace of the ride so much that I'd always forget how fast and far it dropped at the end. And every time we'd make it up to the top, there was that guy whose job was to just sit there and say, 'Are you ready?' or something like that." She laughed. "Every single time I'd say no and beg him to let me get out of the boat."

Jackson laughed. "So you weren't much of a daredevil?"

"Not at all." She smiled at the memory. "I'd forgotten about that. I haven't been to Magic Springs in years. Not since they added the water park." Crystal Falls had opened in the midnineties and had the traditional water slides and wave pools that most water parks included.

"I went last year with my niece and nephew. It was pretty fun."

"So you're an uncle. That's cool."

He pulled the Range Rover into a parking space. "I enjoy it. I probably spoil them more than I should, but they're really great."

"Do you want to have kids of your own someday?" she asked.

He nodded. "I do. Not too many though. My sister and I were pretty close growing up, and I think that's a special bond. So I'd like to have at least two." He glanced over at her. "How about you?"

Violet sighed. "My sister and I are kind of far apart in years. She's nine years younger than me, and I think that's caused a little bit of a division. I grew up babysitting her, and now I think it's hard for us to relate to each other as equals."

"Is that why it's so important to you to have a date to her wedding?"

She nodded. "She's the kind of sister who takes every opportunity to take jabs at me. So I knew the wedding would be brutal. Between her and my mom, they'd probably announce to the world that I'm officially ready to be the new face of the Old Maid deck."

Jackson laughed. "Surely it isn't that bad."

She managed a tiny smile. "You'd be surprised."

He grabbed the picnic basket from the backseat. "There's a blanket behind your seat that we can sit on. Come on." He climbed out of the vehicle, and she followed him to a grassy spot.

Despite their rocky history, she had to admit that Jackson kept surprising her. One thing was sure—the next few months would definitely not be boring.

Chapter 16

Thomas Daniels: Do you want to meet me tonight at the hot air balloon festival? There's a poetry reading taking place that I'd like to go to. (Text message sent September 22, 5:45 p.m.)

Shadow Simmons: I <3 poetry! I will see you there. (Text message sent September 22, 5:46 p.m.)

Jackson pulled a sandwich out of the basket. "It's chicken salad. My mom's recipe."

Violet took the sandwich. "Ooh, on a croissant. My favorite." She grinned.

He hoped that meant he'd finally arrived in her good graces. "I also made deviled eggs and banana pudding." He placed the containers on the blanket between them.

"Wow."

"I know those things probably don't go together." He chuckled. "But this is kind of the extent of my cooking skills unless there is a grill or a frozen pizza involved."

She laughed. "This looks amazing. Seriously. I'm not used to anyone being so nice to me."

"Well you should be." Once he'd distributed the food, he handed her a bottle of water. "Hope this is okay."

"Perfect." She smiled. "Oh, look at that!" She stood up and pointed toward the sky.

Jackson followed her gaze. Hot air balloons in a variety of colors bobbed in the distance. "So cool. Too bad we didn't go up in one, huh?"

She shook her head. "I'd rather just see them while my feet are firmly on the ground. But they're beautiful."

She sat back down on the blanket. If a picnic beneath a sky dotted with hot air balloons didn't get him some bonus points, he didn't know what would.

"I'm glad you talked me into getting out of the house for this tonight."

Jackson nodded. "Thanks for coming. Although I suspect you have a countdown list at home you'll be checking off once the night is over."

She grinned. "Either way, if anyone ever asks if we had a unique date, we'll have one to share."

"True." He watched her for a long moment as she arranged the food on her plate. "Mind if I pray?" he asked once she was situated.

"Please."

Jackson bowed his head. "Thank You, Lord, for the chance to spend time getting to know one another. Please help us keep You in the center of our lives and show us the path You have for each of our lives. Lord, especially be with Violet as she makes this transition in her life. Bless her and be with her as she opens her business. Amen."

Violet caught his eye. "Thanks," she said quietly. "I can't remember the last time I heard someone pray specifically for me."

In that moment, Jackson couldn't help but wonder what had happened to her. She seemed so surprised—grateful almost—like he'd done something extraordinary for her. "Can I ask you a question?"

She took a bite of her sandwich. "Sure."

"Why are you single? I mean, you seem like the kind of girl who would've tied the knot years ago."

Violet daintily wiped her mouth with a paper towel. "I almost got married a few years ago. I met him right after I moved back from DC." She sighed. "It was one of those cases where I just refused to see what kind of person he really was. You know?"

Jackson wasn't sure if he did. "Was he a bad guy then?"

"He was a smooth talker. Always had a line. In hindsight, he'd probably make a great politician." She shrugged. "But he was a lousy boyfriend."

"I'm sorry."

"One thing I hate is being the center of attention. I hate for people to stare at me and to feel like they're judging me somehow. But Zach was always calling attention to us. He'd have the waitstaff at restaurants sing to me because he thought it was funny how uncomfortable I became. And he'd make a big production out of everything—from arguments to terms of endearment. It was like he needed an audience."

"Sounds like he was kind of a jerk."

"He didn't understand me either. I know I like things that are a little weird." She ran a hand along the hem of her dress. "He thought it was dumb for me to like vintage stores. And when I bought that typewriter, he made no effort to hide how archaic he thought it was to even have it in my house." She smiled. "And when he caught on to my weird attachment to old pennies, he couldn't make enough fun of me."

Jackson raised an eyebrow. "Old pennies?"

Violet burst out laughing. "I know it sounds crazy, but hear me out."

"My mind is totally open." He grinned.

She took a sip of water. "I collect pennies that are older than 1984."

"Because. . . ?" He hated pennies. He'd read somewhere it cost more to produce them than they were even worth.

She sighed. "I knew I shouldn't have told you. You probably think I'm as weird as Zach did."

Jackson shook his head. "Nope. Not a chance. I've never met anyone else like you before, but that isn't a bad thing."

"I have this theory that we were all really happier back then. Have you ever watched families today? The next time you're at a restaurant, take a good look. Everyone is looking at their phones. Texting, Facebooking, playing a game." She shook her head. "I'm pretty sure real conversation is on the decline."

Jackson had thought he was the only person who felt that way. "You're right."

"I just worry sometimes that we're so caught up in progress and convenience and technology that we forget what's really important. That's why I save those old pennies. They remind me of a simpler time and of how fast time passes."

"Because you have clear memories of 1984?"

She nodded. "I was five. I still remember my first day of kindergarten. And when I'd get home from school, I'd play outside. We didn't have a computer or a remote control. There was only one TV in the family room, and we didn't get that many channels."

"I remember those days fondly."

She shrugged. "I guess that's partly why I hang on to such old stuff. The clothes, the furniture, the books. . .the pennies." She grinned. "I even have a record player at my house because I think there's nothing quite like the sound of a real record."

Violet continued to surprise him, that was for sure. He'd just assumed she was a little bit quirky. He'd never guessed that there was more to it than that. "That's very cool. I haven't listened to a record in forever. Probably since I was in elementary school."

"Maybe I'll let you listen to mine sometime." She grinned. "I actually have some Beatles albums."

"You just might be the perfect woman." He realized as soon as it left his mouth how it must sound. "For someone, I mean."

"Someone who doesn't mind inside dogs and clutter."

He chuckled. "That's right." He scooped some banana pudding into a bowl. "So did you and this Zach guy just finally realize you weren't meant for one another?"

"If it had only been that simple." She gave him a wry smile. "He cheated on me. A lot. With more than one girl." She sighed. "I had no clue it was going on, but it seems that everyone else did. Finding out was pretty terrible." She shrugged. "That kind of thing does a number on your self-esteem. I haven't dated much since then."

He let out a low whistle. "I'm sorry. You didn't deserve to be treated that way."

"It's really hard for me now to believe I'll find someone who is really trustworthy. Plus I'm sort of scared I'll put my trust in the wrong guy. I've done it once; who's to say it won't happen again."

Jackson shook his head. "I don't have a magic answer. But I do think you deserve the kind of guy who'll treat you like a princess."

"Thanks. Maybe I should've found a fake relationship years ago. It's nice that there's no pressure to be anything but myself. I'm not usually this relaxed on a date." She grinned. "But since this isn't a real date, I can be totally honest."

Not a real date. Why did Jackson keep forgetting that? He smiled. "That's right. Nothing real here except the chicken salad."

"Do you want us to come help you, dear?" Grandma asked after church on Sunday.

"I'm awfully good with a paintbrush," Grandpa said. He winked. "Or is that nice young man we saw you talking to after Sunday school going to be helping?"

Violet blushed. She hadn't expected Jackson to show up at church this morning. They hadn't discussed it last night. "We're going to get the final coat of paint finished. Shadow helped me prime it earlier in the week."

Grandma smiled. "It's all coming together."

"Thanks to a lot of prayers by a lot of people." Violet hugged Grandma. "And you're sure you don't mind helping with Reagan's kids next weekend? They can be a handful." Violet loved them dearly, but each time she watched them for Reagan, it took her two days to recover.

"I'm looking forward to it. And I've got some reinforcements. Betty and Shadow are already lined up to help out." She patted Grandpa's back. "And I wouldn't be surprised if someone else showed up."

Grandpa grinned. "She can't bear to be away from me." He winked at his wife.

Violet hugged them both and hurried toward her car. She loved spending time with her grandparents. She hoped to have a bond like theirs with someone someday.

An hour later, she'd let Arnie have some backyard time and had changed into her painting clothes. She sure wouldn't win any awards today in an old T-shirt and yoga pants.

As she hurried up the sidewalk toward the bakery, she spotted Jackson sitting on a bench in front of Aunt Teak's, wearing a baseball cap and some faded jeans. "Ready to paint up a storm?" she asked, digging in her bag for the keys.

Jackson nodded. "I sure am. I'm even more ready for the kitchen to be functional so I can indulge in some more of those cupcakes."

She pushed the door open and laughed. "You'll be in luck next weekend."

"What's going on then?" He followed her inside and flipped on the light switch.

Violet dusted a speck of dirt from the counter. "Reagan is coming to help with some marketing stuff. One of the things she wants to do is take pictures of cupcakes for the brochure." She grinned. "So there'll be a variety of cupcakes to taste test."

"I like the sound of that," he said.

"Plus I really want to work on the menu. I'm getting really excited. I'm thinking I'll have some basic flavors that are always on the menu. You know—chocolate, vanilla, strawberry, maybe a red velvet." She grinned. "But then I think I might rotate other flavors out on a weekly basis."

"Keep the menu fresh, so people will want to stop in to see what's new." He grinned. "I like that. Smart business."

She blushed. "Just an idea."

"It's the kind of idea that will help make you very successful."

Violet sighed. "I hope so. The closer I get to the opening, the more nervous I get."

"I think we need to work on your self-confidence a little bit." Jackson took her by the shoulders and looked into her eyes. "You are brilliant. You're smart and funny. People are going to love to stop in here just to talk to you. Your cupcakes are amazing, and your sales are going to be off the charts."

She blinked. He really thought those things about her? "But what if—"

He put a hand over her mouth. "No buts. You need to believe in yourself and your abilities." Jackson removed his hand and smiled. "I believe in you. Your grandparents believe in you. Reagan believes in you. It's time for you to believe in yourself. Otherwise you're going to worry yourself silly trying to open this place and being too afraid of failure."

Tears filled her eyes. Was it really that obvious that she struggled with self-doubt? "Thanks for the pep talk," she whispered. "I guess I needed it."

Jackson grinned. "Anytime." He motioned toward the paint cans sitting on the floor. "Now let's get this party started." He opened a paint can and poured the creamy yellow paint into a tray. "That's going to be awfully cheery."

"I hope so." She picked up a foam paint roller. "I considered just painting it white, but decided a pop of color would be better."

"You definitely seem like the type of person who would do better surrounded by color. Plain walls just don't seem to go with your personality." He dipped a brush into the paint and climbed up on the step ladder. "I'll start cutting in, and you can roll behind me. Is that good?"

Violet nodded. "Works for me. I'm not that great at cutting in. You can always see my brush strokes." She watched him work for a long moment. "So I'm thinking about bringing my record player to use in the shop. What do you think?"

"That could be fun. Kind of a retro feel."

She laughed. "Plus then I'll have an excuse to look for records at thrift stores and yard sales. I might use some as decorations."

"Sounds like a plan." He concentrated on the corner. "And that girl we saw last night is going to work here?"

"Shadow. Yeah. Her grandmother owns the antique store next door and lives next to my grandparents."

"So she lives with them?"

Violet rolled the roller in the tray and let the excess paint drip off. "Her mom—their daughter—was killed in an accident a couple of years ago. Her dad remarried, and I think she's just had a really hard time adjusting."

Jackson let out a low whistle. "Such an awful thing for a kid that age to deal with." He stepped down from the ladder to dip his brush into the paint. "Really for any age to deal with."

"I can't imagine."

He looked at her with pain in his eyes. "I can. My dad passed away last year. It was completely unexpected. He'd always been the picture of health."

Violet put the roller down. "I'm so sorry to hear that."

Jackson nodded. "Heart attack. It's been a pretty awful year." He turned back to the wall. "And now my mom is dating again." He laughed bitterly. "I'm having a hard enough time coping with that—I can't imagine if I were still in high school."

Violet watched him work and couldn't help but feel an ache in her heart. Part of her wanted to hug him, to try and take away the pain he obviously still felt.

But it wasn't really her place. They were only together for show, not to be part of each other's lives.

So she kept quiet and turned her attention back to her painting.

Dear Mama,

This was an awesome weekend. I got to see hot air balloons and listen to Thomas recite some of his poetry. He's so cool.

Nana and Granddaddy would only let me meet up with him for an hour though. I'm tired of them treating me like a baby. I read in your journal that they didn't let you date until you were seventeen. Well, I'll be seventeen in five months. And I can't wait.

Thomas and I ran into Violet and her boyfriend at the festival. She wants me to start working regular hours at the bakery pretty soon! I helped her do some painting after school earlier in the week. I think she was surprised that I was actually good at it. I hope she'll let me put icing on the cupcakes once the bakery opens.

I got another e-mail from Daddy asking me about Thanksgiving. It seems like I don't really have much of a choice but to go.

I miss you so much, Mama. If you were still here, I wouldn't have such a big hole inside me. Thomas says I should draw on my pain to create poetry, but I don't know.

Ily,
Shadow

Chapter 17

Jackson Stratford: How does the paint job look today? And what's your favorite movie? (Text message sent September 26, 4:13 p.m.)

Violet Matthews: The paint job is fantastic. And I'm a John Hughes fan, so either The Breakfast Club or Sixteen Candles. Or Ferris Bueller's Day Off. You? (Text message sent September 26, 4:19 p.m.)

Jackson Stratford: You get more impressive by the day. Nice choices. I've got to go with Indiana Jones though. Either Raiders of the Lost Ark or Temple of Doom. Can't go wrong there. (Text message sent September 26, 5:03 p.m.)

Reagan paced the floor Wednesday night. They'd just gotten home from church and put the kids in bed. She'd hoped she and Chad would finally have the chance to sit and talk, but he was flipping through the channels.

Ever since he'd dropped the bomb about his trip to Miami, she'd been trying to figure out the best way to broach the subject. Except that she wasn't totally sure she wanted to know who all from his office would be attending the conference.

"So are you still on for Miami?" she asked, sitting down beside him on the couch.

He glanced up. "Yeah. I'll be leaving Friday afternoon and be back on Monday."

"What kind of thing is it, anyway?" She brushed some dirt from her pants. No telling where that had come from.

"It's a continuing education thing put on by SHRM. Nothing exciting, believe me." He grinned.

"Are you the only one that has to go?"

Chad furrowed his brow. "No. There are six or seven of us I think. And even that won't make it more exciting. In fact, I'm on a different flight than they are because I have a meeting Friday morning that couldn't be moved."

That set her mind at ease, at least to a certain extent. At least it wouldn't just be him and Reese. "How's your new assistant working out?"

"Reese? She's great. You should come by and meet her sometime. She reminds me a lot of you when you were that age."

Reagan froze. "When I was that age? What, like I'm some old lady now?"

Chad chuckled. "Of course not." He reached over and squeezed her knee. "But when you were in your midtwenties you were all about your career. She's like that."

His explanation didn't make her feel any better. "So is Reese going on this trip?"

"Huh?" He pulled his gaze away from the TV to glance at her. "Oh. Yeah. She's going."

No remorse. "Don't you think it's a little inappropriate for you to be heading to Miami with your single assistant?"

Chad clicked off the TV and glared at her. "What are you getting at? That I'm lying about having to be there and am instead planning some rendezvous?" He shook his head. "When did you get so paranoid?"

She should've kept her mouth shut. "I don't know. When you started working around the clock. When I found myself stuck in the house all the time taking care of your children while your life just goes on like normal. When you don't even notice anything about me anymore." She ticked them off on her hand. "Take your pick."

Chad stood up. "You're being ridiculous. I love you. I adore the kids. I'm the same guy I've always been. And the fact that you'd even insinuate that there might be something inappropriate going on between me and Reese is a huge insult." He tossed the remote on the coffee table. "I thought you knew me better than that." He jerked his chin toward their bedroom. "I'm going to bed."

Without another word, he walked out of the room.

Was it true? Was he the same guy he'd always been? And if so, did that mean she was the one who'd changed?

Reagan curled up on the couch and closed her eyes. *Lord, I need help. In a major way.*

Thursday afternoon the door to the bake shop burst open, and Violet looked up from the supply list she was working on. "Hi, Shadow. Thanks for coming by today."

The teenager nodded. "No prob." She put her backpack on the floor next to the counter and glanced at the walls. "It looks really pretty now. I love the yellow. It makes everything much brighter."

"Thanks. I'm really happy with the way it turned out." Violet admired the wall. "I especially like the way the yellow looks against that white crown molding."

Shadow nodded. "So what do you need me to do today?"

Violet took a good look at Shadow. "Those are cute glasses." She hadn't been wearing them last week when they primed the walls.

"Thanks. They're just reading ones."

After running into Shadow and a boy named Thomas the other night at the Legends Balloon Rally, Violet had a pretty good idea of what was going on. "And that sweater vest is adorable. Different from your normal style." But very similar to the way Thomas had been dressed on Saturday.

Shadow shrugged. "I like plaid."

"Argyle. It's Argyle."

"Whatever."

Violet fought back a grin. She didn't want to push the girl away. "I was thinking you could help me take inventory this afternoon. I had a delivery earlier today of some of the things we'll need during the next few weeks." She handed Shadow a list. "The delivery guy put the boxes in the storeroom. Just check to make sure everything on this list is there and in the quantity this paper says."

"Sure." Shadow looked at the list. "Have you decided when to open?"

Violet smiled. "My friend Reagan is coming to town this weekend, and she'll be starting on the logo and some marketing materials. Once she's got some of that figured out, we'll have a better idea. I'm hoping for Halloween though."

Shadow gave her a tiny grin. "Really?"

"Wouldn't that be kind of fun? We could wear costumes and everything. Plus we might be able to come up with some neat Halloween-themed cupcakes."

Shadow bit her lip. "Um. I'm pretty good at drawing stuff. Maybe I could help with some of the decorations."

Violet nodded. "Of course." As far as she was concerned, Shadow even showing interest in the bakery was progress. The first few times she'd been around the girl, she'd barely acknowledged anyone or anything. But Mrs. Kemp had mentioned that she thought Shadow was really excited about the bakery opening and about working there.

"I'll be out here if you need me," Violet called as Shadow went into the storeroom.

Her phone buzzed against the counter, and she glanced at the caller ID. "There's my favorite graphic designer. Are you ready for a weekend of chaos?"

Reagan laughed. "Have you forgotten who you're talking to? My *life* is chaos. Not just my weekends."

"True. Any idea when you'll be arriving?"

"Tomorrow afternoon. I'll pick Izzy up from school, and then we'll be on our way."

Violet couldn't wait. "We'll have so much fun. And by the way, Grandma, Mrs. Kemp, and Shadow are on board for a little Saturday afternoon babysitting. I think Grandpa might even pitch in as long as he can watch the Razorback game." Grandpa had called her yesterday to make sure she had ESPN. She hadn't pressed, but she figured he was trying to arrange his Saturday around his favorite team.

"You're kidding. They don't have to do that."

"Oh, but they do." Violet grinned. "Because not only will we be working on the design of the store logo, but I've booked us two hours at one of the spas."

"Time at a spa? You're going to make me cry."

Violet laughed. "You deserve it. A massage and a facial are probably just what you need. And I even booked us for the bath package."

"You did?" Reagan laughed. "What is it they used to call it? Taking to the waters?"

"That's right. The waters have healed and rejuvenated people since Hot Springs was discovered," Violet said. "So why shouldn't we partake in some of that therapy?"

"I'm game, especially if it will take my mind off the fact that my husband will probably be poolside in Miami this weekend with his twenty-six-year-old assistant." Her bitterness came through the phone.

"I thought you talked to him about it."

"I did. But what's he going to say? Of course he denied it."

Violet exhaled. "Please try not to worry. Just come to Hot Springs and relax. Maybe just having a bit of a break will give you fresh perspective."

"Maybe." Reagan obviously wasn't convinced. "Or maybe I should just face the facts. Something is off in my relationship with Chad. Something big. And I can't figure out what that is."

Violet had no advice for her friend. She'd always felt that if your instincts told you something was wrong—it usually was. So where did that leave Reagan and Chad? "I'll be praying."

"That's all you can do."

Violet hung up and went back to her list, but Reagan's words kept playing in her head. *That's all you can do.* How many times did Violet have to learn that lesson? She'd often been guilty of trying to fix things herself. She'd make lists and anticipate problems and worry about her decisions. Prayer was her last resort. Her fallback plan. What she did when she couldn't do anything else.

She couldn't help but wonder how things might be different if prayer came first. Before she stepped in to offer advice or to try to solve things. Maybe she'd gotten it backward all her life.

Lord, from now on, I'll go to You first. And not just when there's a crisis or a problem.

Dear Mama,

You're not going to believe it. Nana is letting me go to the school dance this weekend. She wasn't super happy about it, but I think Granddaddy talked her into it.

I'm so excited that I finally get to go and do something. I made a friend at school named Rachel, and we're going to get ready together. I think her mom is going to take us for manicures. I wish you were here to take us instead.

I'm a little bummed that Thomas didn't ask me to go with him, but he told me he thinks school functions are stupid. He says he isn't even going to walk at graduation. I think that's kind of weird, but I didn't tell him that.

I love you,
Shadow

Chapter 18

Violet Matthews: THE TASTE TESTING IS TONIGHT AT
THE SHOP. SHOULD I SAVE YOU A CUPCAKE? AND TELL ME
SOMETHING ABOUT YOURSELF THAT WOULD SURPRISE ME. . . .
(Text message sent September 29, 10:02 a.m.)

Jackson Stratford: I'LL BE THERE WITH BELLS ON. 7ISH?
AND HOW ABOUT THIS: I TRAVEL TO PANAMA EACH
SUMMER WITH A GROUP FROM CHURCH AND VOLUNTEER
AT AN ORPHANAGE. YOU? (Text message sent September
29, 10:22 a.m.)

Violet Matthews: 7 IS FINE AND THAT IS A SURPRISE. I NEVER
WOULD'VE PEGGED YOU FOR A MISSIONARY. HERE'S MINE:
ONCE WHEN I LIVED IN DC, I HAD DINNER AT THE WHITE
HOUSE. (Text message sent September 29, 10:29 a.m.)

Jackson tossed his phone on his coffee table. This arrangement
with Violet was starting to get dicey. More and more, he found

himself looking forward to her texts or to checking off another date from their list. And it had nothing to do with being ready for their date balance to be zero.

And Kathleen had been after him to bring his new girlfriend to Memphis for the weekend, something he wasn't totally sure he could do. He and his sister had always shared everything. Even through some of the darkest days of his life, she'd known what was going on with him.

The idea of parading a fake relationship in front of Kathleen and her family didn't sit well with him. The deal had started out with the best of intentions, but Jackson was starting to wonder if it was worth it.

The doorbell rang and put a welcome end to his worrying. He wasn't expecting company though, especially on a Saturday morning. He peeked out the window.

His mother stood on the porch, a big smile on her face.

He swung open the door. "Hey, Mom. I didn't expect to see you today."

"Sorry for stopping by without notice." She stepped over the threshold and into the living room. "But I was nearby and wanted to speak to you."

"Come on in," he said, motioning toward the couch.

Donna Stratford sat down on the leather couch and crossed her ankles. "I'm just going to cut right to the chase."

"Of course." Mom always had been direct, a quality Jackson had inherited. When Kathleen and Jackson had gotten in trouble as kids, they'd always joked that Dad was the good cop and Mom was the bad cop. They'd been a great team.

"Your sister tells me you aren't happy that I'm seeing Roger." She leveled her blue eyes on him. "If you have a problem with things, now is the time to speak."

Jackson exhaled loudly. He sure didn't want to get into this with his mother. For one thing, he completely realized how childish it seemed for him to be upset that Mom was moving on. "I'm just worried, that's all." He shrugged. "What do we really know about this guy anyway? Nothing."

Mom smiled. "Actually I know quite a bit about him. Your dad and I were friends with Roger and his wife, Melinda."

It was even worse than he thought. "Don't tell me he left his wife."

"For me?" Mom laughed and shook her head. "Don't be silly, dear." She frowned. "Actually, Melinda passed away a couple of years ago. Cancer."

Jackson sighed. "I'm sorry for his loss. . .but still."

"What do you want me to do?"

"I don't know. Isn't there a nice book club you can join? Or a ladies bowling team?"

Mom shut her eyes and shook her head. "Jackson, you know I love you. And I'm sorry that my dinners with Roger upset you so much. But he understands how it feels to lose a spouse. He's been a great support for me, and frankly, it's nice to have someone to go out and do things with sometimes." She shrugged. "Plus he makes me laugh. And there was a time I didn't know if I'd ever laugh again."

Now he felt terrible. "I'm not trying to cause problems. I just feel like it's a little soon—that's all."

Mom frowned. "Your dad's been gone for more than a year. And

I spent so much of that time too upset to even get out of bed. But Roger has given me a reason to get up and to leave the house. I think that's what your dad would've wanted."

Jackson bristled. There it was again. That phrase he loathed. "Or telling yourself that's what Dad would've wanted is a way to ease your conscience."

"That was uncalled for. You might be a grown man, but I'm your mother and I deserve your respect." Mom stood. "Your sister is happy for me. I suggest you find a way to be on board with this."

Jackson stood up and rubbed his jaw. "I'm sorry. I don't mean to seem unsupportive. I'm just worried." He shrugged. "I don't like change."

Mom smiled. "I know, dear. It isn't easy for any of us. But really try to keep an open mind where Roger is concerned." She walked to the door and turned to face him. "If things go well, he'll probably be at our family Thanksgiving. And I'll expect you to make him feel welcome."

His earlier doubts about the contract he and Violet had flew out the window. Her being there might be the only thing that would get him through. "I'm probably bringing someone, too." He grinned at Mom's expression. He'd never brought a girl home to meet his family. "So I'll expect you to make her feel welcome, too."

Mom gave him a hug. "Deal." She kissed him on the cheek and hurried toward her car.

Reagan leaned her head against the passenger seat and tilted her face toward the sun. "Thanks for driving," she said as Violet got behind the wheel. "I just felt better leaving the van and car seats behind in case there is an emergency."

"No problem. We'll go to the spa, and then I'll show you the space." Reagan headed toward town. "Was the guest room okay?"

Reagan laughed. "It was more than okay. You're the one I should worry about. Sorry that Izzy insisted on sleeping with you. Did she kick you a lot?"

"Only a few times." Violet grinned. "No more than Arnie usually does."

"Oh, that dog." Reagan shook her head. "He is just the sweetest. Have you noticed how he wants to be wherever the babies are? He slept in the doorway of our room last night."

"I wondered where he went. Sometimes he stays in the living room now because it's too much trouble to get up and move to the bedroom."

"He actually makes me think a dog wouldn't be a bad addition to our family," Reagan said. "But not for a couple of years so Izzy and Ava Grace are old enough to help take care of it."

Violet slowed down as she reached Central Avenue. "I'm considering getting a puppy. I know Arnie won't be around forever. The last time we were at the vet, I found out his kidneys aren't doing too well." She sighed. "I'm thinking maybe a puppy will help lessen the blow when his time comes."

Reagan reached over and patted her arm. Arnie had been part of Violet's life since they were right out of college. "I'm sorry. And I think a puppy would be a great idea, if you're sure you have time for the training that goes along with that. Opening a business is going to keep you pretty busy though."

Violet pulled into an empty space near Bathhouse Row. "I know. I just worry about how empty my house will be without a dog in it."

There were days Reagan fantasized about her house being totally empty and quiet. A whole day of quiet sounded heavenly. But it would get old and lonely soon. "Maybe Arnie will pull through the kidney thing and have a lot more great years."

"That would be nice, but he's fifteen. I'm not living under the delusion that he's going to be here forever." She reached into the backseat and grabbed her bag. "You ready for this? No stress. No worries."

Reagan slung her bag over her shoulder and followed Violet to the crosswalk. "Where are we headed?"

"Quapaw Baths and Spa. I haven't been inside since they renovated, but Grandma said it's nice." The bathhouse was built in the 1920s and derived its name from the tribe of Indians that lived in the area. "Did you know there's a cave in the basement near the spring that gives the spa its water? Legend has it that the cave and spring were discovered by the Quapaw Indians when they inhabited this area."

"Cool." Reagan grinned. Violet's love of the past never ceased to amaze her. For as long as they'd been friends, Violet had been providing her with interesting historical tidbits or encouraging her to hold on to the past.

Twenty minutes later they were in full spa mode, complete with robes and slippers. "This is exactly what I needed," Reagan said. "These last months have been so stressful. Just getting away from the house is kind of nice."

"I'm sorry I haven't come over to keep the kids and let you have some time off."

Reagan shook her head. "Don't be silly. It isn't your place."

"Have you told Chad how you feel? That you need some help?"

She couldn't imagine having that conversation with Chad. "He has to know I'm overwhelmed. Everyone with eyes knows I'm overwhelmed." She flipped through a *People* magazine. "Besides. It makes me feel like a terrible mother. I mean, I should be able to manage four kids with no problem, right?"

Violet raised her hands in surrender. "You're asking the wrong person. I don't think I could do it, especially once the twins came along. I'd definitely need some help." She closed the magazine she'd been reading and tossed it on the chair next to her. "And I really think you need to figure out a solution."

"This woman at my gym thinks I should plan a romantic date night with Chad. She says we need some time alone together in a major way."

"I might not be married, but that sounds right to me. You guys used to have date nights, didn't you?"

Reagan nodded. "It was before the twins came along. My mom was really good about offering to keep Izzy and Ava Grace."

"So find someone else. Figure it out. Because I don't think you can go on like this for much longer. Even if you have to get two sitters—maybe someone from church can watch Izzy and Ava Grace and Chad's mom can watch the twins. But you need some help."

Reagan had been thinking the same thing lately. "Chad's mom called earlier in the week and offered to let the kids stay the night with them. I declined the offer since I hated to impose like that."

"She offered. Do it. Impose." Violet grinned. "You and Chad have some stuff to work out. Who knows? Maybe a romantic date night is just what y'all need."

True. She could make a reservation at one of their favorite places. It would be so nice to take some time to reconnect without worrying about the kids. "As soon as he gets back from Miami. . . I'll run it by him."

Violet grinned. "Perfect."

A woman in a white coat walked into the waiting area. "Ladies, if you'll follow me, I'll take you downstairs to the baths." She led them down a hallway and to a staircase. "Watch your step. Once you're finished with the baths, you'll come back upstairs for the massage and facials. The warm water will loosen your muscles," she explained.

They walked past the public baths where bathing-suit clad people lounged in the steamy water. "Look at that," she whispered to Violet. "I've read about the public baths, but didn't realize it would look like a big hot tub."

Violet giggled. "That's why I booked us each a private bath. It will be like we each have a personal hot tub."

It sounded divine.

Another spa worker in a white coat met them at the doorway to the private baths. She held two cups of ice water. "Here you go." She handed one to each of them and motioned for them to follow her into the room.

"Your water is running now," she said, consulting her clip board. "Reagan?"

Reagan stepped forward. "That's me."

"Right this way." She led Reagan into a tiny room with an antique-looking tub in the corner. "I'll start your bubbles," she said. She bent down and flipped a switch, and the water started bubbling. "Is this your first time in the Spa City?"

Reagan shook her head. "I've been here before, but never to the thermal baths."

"Well you're in for a treat. The thermal waters have been used therapeutically for thousands of years. The water is high in silica, calcium, magnesium, free carbon dioxide, bicarbonate, and sulfate." She smiled. "Try to say that fast."

Reagan laughed. "I'm sure I'll enjoy the experience."

"The timer will start when I close the door. You'll hear me knock when it's time to get out." She motioned toward a tray next to the tub. "There's an extra ice water for you to drink. It's recommended that you hydrate your insides as well."

"Okay, thanks."

"There's a bell on the tray—ring it if you need anything and I'll come in." She poured a cup full of salts into the tub. "Green tea to help with relaxation," she explained. "Enjoy." She closed the door behind her.

Reagan sank into the bath. This was heavenly. She could barely remember the last time she was alone without someone banging on the door or having to keep her ears open for the baby monitor. She leaned her head back against the rolled towel and closed her eyes. There was even a bell to ring in case she needed something. Not that she'd ring it, but the thought made her smile.

Tomorrow she'd corral her children back into the van and they'd head back to their home and their full week. Monday, she'd drop Izzy off at school and take Ava Grace to gymnastics and call the pediatrician to schedule Scarlett and Simon for their yearly check up. She'd pick Chad up from the airport and send her mother the new pictures she'd just gotten from the photographer.

For now though, all that could wait.

Now she could just be Reagan, woman at the spa with no responsibilities.

Bliss.

Chapter 19

Reagan McClure: Just left the spa. Hope Miami is nice. Your mom offered to keep the kids next Friday so we could have a date. Does that work with your schedule? (Text message sent September 29, 3:02 p.m.)

Chad McClure: Glad you're having fun. Miami is rainy. Next Friday sounds great. Love you, babe. See you soon. (Text message sent September 29, 3:15 p.m.)

Violet pulled a pan of cupcakes from the oven. "Here's the first batch from the bakery kitchen."

"The first of many," Reagan said. "And they smell amazing."

"Thanks. While I wait on them to cool, let me show you what I have in mind for the rest of the shop." Violet motioned for Reagan to follow her to the counter that held the cash register.

"Can I just say that I think this is a terrific setup? You have so much space behind the counter, and having a station to ice cupcakes and an oven and everything right there. . .I think people will love it," Reagan said.

Violet nodded. "I was afraid it would be weird at first because customers will literally be able to see the whole process. But I think it will go really well. In the afternoons, Shadow will work the register while I do any baking or icing. But mostly I'm going to try and get several batches baked each morning before I open."

"What time?"

Violet sighed. "I'm thinking we won't open until ten. And then I'll probably stay open until seven. It might all depend on the season."

"Good plan," Reagan agreed.

"I'll be closed on Sunday and Monday." She glanced over at Reagan. "Do you think that's a bad business decision?" Being closed on Sunday was very important to Violet. She didn't like the idea of having to miss church for work, and she didn't want to have employees that had to make that kind of sacrifice either. The sales she might make just weren't worth it.

Reagan shook her head. "It sounds like a smart idea to me. I totally get where you're coming from. I'm sure there are others who might disagree, but I think it is probably the best choice for you. Besides, I'll bet Saturday will be one of your busy days and you'll be glad you have Sunday and Monday to recover."

Violet nodded. "That's what I'm guessing. I visited one of my favorite cupcake shops in Little Rock a couple of weeks ago and asked them some questions. Their hours are nine until six, which I guess could be a possibility for me in the winter. And they told me Saturday is so busy sometimes they actually sell out." Violet couldn't imagine her cupcakes selling out, but it was a nice dream.

"Have you settled on a name yet?"

Violet groaned and shook her head. She'd been brainstorming names for two weeks and was finding it one of the toughest decisions of her life. "I need something simple. Something that looks good on the sign out front. Something that's fun." She shook her head. "I'm having a terrible time deciding."

"What are your top choices?"

"Icing on the Cake." Violet raised her eyebrows in question.

Reagan shook her head. "Too cutsey. What else?"

"Hot Springs Cupcakes."

"Too boring. Next?" Reagan grinned.

"Cupcakes by Violet."

Reagan made a face. "Too cliché."

"Central Avenue Cupcakes."

Reagan's eyes lit up. "Definitely that one. Central Avenue Cupcakes. That's perfect! It tells the location—and everyone who visits Hot Springs visits Central Avenue. It's simple and catchy." She nodded. "And I think we can definitely create a great logo."

"I hope so." Violet ran her hand along the counter. "Central Avenue Cupcakes. I like it. Thanks for helping me figure it out." She'd been leaning toward that one all week but kept second-guessing herself. It was nice to have her pick reinforced by Reagan.

"You're welcome. Remember that I do have a little bit of experience with that kind of thing," Reagan said.

Violet motioned for Reagan to follow her around the counter and into the large open space right inside the entry door. "I'll leave space for a line to form here." She pointed. "And then I'll get four or five tables to fill the rest of the space. How do you think that will look?"

"Amazing. What kind of tables?"

"Probably mix and match. I found a couple of options at a thrift store last week. I'm going to go back tomorrow and see if they still have them." She knew some people would think it was weird to have tables and chairs that didn't exactly match one another. But she'd been to shops with décor like that and thought the effect was quaint.

"What color?"

Violet grinned. "You know me and my funky style. I'm going to get Shadow to help me paint them. We'll probably do the tables white and then paint the chairs in a variety of fun colors. I may even see about putting some kind of different design on each table." Shadow had mentioned being a good artist, and next week Violet would put that to the test.

"That will look amazing next to the yellow wall." Reagan looked around. "This place will definitely be 'you', if you know what I mean."

Violet laughed. "I do. I'm planning to bring my record player up here and put it in the corner." She pointed to a little nook. "And I have my great-grandmother's quilt squares I'm thinking of framing and putting on the wall." The quilt squares would give it a personal touch, plus knowing she had a family heirloom in her store would make her happy.

Reagan clapped her hands. "This is really going to be an awesome place. I'm so happy for you."

"Thanks. I'm still a little shell-shocked that I'm actually doing it. And I'm so scared of the place tanking." Her mother's words about her impending financial ruin rang in her head every night when she went to bed.

"You didn't buy the building, right?"

Violet nodded. There'd been no way she would've bought the place without a trial run as a renter. What if the business failed and she was stuck with payments on a building? "Just renting for now."

"So if something crazy happens and the place isn't all it's cracked up to be, you'll sell your equipment and move on. But I'm putting my money on you and the shop being a smashing success." Reagan leaned against the counter. "I'm the last person who should be saying this because I'm so guilty of it, but stop worrying. Pray about it and do your best on the shop, but don't worry so much."

Violet smiled. She thought about Jackson and his little pep talk the other day. So many people believed in her. So why did she have such a hard time believing in herself?

Jackson paused on the sidewalk outside of the bake shop. He should've asked more questions about who would be in attendance tonight. The only thing he knew for sure was that Violet had texted to make sure it would count toward their date number.

"Jackson?" a voice called from behind him.

He turned around to see a blond woman striding toward him. "Reagan. Long time no see."

"It's been a long time," Reagan agreed. "I came to see Violet graduate from college—you know, after she had to attend the summer semester. Seems like you graduated that day, too."

He might be making some progress in getting back in Violet's good graces, but clearly Reagan would take more time. "I did. You look well."

She raised an eyebrow. "We went to the spa today. It's been a nice day." She gestured toward the bake shop. "Have you seen the place yet?"

"I helped paint the inside."

The surprise on her face was unmistakable. "I see. I didn't realize you and Violet were such friends."

Jackson winced. So Violet wasn't telling her closest friend about their "relationship" yet? That seemed strange. And kind of hurtful. "We see each other now and then."

Reagan nodded. "She mentioned a while back that you'd let her stay at your lake house, but I didn't know that meant the two of you were actually friends."

"Well we are. She's a great girl."

Reagan leveled her blue eyes on his. "She is. And your antics in college drove her crazy. To tell you the truth, I'm surprised she gives you the time of day."

Had he really been that bad? Sure, he'd messed up their presentation. And caused her boyfriend to dump her. "I don't remember it being that bad."

"Jackson, you told all the guys in your dorm that she put the moves on you. And you printed up a T-shirt with a very unflattering picture of her on it. Do you remember that?"

He'd forgotten. At the time he'd thought it was one of his best, most memorable pranks. "I wore it under my team jersey and told her if she didn't come to all of my intramural basketball games I'd take my jersey off so everyone would see the picture."

Reagan nodded. "And I'm pretty sure you're the one who managed to put her name and phone number with a 'call me, I'm desperate' message on the big screen in the auditorium that showed up during chapel announcements."

Their school had a daily chapel service, which meant Violet had been effectively humiliated in front of the entire student body. He'd forgotten about that one as well. "I guess I gave her a pretty hard time. Honestly, I'd sort of blocked that stuff out of my mind."

"Well I can guarantee you she hasn't. Violet has always felt like an outcast. She's lived her life marching to the beat of her own drum. Because of that, she's never had the best self-confidence. And the one thing that she's always hated is to be the center of attention."

Jackson could admit that he'd been horrible to her. He'd been horrible to a lot of people. But Reagan would never understand his frame of mind at the time, and she obviously didn't think people could change. "I'm trying to make up for all of that now."

They stared at each other for a long moment.

"Just don't hurt her again," Reagan said finally.

Jackson nodded. "Of course." He opened the bake shop door and held it open for Reagan. If she had that much animosity toward him, it was no wonder Violet was counting down the days until their deal was over. Those pranks hadn't seemed so major to him at the time, but looking back now, maybe he had more to make up for than he'd first thought.

"Thanks," Reagan said softly.

He followed her inside the shop and was greeted by the

wonderful aroma of freshly baked cupcakes. He spotted Violet arranging cakes on a platter. "Those look wonderful and smell even better."

She looked up and grinned. "Thanks. Today has been amazing. We got a ton of work done on the marketing stuff." She threw her hand up like a spokesmodel. "Welcome to Central Avenue Cupcakes."

"Nice name. I like it a lot."

She beamed. "Reagan helped me decide which one would be best. And I think she has some really cool ideas for the logo. Hopefully by this time next week, the signage will be ordered for the front of the store and I'll have business cards and flyers." She pointed to the arrangement of cupcakes. "Reagan took a ton of pictures today that I think are going to look awesome on a website. There's just so much to think about."

"Just take a breath. You don't have to have absolutely everything done for the opening. Think of it as a soft opening—just for locals. Then you have the rest of the fall and winter to really beef up your marketing in time for the spring and summer tourist season."

Violet nodded. "You're probably right. I just keep thinking of things I need to do. It's easy to get overwhelmed."

"In my experience, the thing you should concentrate on first is making the best cupcakes possible. Get the inside of the store finished. Then after you've opened and people have sampled the cupcakes and soaked up the atmosphere here, they'll tell their friends. I predict you'll do a lot of word-of-mouth business."

She frowned. "I really hope so."

"Do I still detect some worry?" he asked.

Violet shrugged. "Maybe a little. There's definitely a fear of the unknown."

"But that's what makes it exciting, right? The fact that life is full of surprises."

"Listen to you being all philosophical. What's gotten into you?"

He chuckled. "I've always been philosophical. Maybe you never noticed it till now."

"Whatever. Sometimes I think you're just trying to butter me up."

"Nah, just trying to be the best fake boyfriend I can be," he whispered in her ear. It was the closest he'd ever been to her, and he could smell the sweet scent of her shampoo.

She laughed. "I guess." She motioned to where Reagan stood, talking to an older lady. "That's Mrs. Kemp. She owns the shop next door. And did you get to speak to Reagan?"

"She's not exactly a fan of mine."

Violet shrugged. "Sorry. She has a really good memory, so it's kind of hard for her to accept you and me as anything other than enemies." She grinned mischievously. "I mean, we've always been really good at being enemies. So I can see how she'd be confused."

"I guess. Maybe you should put in a good word for me though." He grinned.

"Maybe I will." Violet returned his grin. "Maybe I will."

Dear Mama,

Thomas broke up with me. It's all Rachel's stupid fault. She put a picture on Facebook of the two of us getting ready for the dance. Thomas told me he couldn't possibly go out with someone who was such a conformist.

I don't think me wanting to go to a school function with my friends makes me a conformist, do you? Either way, I'm not speaking to Rachel right now. I told her not to post it because I didn't want him to see.

She said it was silly of me to be that way and that Thomas is the one who is stupid. Actually she called him pretentious.

Oh well. Next week is the week I start working normal hours at the bake shop. It has a name now—Central Avenue Cupcakes. I think that's a pretty good name. Violet told me at church yesterday that my job this week is going to be helping her paint the tables and chairs! I told her I was fine doing whatever, but to tell you the truth, I'm pretty excited about painting.

I kind of like hanging out with her, too. She's not like Stephanie. She doesn't try to force me to be her buddy or whatever. She just treats me like a normal person.

I miss you,
Shadow

Chapter 20

Violet Matthews: THANKS FOR YOUR HELP! THE LOGO IS AWESOME. ARE YOU OKAY? (Text message sent October 3, 10:22 a.m.)

Reagan McClure: I'M SO GLAD YOU LIKE IT! I'M AMAZINGLY PRODUCTIVE DURING NAP TIME AS LONG AS I IGNORE MY DIRTY LAUNDRY AND DISHES. CHAD'S MOM IS COMING TO GET THE KIDS FRIDAY MORNING. WE'LL SEE HOW THIS GOES. . . . (Text message sent October 3, 10:30 a.m.)

Violet unloaded the last of the chairs from Grandpa's truck. It was a good thing he still had the old thing, otherwise she'd have made fifteen trips from the thrift store.

She dusted off her jeans and looked around her garage. She and Shadow had a lot of painting ahead of them.

"Is that the last one?" Shadow asked.

Violet nodded. "Yes. Now the real work begins." She pointed to a table and four chairs in the corner. "Those are ready to paint.

They've been sanded and primed. Do you want to give it a try while I start sanding the rest?"

Shadow beamed. "Yes, yes, yes."

Violet grinned. "It's nice to see you so enthusiastic about the project." She was a little surprised at the teenager's attitude. When Mrs. Kemp had first mentioned her hiring Shadow, she'd been a little hesitant. The first couple of times she'd been around Shadow, the teenager had been so sullen and sarcastic. It seemed to be lessening now. "And that's a cute outfit. Are those . . .cowboy boots?"

Shadow held out a foot encased in a red cowboy boot. "They are. Aren't they darling?"

Between the boots, dark jeans, and flannel shirt, Shadow looked like she'd just stepped out of an ad for a dude ranch. "The braid is cute, too. You look like you belong on the show *Hee Haw*."

Shadow wrinkled her nose. "What's that? I've never heard of it."

Violet groaned. She hadn't felt too old until she started spending regular time with a sixteen-year-old. "It's a TV show that was based in Nashville. I used to watch it with my grandparents."

"Oh." Shadow knelt down to look at the variety of paints. "These colors are awesome. Are we really painting the chairs different colors?"

Violet nodded. "We are. I have spray paint for the chairs."

Shadow made a face. "Are you sure that will work?"

"I saw it on HGTV. It worked for them, it'll work for us." At least she hoped so. "Before you get started, do you want to change clothes? I have some old T-shirts and sweatpants. I'd hate for you to get your clothes messed up."

Shadow shrugged. "I guess so."

Violet led her into the house. "Hang on a second and I'll go grab some clothes for you."

"Cute dog." Shadow sat down next to Arnie on the couch.

"Thanks. He's fifteen and almost totally deaf."

"Wow. He's almost as old as I am."

Violet nodded. That really put Arnie's age into perspective. "I've had him for a long time. But he's not doing too well right now."

Shadow leaned her face close to Arnie and talked to him softly. "Sweet, sweet dog. I have a dog in Texas, and I miss him very much." The sadness in her voice was evident.

Violet hurried to grab the clothes then went back to the living room. "These should do fine." She tossed them to Shadow. "You won't have to worry about getting them messed up. If they get paint on them, it might improve their looks." She grinned and pointed to a door in the hallway. "There's the bathroom."

Shadow gave Arnie one last pat and went to change clothes.

Violet thought about how judgmental she'd been when she first saw Shadow in her Goth attire. She'd never imagined all the trials the girl had faced. Her mother's death, her dad remarrying and having another child, leaving her pet behind to come live with her grandparents. . .it was no wonder she seemed so lost.

Lord, give me the wisdom to know how to help Shadow. Open her heart to letting me be her friend and mentor, and help me to guide her down a path that will lead her closer to You.

Jackson slid into the booth at Chili's and grinned. "Sorry I'm late. Traffic was terrible."

Jeff shrugged. "Don't worry about it." He motioned toward the appetizer platter. "More for us."

"Oh, you two. Stop with the small talk. Tell us about the girl." Lauren banged her hand on the table like she was calling a meeting to order. "I'd kind of hoped she'd be with you tonight."

Jackson smiled. "Patience doesn't mean anything to you, does it?"

Lauren scowled.

"Okay, okay. I didn't ask her to meet us because she's really busy right now getting ready for the grand opening of her bakery."

"Fine. Just as long as she is in fact a real person and we will get to meet her soon." Lauren popped the rest of her mozzarella stick into her mouth.

For a moment Jackson wished he could come clean to them about the arrangement he and Violet had. He'd love to hear their advice. Ever since his run-in with Reagan last weekend, he'd felt remorseful for the way he'd treated Violet all those years ago. "You will definitely get to meet her, and I promise she is one-hundred-percent real." Their relationship, on the other hand, was not.

"Fair enough."

Once they'd placed their orders, Jeff nudged Lauren. "Can we tell him now? Please?"

"Tell me what?"

Lauren smiled broadly. "We're pregnant. You're going to be a faux uncle again."

"Congratulations! That's very exciting news. I didn't realize y'all were going for number three."

Jeff beamed. "With Bennett in school now and Levi starting

next year, we figured it was the right time."

"I'm hoping for a girl to even out some of the testosterone in my household." Lauren grinned. "Maybe a little less rough and tumble would be nice."

"Levi has his arm in a cast right now because Bennett convinced him to try jumping from the top bunk." Jeff shook his head. "It's always something."

"We're on a first-name basis with the nurse at the walk-in clinic." Lauren laughed.

Jackson was happy for his friends. Lauren and Jeff were great parents. They seemed to have found just the right balance between too worried and too laid back.

"So. . .not to pry, but do you think this girl could be 'the one'?" Lauren made quote marks in the air with her fingers. "Or is she just a way to pass the time?"

Jackson took a sip of sweet tea. "Violet has a lot of wonderful qualities. She's smart and funny and very pretty." He grinned. "And she's a good person. She lives her life striving to do God's will." He shrugged. "But I don't really know where things will go with us." Actually, he was pretty certain they'd lead to a breakup the third week of January, but he didn't dare mention it.

"Sounds like a keeper to me," Lauren said. "And it's about time. You haven't had the easiest road."

Jeff sent his wife a dirty look.

"What?" she asked. "He hasn't. We all know how tough things have been at times."

Jackson shrugged. "I don't like to dwell on the past. You know that. By the grace of God, I got through the bad stuff and I'm here now. But everyone has had difficulties. Not just me." He'd always tried to downplay the bad parts of his life, preferring to look at the bright side.

"How's your mom?" Jeff asked, going for a swift subject change.

"Dating." Jackson couldn't help but roll his eyes. "Can you believe that? It's something you don't think you'll ever have to deal with. One of your parents having a love life."

"Yeah, Kathleen mentioned it," Lauren said. "She's good with it though. Says she's glad your mom has someone to talk to and go out and do things with." She grinned. "And for the record, I think it's great, too. I mean, if something ever happened to me, I'd want Jeff to move on." She gave Jeff a wink. "After a very lengthy grieving period, of course."

Jeff laughed. "I'll keep that in mind."

Were they right? Was Mom dating again just the natural order of things? "I've met the guy once at church, but it was only briefly. I don't usually attend where Mom does, so I haven't really been around him. But she says he'll be at our family Thanksgiving."

"Will your girlfriend be there, too?" Lauren asked.

He nodded. "She will."

Lauren shot him a cat-that-ate-the-canary grin. "I'm liking this more and more. I cannot wait to meet her and see how cute you guys are together."

"I think I may have the perfect time for us to hang out." Jeff scrolled through his phone. "The Razorbacks are playing at War Memorial in a couple of weeks. Does your girlfriend like football?" The University of Arkansas football team played most of their games at the Fayetteville campus, but one or two games each year were played at Little Rock's stadium.

Jackson had no idea if she liked it, but she'd signed a contract agreeing to attend a game. "We've actually talked about going to that game."

"Let me see what I can do. I think I can get us four tickets together. We can tailgate before the game and get to know her."

Jackson nodded. "Sounds like a plan. I'll talk to her later and make sure her schedule is clear." So far they hadn't tried to convince anyone of the nature of their relationship. He hadn't stayed at the taste testing long the other night, and from what he could tell, Reagan thought they were just friends with potential. But if they went to a Razorback game with Jeff and Lauren, their every move would be under constant scrutiny.

They'd have to come off as a convincing couple. Jackson knew he was on board—he looked forward to it. He was just afraid Violet would balk at the idea. Especially if he held her hand or hugged her. So far when he'd gotten close to her, she'd tensed up.

Was that because he repulsed her? Or was she becoming aware that he was attracted to her?

Only time would tell, but Jackson knew one thing—he was looking forward to playing the role of her dutiful boyfriend in public.

Just how much he looked forward to it surprised him.

Dear Mama,

I met the cutest boy the other day at the feed store. What a strange place to meet a boy! I went with Granddaddy to get some weed killer for his garden and there, standing next to a display of fake turkeys, was the cutest boy I've ever seen.

His name is Dale, and he had on a cowboy hat and everything. He rides horses in competitions. He asked me to go watch him ride a bull sometime, and he got my phone number.

Granddaddy embarrassed me though because he came over to meet him and asked a million questions.

Anyway, he texted me today, so I think he really likes me.

Oh—Violet and I got the tables and chairs painted for the bake shop. They are so pretty. We painted the chairs all different colors—yellow, pink, blue, orange—you name it! And then we did the tables white, but Violet let me do some free-hand painting on the top. I mostly did little swirly designs and stuff to match the chair colors. It looks so neat.

Violet thinks I should take an art class, but I don't know.

Love you,
Shadow

Chapter 21

Jackson Stratford: Two questions: Do you have plans tomorrow night and what's your favorite color? (Text message sent October 5, 9:09 a.m.)

Violet Matthews: Working at the shop I guess. Why? And purple is my favorite color. Did you really have to ask? How about you? (Text message sent October 5, 9:15 a.m.)

Jackson Stratford: How about dinner at 7? And yeah, I guess that one should've been obvious. Mine's green, although violet is a close second. (Text message sent October 5, 9:18 a.m.)

Reagan stood in the driveway and waved good-bye to the kids. There'd been a few tears from Ava Grace, but when Chad's mom had promised that she and their Paw Paw would take everyone for ice cream later, the tears had miraculously disappeared. Ava

Grace was a girl after her mom's own ice-cream-loving heart.

She glanced at her watch. It wasn't quite three yet. She'd be able to take her sweet time showering and getting ready for her date with Chad. In some ways, she was as nervous as a teenager. They'd spent so little time together during the past few months, and when they had, their conversation centered on the kids. What if they didn't have anything to say to each other anymore? What if Chad couldn't help but compare her to Reese?

Reagan pushed the thought from her mind and took the longest, steamiest shower she'd had in a very long time. It was pure joy to get to wash *and* condition her hair and even shave her legs. Motherhood trumped things like personal pampering.

She wrapped herself in the plush robe Violet had given her when Ava Grace was a baby. She'd called it a spa robe. Whatever the name, it was made from the kind of material that seemed to envelop her in a warm, fluffy cocoon.

Reagan took her time drying her hair, making sure all the kinks were straightened out. Her long blond hair was her one throwback to her pre-mommy days. Chad's mom had chided her for not getting it cut short when she had kids, claiming it would be so much easier to care for, but Reagan had resisted.

Chad had told her once that her hair was the first thing he'd noticed about her. So she'd kept it long, even though it meant more trouble.

And as her family grew, it became more of a hassle, yet she still kept it as a reminder to herself that she was still in there somewhere—the girl Chad had fallen in love with.

She painted her fingernails and toenails red and sat down on the bed for a moment. Still plenty of time left.

She couldn't resist leaning back and resting her head on the pillow just for a second. Last night she'd been up almost every hour with someone, and by the morning when it was time to get Izzy to school, she'd been exhausted.

Reagan burrowed into the soft robe and closed her eyes, thinking about the fun she and Chad would have tonight.

Just like old times.

She heard a loud noise and sat upright. The bedroom door was closed. That was weird. "Chad?" she called. "Are you home?"

The door cracked open, and Chad peeked inside. "Hello, Sleeping Beauty. It's about time you joined the land of the living." He grinned.

She stood up. Her brain felt so foggy. No wonder she didn't nap anymore. "Sorry. I'll be ready in just a sec."

Chad laughed. "Ready for what? The kids will be back soon. You were asleep when I got home last night so I cancelled our reservation and closed the bedroom door." He grinned. "I slept in the guest room so I wouldn't wake you."

Reagan sank onto the bed. "Wait. It's tomorrow? Already?" She closed her eyes. "I don't understand how this happened."

"Babe, you're exhausted. There was no way I was going to wake you up. No dinner was that important." He sat down next to her. "You look upset. Are you mad?"

"What? No." She bit her tongue. "Actually yes. I'm mad." She stood up. "I can't believe you didn't wake me up. You know how much trouble I'd gone to. I arranged for your mom to take the kids, I made a reservation." She frowned. "I even made chocolate-dipped strawberries for dessert."

"I know. I had them as a little snack while I watched *SportsCenter* last night."

He thought he was being funny. "It's me, isn't it? You didn't want to have a romantic night with me." She'd planned to fill him in on her gym membership last night. She'd expected that if they actually had some time alone together, he'd finally notice that she'd lost almost ten pounds. But he hadn't. Because he hadn't woken her up.

"Don't be silly. I was looking forward to the night, too. But you looked so cute asleep, I didn't want to wake you up."

She glared. "Don't try to make me feel better by saying I looked cute." She sighed. "You aren't attracted to me anymore." Hot tears sprang into her eyes. "Are you?"

Chad groaned. "Reagan, that's crazy. And you know it."

The doorbell rang.

"That's Mom with the kids." He stood up. "This conversation is not over." He walked out of the bedroom.

As far as she was concerned it was over. Ten years ago, there was no way he would've just let her sleep through what was supposed to be their first romantic night together in months. No kids. Just the two of them.

It was just as she'd suspected. Something was off between them. And she had no idea how to fix it.

Violet glanced around the shop. It was amazing how much she'd gotten done this week. The taste testing had sent her into full-on panic mode, and she'd felt like she was moving in fast forward all week.

Shadow had turned out to be a huge help, painting and then helping to transport the furniture.

Violet sat down in an orange chair and ran her hand across the smooth tabletop. The multicolored swirls added an extra kick. She couldn't help but smile. This place was a dream come true.

A tap at the door startled her. She glanced up to see Jackson on the other side of the glass, a grin on his face.

"I didn't mean to lock it," she said, opening the door.

He chuckled. "With you up here alone, I think I feel better knowing it was locked. Most everything on this street is closed or closing for the night." He walked past the tables. "Someone's been busy. It looks incredible."

"Thanks. I'm really happy with the way it all turned out."

He pulled back a turquoise chair and sat down. "Can I be honest?"

She nodded. "Always."

Jackson grinned. "When you first told me the plan—the yellow walls and the multicolored chairs and mismatched tables—I couldn't imagine how that would possibly look okay." He glanced around. "But you had a real vision. It looks perfect for a cupcake shop. People are going to love it."

She sat down across from him. "I hope so."

"Still a doubter, huh?" He shook his head. "What am I going to do with you?"

Violet shrugged. "Give me a guarantee."

"There are no guarantees in life. You know that. Put your trust in the Lord. Do your best." He smiled. "And pray a lot. I guess that's my best advice." His blue eyes were the same color as his sweater.

"Pretty good advice I guess." She pushed a strand of hair from her face. "Did anyone ever tell you that your eyes are nearly the same color as denim? Kind of a gray blue?"

He laughed. "Can't say that they have." He raised his eyebrows up and down. "But thanks for noticing."

She blushed. Great. Now he thought she was checking him out. "Just an observation." She stood up. "What are you in the mood for tonight?" As soon as she asked the question, she wished she could take it back. The gleeful expression on his face told her he was about to make an off-color joke.

"Well. . ." He trailed off and chuckled at her dirty look. "What?" He held up his hands in surrender. "I was just going to say pizza. I'm in the mood for pizza."

"Right." Their stupid contract with that ridiculous first kiss flashed through her mind. She knew he might spring it on her any time. Every time she thought about it, she grew uneasy. She liked surprises, but not that one. Not from him.

"Or something else if you don't want pizza." He shrugged. "I'm flexible."

"Actually, pizza is good with me. Would it be weird to just go back to my house and have it delivered? Arnie isn't doing all that great, and I've been gone a long time today." Her voice caught at the mention of Arnie, and she hoped he hadn't noticed. His stance on inside dogs still angered her.

"That sounds like fun. I'll follow you there."

She grabbed her bag and turned off the lights. Just a few more weeks and the shop would be bustling.

Hopefully.

Jackson stood on Violet's front porch and waited for her to get out of the car. It sure was dark out here. She'd been excited to find a place outside of town, but he wasn't sure if it was such a good idea. Her nearest neighbors were pretty far down the road, and there wasn't much of a light out front.

"You look lost in thought," she said as she walked toward him.

He frowned. "I was just thinking about how dark it is out here."

"Funny how that happens at nighttime," she said with a smirk.

Jackson groaned. "I'm serious. Why don't you let me put one of those motion sensor lights out here? You're awfully far from the road, and you don't even have neighbors nearby."

"Are you worrying about me?"

He shrugged. "I guess."

"I'm flattered. But I'm fine." She grinned and stuck her key in the lock. "Really. I haven't been scared once since I moved in."

He followed her into the living room, and she flipped on the light.

"Arnie boy, do you want to go outside?" she asked, bending down and shaking the dog lightly.

Arnie slowly opened his eyes then jumped up, startled at the sight of Jackson. He barked a few times in Jackson's direction.

Violet put her hand on the dog's head. "It's okay," she said. "Come on." She steered him toward the back door.

"Everything okay?" Jackson asked once she came back into the room.

She shrugged. "He's not doing that well. I need to take him to the vet to get his kidney function checked again, but I'm afraid of what I'll find out." She frowned. "I'm giving him a special kind of food and also cooking for him some."

"You cook for him? Like on the stove?"

Violet glared. "Yes, I do. I know you can't possibly understand the attachment I have to him, but rest assured that it's a big one. He's been with me for a lot of years. When people have let me down, Arnie has been by my side. Happy to see me when I come home—whether after a day at work or a trip that lasted a week. It's hard to find unconditional love anymore."

That was true, he'd give her that much. But still. . .the dog hair and dirt and messy yard seemed like a real pain. "I'm sorry. I didn't mean anything by that. My sister is the same way about their Lab. Her husband jokes sometimes that Max is the real love of her life."

Violet's mouth quirked into a smile.

Finally. "Speaking of my sister. . ." He trailed off. He'd been putting this off because he wasn't sure what her reaction would be. "She's invited us to come to her house in Memphis next weekend. I know you're busy with the shop, but if we don't go before you open, it will be almost impossible for you to find a free weekend."

"Memphis for the weekend?" She sat down on the couch. "I don't know."

Was she torn about going somewhere with him, or was it just because she was so close to the opening? Jackson wasn't sure he wanted to know the answer. "I can tell her no if you can't make it."

"Yes. I'll go." She gave him a tiny grin. "It was part of the contract after all. I know we're going to have to be around our friends and families soon, and this thing between us needs to look believable."

Jackson let out a breath he hadn't realized he was holding. "So you'll go?"

She nodded. "Count me in. I'm sure it will be a blast. I love Memphis. Grandpa can come over and let Arnie out."

"We'll leave next Saturday morning and be back Sunday afternoon." Jackson couldn't remember the last time he'd taken a woman on a road trip. And he'd never taken anyone to his sister's house.

"I'd better order the pizza." Violet stood up and grabbed her phone. "Pepperoni okay with you?"

He nodded and watched her dial the number. He knew without a doubt that Kathleen and Violet would get along wonderfully. They could probably be pretty good friends.

A sinking feeling washed over him. He couldn't risk Kathleen letting the truth about his past slip to Violet.

And that meant one thing.

He'd have to tell her himself.

Chapter 22

Violet Matthews: THE SIGN FOR THE FRONT OF THE STORE
ARRIVED TODAY! I HAVE THE MOST AWESOME DESIGNER
EVER! ACTUALLY, I'VE ALREADY HAD SOMEONE ASK FOR YOUR
CONTACT INFORMATION. ARE YOU UP FOR ANY FREELANCE
WORK? (Text message sent October 9, 1:23 p.m.)

Reagan McClure: ARE YOU SERIOUS? I'VE NEVER THOUGHT
ABOUT IT, BUT I LOVED CREATING YOUR STUFF SO MUCH.
HADN'T REALIZED HOW MUCH I'D MISSED IT. SO SURE!
FEEL FREE TO PASS MY INFO ALONG! (Text message sent
October 9, 1:35 p.m.)

Violet hung the last of the framed quilt squares in the bakery's
dining area. Perfect.

"What do you think?" she asked Grandma. The older woman
had stopped by the shop on her way to the grocery store.

Grandma looked at her with watery eyes. "My mother would
be so proud that she's part of your store." She smiled and wiped her

eyes. "I'm just glad I saved them." She held up a bag. "And even happier about this." She handed the bag to Violet.

"What's this? Grandma, you didn't have to get me anything."

Grandma shrugged. "It isn't anything I paid for."

"Grandma, are you stealing again?" Violet teased.

The older woman burst out laughing. "I guess that did sound pretty bad, huh? It's just something that I think you can use."

Violet reached into the bag and pulled out a purple and yellow apron. It was a little faded, but that added to its character. "I love it."

"It was mine. A gift from your grandpa in the early fifties." She smiled. "I always thought I'd pass it on to whichever of my granddaughters married first, but I believe you will cherish it a lot more than Amber." She smiled. "I'll buy her a brand-new apron, and she'll be thrilled."

Violet slipped it over her head and quickly tied the ribbon in the back. "What do you think?" She twirled around the shop.

"Perfection." Grandma smiled.

Violet walked over to the counter and checked her list. Things were surprisingly on target. "I'm set to open the week of Halloween," she said. "What did you think of the sign?"

"I think you're going to be very busy. It looks wonderful."

Violet handed her the mock-up of the flyer and business cards. "Here are the other things Reagan worked on. They're at the printer now."

"She's very talented. These look great." Grandma tapped the paper. "And these cupcakes look delicious even in the photo." She handed them back to Violet. "Is there anything I can do to help?"

Violet shrugged. "Just spread the word. I'll give you the grand opening flyer and some business cards, and you can help me distribute them." She sighed. "And there's the possibility I might need a little help behind the counter. I'm not at all sure what to expect." She grinned. "But I'll be looking to hire someone before it gets out of hand, so don't think I'll be calling on you all the time."

Grandma chuckled. "I'll be glad to help out however I can, even if it's just going to the grocery store for you or running other errands. But I think working behind the counter sounds fun."

"I was hoping you'd say that." Violet grinned. "And I think Shadow will be a great help."

Grandma nodded. "Betty's just thrilled that she seems to be blossoming a little bit. She's made a couple of good girlfriends at school who are in the youth group with her at church."

"She's becoming a little more talkative here, too. I think she likes the creative side of working here. Her painting is beautiful, and she told me yesterday she'd like for me to teach her how to ice the cupcakes." Violet had been thrilled that Shadow might want to learn some of the baking. When she'd hired her, she'd expected that the teenager would only be interested in packaging preorders and working the cash register.

"That's wonderful." Grandma bit her lip. "Can I ask you something?"

Violet stopped checking things off her list and nodded. "Of course."

"Now I don't mean to pry, but Betty says she met your young man the other night. And your grandpa tells me you've asked him to care for your dog this weekend." She patted Violet's arm. "Are you going somewhere with him?"

Violet felt the heat rise up her face. "We're going to Memphis to visit his sister."

"Meeting the family. . .that sounds serious."

She didn't want to mislead her grandmother. "It's complicated. Jackson and I—we haven't always gotten along. Sometimes we still don't." She shrugged. "We knew each other in college."

"Betty was quite taken with him. Said he was very polite and charming." Grandma raised an eyebrow, an ability Violet had never quite mastered. "And I just wondered if you thought it was going anywhere."

The last guy she'd dated who was polite and charming had lied to her, cheated on her, and turned out to be a world-class jerk. She could see why Grandma might worry. "I think that for now we're just learning to be friends." It was way too complicated to try to explain. And even if she admitted the agreement she and Jackson had made, she knew her grandma would probably think it was a terrible idea.

"Being friends is nice." Grandma smiled. "You know, your grandpa and I weren't exactly friends from the beginning. He thought I was way too headstrong, and I thought he was too uptight." She chuckled. "But we worked that out and figured out our differences only made our relationship more interesting." She gave Violet a hug. "I pray that you'll find the same thing someday."

"Thanks." Violet watched her grandmother go. It was hard to wrap her mind around people thinking she and Jackson might actually be a real couple. But she'd better get used to it because in two days they'd be in full-on couple mode.

Reagan collapsed on the gym floor. "Is it my imagination, or is today's workout harder than last week's?" she asked Maggie.

"This instructor is used to teaching the advanced class."

"*Now* you tell me." Reagan grinned. "I was beginning to think I'd gone backward on my fitness goals."

Maggie shook her head. "I'd say you're just right." She nodded her head toward Reagan. "You look great. How do you feel?"

Reagan sighed. "I feel better about everything except for Chad. He let me sleep through our date night last week."

"Maybe you needed the rest."

"I'm sure I did, but it still stings that he'd do that. I mean, we haven't had time alone in eons." She'd refused to discuss it anymore with Chad, but he'd claimed he was only trying to do what was best for her. "And I can't shake the feeling that he's hiding something."

Maggie narrowed her eyes. "Have you told him about the gym yet?"

"No. But only because I want him to *notice* that there's something different about me. He lives with me. He sleeps in the same bed as me. You'd think he'd catch on that I've lost nearly ten pounds."

"Oh, he probably notices. He might not know what's different, but I'm sure he knows something is." Maggie chuckled. "But why don't you just schedule another date night? Now that you know you can let someone else watch the kids for a while, maybe you should take advantage of that."

"Maybe you're right."

Maggie nodded. "I am. Trust me." She grinned. "I was right about Zumba, wasn't I?"

"I guess. Although if I shimmy much more today, I might have to be carted out of here on a stretcher."

"Don't sell yourself short. Here *or* at home." Maggie took a sip of water. "By the way, the family I work for is moving at the end of December. You know anyone who might need a nanny?"

Reagan laughed. "I wish. But I'm pretty sure Chad would never go for that. His mother has told me a million times how the best decision she ever made was leaving her job so she could stay home. He's always wanted me to stay home with our kids."

"But don't you think that's something the two of you should agree on? I'm not even saying you shouldn't stay home. I'm saying that maybe you need some help. Even another mom you can trade some time with."

"Well, I do have some exciting news that might mean I need a little bit of time without the kids." She filled Maggie in on the design work she'd done for Violet. "And I got an e-mail this morning from a business just down the road from Violet's shop that sells soaps and lotions. They're interested in having me design a new logo for them and possibly renovate their website."

"And is that something you're passionate about?"

She nodded. "I'd really like to accept the job, but I'm not sure how I'd swing it. I did Violet's project because she's my best friend, but I had to let a lot of stuff slide at home. I'm still catching up on laundry."

Maggie laughed. "It's a black hole, isn't it?"

The instructor called everyone back from the break.

"Just think about it, okay? I think it's time you and your husband had an honest conversation about things."

Reagan pondered the advice. Maybe Maggie was right. But what if it drove an even bigger wedge between her and Chad? She wasn't sure the distance between them could get any farther. Because if it did, they'd be dangerously close to being two strangers who happened to share a house and a last name.

Dear Mama,

I am so excited about this weekend! Rachel and I are going to watch Dale in some kind of bull-riding competition. I think it will be so cool to see him ride.

I'm working on my schedule for next semester, and I'm considering taking an art class for one of my electives. Violet and I had a talk the other day about my classes, and she told me all about how she became a lawyer for all the wrong reasons and how excited she was to finally be going after her dreams. She thinks I should try different things to see what kind of stuff I'm good at and enjoy. It makes sense, I guess, but I don't know how I'll feel about getting a grade for my artwork.

You know that's always been something I just did for fun. What if I'm not really talented?

I guess there's only one way to find out, but it's kind of scary.

ILY,

Shadow

Chapter 23

Jackson Stratford: WE'LL BE THERE AROUND NOON
TOMORROW. WHAT'S THE PLAN? (Text message sent
October 12, 8:22 a.m.)

Kathleen Morgan: YAY! WE'RE SO EXCITED. THE KIDS HAVE
MADE WELCOME DRAWINGS FOR VIOLET. LUNCH WILL
BE READY WHEN YOU GET HERE. LOOKING FORWARD TO
GETTING TO KNOW VIOLET! (Text message sent October
12, 8:34 a.m.)

Jackson stood outside Violet's house, wondering if this was
a huge mistake. Showing up unannounced wasn't usually his
style, but he really needed to see her. He knocked on the door.

She opened the door, the surprise evident on her face. "Jackson!
What's wrong?"

"I know we aren't leaving until tomorrow, but, uh, I kind of
needed to talk to you." He shifted uncomfortably.

"Of course." She opened the door wider. "Come on in." She

smiled. "And excuse the mess. I'm trying to go through my giant collection of paper."

"Paper?"

Violet laughed. "I can't seem to throw it away. I'm seriously drowning in stacks of paper." She gave him a sheepish look. "Something I'm sure you can't understand."

"I don't hold your paper hoarding against you in any way," he said with a laugh. "At least you know you have a problem." He flipped through a stack of magazines.

"So what's up?" she asked.

He sighed. He'd known when she accepted his invitation to Memphis that he'd have to come clean about his entire past, but it might be harder than he'd expected. "Let's sit." He motioned toward the couch.

Once they were settled, he took a deep breath. "Violet, I'm really sorry for the way I treated you when we were in college. I'd sort of forgotten most of it until I ran into Reagan the other day. She was more than happy to refresh my memory."

Violet shook her head. "You don't have to apologize. That was a long time ago."

"I do." He frowned. "You need to know how genuinely sorry I am."

She furrowed her brow. "I appreciate you telling me."

"There's more." He cleared his throat. "I think there was a rumor in college that I'd taken a gap year or something and gone to Europe." He shook his head. "That wasn't the truth."

Violet widened her eyes. "Yeah, I'm pretty sure I heard something like that."

"I actually started college at the U of A with some of my friends. Summer after my freshman year, I lived there in an apartment with some other guys." He chewed on the inside of his lip. "We were dumb guys, you know? It was the first taste of freedom for many of us, and we did some really stupid stuff." He sighed. "The stupidest by far was one night toward the end of the summer when I got in the car with one of my buddies. He'd been drinking." He swallowed. "We both had."

She shook her head. "What happened?" she whispered.

"There were several of us in the car. We were so stupid." He'd never had to tell anyone the story before. It was much harder than he'd expected. "Richie lost control going around a curve. I was thrown from the car. The last thing I remember is hearing the girl I'd been seeing—her name was Jenna—scream." He took a deep breath. "Jenna didn't make it. I barely did."

"I'm so sorry." Violet reached for his hand and squeezed it.

"I had a lot of injuries. I went through multiple surgeries and a lot of rehab. It was terrible." He sighed. "Not only that, but I felt immense guilt over Jenna's death. I hadn't dated much before college, so she was my first real relationship. And it was my fault that we were in that car. I knew better. I'd been brought up better."

"You were young."

He shook his head. "That's not really an excuse." He cleared his throat. "Anyway, it took me a long time to recover. And there was a lot of pain—so much that I was on a lot of pain medication." He shrugged. "My parents were so upset with me over my behavior at the U of A that they insisted the only school where they'd pay tuition was Harding. They wanted me surrounded by Christians in the hopes that it would help turn me back to the straight and narrow."

"And did it?"

He shrugged. "It was definitely better for me to be in that environment after everything I'd been through. But in some ways, it caused me even more problems. I felt like I wasn't good enough to be there."

"I'm sorry you felt that way."

"It just felt like everyone I met had these perfect lives. They did and said the right things. And then there was me, with this big, awful secret. Even worse, I had a very hard time getting off the pain pills. Probably a lot of the time you had interaction with me, I was refusing to face the fact that I might be addicted. That made me feel even worse about myself."

"It sounds like you had a really rough time. I had no idea."

"I was miserable, and I tried to make everyone around me miserable. I came to that campus acting like I was some kind of hotshot. I picked on anyone who might be an easy target just to make myself feel better."

"Including me."

He squeezed her hand. "I'm really sorry. You have to understand that I'm a different person now. I've worked really hard to put all of that behind me."

Violet regarded him for a long moment, and Jackson couldn't help but wonder if she was going to dissolve their contract and send him on his way.

Violet's mind reeled. Jackson's story was not at all what she'd expected when he'd shown up on her doorstep. She'd thought he might want to prep her for the visit to his sister's house. But she'd never expected anything like this. "I can't imagine what you've gone through."

He sighed. "I don't want pity or anything. I just need you to understand that the guy you met fifteen years ago was carrying a lot of burdens. I was in pain—both physical and emotional—and nothing helped. I think it was during that time that I lashed out at those people I saw as having it all together. People like you."

"You thought I had it all together?"

He gave her a tentative smile. "Yeah. You were the kind of person who just floated through life. You never seemed to care much about fitting in with a certain crowd. You just did your own thing."

"I dealt with stuff of my own. Nothing like you did, but still. My life was far from perfect."

"I know that now. It's something I guess you learn with age. We all have our own issues, our own insecurities."

She nodded. "So how did you get your life back together?"

"After graduation, I went to grad school. I worked hard to get off the pain meds completely. It was hard. Very hard. But I had a good support group at the church I attended. I think I told you that grad school was when I feel like I really formed my own relationship with the Lord and developed my own faith. That had a huge part in my recovery and eventually helped me to become a better man. It's hard knowing I hurt people."

"It's weird how you never know the things a person might be dealing with just by looking at them, isn't it?" She glanced at him. "When I met Shadow and she was all decked out in black clothes and had fake tattoos and piercings, I jumped to a conclusion about her. And back in college when I met you, I thought you were a pretentious frat boy who made fun of everyone and everything." She shrugged. "I was wrong in both cases. Shadow has dealt with tremendous loss for a child so young. And you must have felt such remorse over the accident and the fallout that it's no wonder you lashed out."

Jackson nodded. "I think for me, one of the worst things was the division it caused within my family. My parents fought a lot during those years, and I know a big reason was because of the stress I put on the family. It can't be easy to see your child make terrible decisions and almost get himself killed. And my parents knew about my problem with pain meds, but they were helpless to stop it." He shook his head. "I finally realized that the pain I was trying to end wasn't really from my physical injuries—but it took a long time to figure that out." He gave her a sheepish look. "Now that you know the truth, do you think I'm too messed up to deal with?"

She smiled. "Not at all. I know it wasn't easy for you to tell me all of that. But look at you now. You have your life together, you're successful in your career, and you're about to receive an award from your alma mater." She bumped against him with her shoulder. "And you have the best fake girlfriend in the history of fake girlfriends."

Jackson chuckled. "That I do."

Violet could tell he was glad to have gotten it off his chest. And she was glad for him. Sometimes it seemed like harboring secrets wound up causing more hurt than just letting them out in the open.

She wondered what that meant for their arrangement. Would the secret they shared come back to haunt them? She certainly hoped not.

Chapter 24

Reagan McClure: GUESS WHAT? I AGREED TO DO THE FREELANCE JOB. WHAT DO YOU THINK OF REAGAN MCCLURE DESIGNS? (Text message sent October 13, 8:14 a.m.)

Violet Matthews: THAT'S AWESOME! WHAT DOES CHAD THINK? WE'RE ON OUR WAY TO MEMPHIS TO VISIT JACKSON'S SISTER. . . . (Text message sent October 13, 8:22 a.m.)

Reagan walked into Ava Grace's room to see what the commotion was about. "What's going on in here?" she asked. Blankets were spread all over the floor, most of them with dolls or stuffed animals on them. Two of the blankets were empty.

Ava Grace cast a woeful gaze at her mother. "They're in time-out." She pointed to a stuffed bear and a doll missing an arm.

"You're putting your babies in time-out?" She couldn't hide her smile. Time-out was a concept Ava Grace had picked up at Sunday school. "Were they bad?"

The little girl nodded. "They didn't share." She put the back of her hand to her forehead. "It was terrible."

Reagan burst out laughing. "Oh, drama."

"I'm not drama. I'm Ava Grace." She lifted her chin defiantly.

"That you are," Reagan said. Her kids were so funny. She knew every mom in the world must think they had the funniest kids, but she was pretty sure hers really were.

"Mama, I can't find my gymnastics bag," Izzy yelled.

Reagan hurried to help hunt the lost bag. Chad had promised to take Izzy to gymnastics today, which would help out a lot. Once Ava Grace and the twins were down for their naps, she could get some housework done and maybe play around with a few ideas for her freelance job.

"When was the last time you saw your bag?" she asked Izzy. In the span of a couple of hours, she'd managed to tear her room apart. "And what happened to your room? It was clean this morning."

Izzy shrugged her shoulders. "I'm trying to find my bag."

"Is your version of trying to find your bag tossing everything off the shelves and onto the floor?"

"Pretty much." Izzy grinned, showing the gap where her two front teeth were missing. Soon she'd have her permanent teeth. She was sure growing up fast.

"Want me to put your hair up for class?"

Izzy thought for a moment. "Can you do a bun? Like a ballerina?"

"I can try." She grabbed a brush from the bathroom. "Come here."

Izzy stood in front of her and watched in the mirror.

Reagan brushed her long, straw-colored hair. "You've got some tangles today. Did you sleep standing on your head?"

Izzy giggled.

Reagan quickly wound her daughter's hair into a bun. "There you go. You look like a princess." She hugged her. "Now let's go see if your bag is in the laundry room. I think I remember seeing it there."

They walked past Ava Grace's room where she'd put two more dolls in time-out and was fussing at them for arguing with each other.

Just a typical morning at the McClure house.

"We're going to be late," Chad said as Reagan and Izzy walked into the kitchen.

"There's a missing bag. You'll have to hold on one second," Reagan said. She scanned the laundry room that also served as the entry room from the garage—and thus the catchall room. Shoes, bags, blankets, toys. You never knew what you might find in there. "Here it is." Reagan handed Izzy the bag and kissed her on the forehead. "Have fun."

Chad walked past her and grinned. "We'll be back soon." He gave her a quick peck on the cheek and ushered Izzy out the door.

Once she had put Ava Grace, Scarlett, and Simon down for naps, she sat down at the computer. Reagan McClure Designs. It had a nice ring to it. She should talk to Chad tonight.

Unless she waited until she had a couple of clients. If her freelancing didn't pan out, there was no need to have started an unnecessary argument.

Yes, that was a much better plan. She'd do a couple more jobs, and then if she had success, she'd tell him her plans.

Even though she hated keeping things from her husband, she was pretty sure there was something he was keeping from her. He'd never been good at keeping things from her, and the past few weeks he'd been very closemouthed about meetings and had been constantly glued to his iPhone. She wasn't sure what was going on, but she feared the worst.

Jackson took Violet's hand and helped her out of the car. "Ready?" he asked.

"Ready as I'll ever be. You?" She'd had fun on the trip to Memphis. Now that Jackson had gotten the news about his accident and bad behavior off his chest, it seemed he'd loosened up some. They'd discussed everything from their favorite movie moments to the next presidential election.

Violet had never been so open with a guy before. She knew part of that was because their relationship wasn't what they claimed it to be. So she felt like she could be herself. She could say anything.

"Uncle Jack!" A brown-haired girl who looked to be about five raced toward them.

Jackson picked her up and tossed her in the air. "Hello, sweet Olivia. When did you get so grown up?" He put her down, and she gave him a gap-toothed grin.

"I'm not grown up, silly. I'm in kindergarten." She looked at Violet. "Tyler and I have presents for you," she said shyly.

Violet knelt down. "I'm Violet. Thank you for letting me stay in your house tonight."

"Oh, you'll have to thank my mommy for that." She grinned again. "I'm not allowed to have sleepovers yet."

Violet laughed.

Olivia took Jackson's hand and then held her other hand up to Violet. "Can you swing me?"

They walked the rest of the way to the house swinging Olivia between them. She giggled each time they lifted her in the air.

"She's great," Violet murmured to Jackson as they reached the porch.

"There you are." A petite woman with the same steely blue eyes as Jackson opened the door. "Olivia has been sitting out here waiting." She grinned at her daughter. "She was supposed to come tell us when you got here, but I'll bet she was too excited." She held out a hand to Violet. "I'm Kathleen Morgan."

Violet introduced herself and followed her into the house. Meeting the family was a new experience for her. Zach's family had lived out of state, and she'd never met them. "Thanks for having me."

"Are you kidding?" Kathleen grinned and gave Jackson a side hug. "We're thrilled that Jackson has found someone he wanted to introduce to us." She nudged him with her elbow. "But Mom is jealous that we're meeting Violet first and she lives right there in town."

Jackson chuckled. "Thanksgiving will be here before you know it."

He'd filled Violet in on his mom's dating life. She'd tried to be supportive of his feelings, but had finally pointed out that he might be overreacting a bit. "I'm looking forward to meeting her though," Violet said.

Kathleen led them into the kitchen. "The guys are gone to get Tyler a new pair of soccer cleats, but it could take a little while to find just the right pair. Let's go ahead and eat while it's hot."

An hour later after the dishes were cleared, Jackson went to the backyard with Olivia so he could see her new swing set.

"Would you like a cup of coffee?" Kathleen asked.

Violet smiled. "That would be wonderful."

"That's why I love my Keurig. I can have fresh coffee at the touch of a button." Kathleen handed Violet a steaming cup. "There's creamer in the fridge and here's sugar and Splenda, whichever you prefer."

Violet poured cream and sugar into her cup and stirred. "Thanks again for the hospitality."

"I'm just glad to finally meet you." Kathleen motioned for Violet to follow her to the kitchen table. "Jackson says you guys knew each other in college."

Violet nodded. "Not well." She smiled. "And we didn't get along."

"No one got along with Jackson back then." She met Violet's eyes. "He's changed a lot."

"Seems that way." Violet took a sip of coffee and stared out the bay window at Jackson pushing Olivia in the swing.

"He speaks very highly of you. He's really excited about your bake shop."

Violet grinned. "The grand opening is just a little over two weeks away." Butterflies swarmed her stomach. Soon it would be time to sink or swim as an entrepreneur.

"Jackson seems to think it will be a raging success. And being able to spot good business opportunities is kind of his specialty."

"True. That does make me feel better."

"I'm glad you're here, Violet." Kathleen grinned. "I hope we see a lot more of you."

Violet's heart sank. This was part of the deal she hadn't bargained for. She actually *liked* Jackson's family. It made her sad to think that in a matter of months, they'd learn there'd been a breakup and never hear from her again.

Maybe she should just enjoy one day at a time and not worry that she was becoming attached to Jackson and his life.

"Told you they were going to love you," Jackson said once they were alone in the car. "Kathleen pulled me aside earlier and told me I'd found a winner."

Violet laughed. "Did you tell her I'm really just a loser masquerading as a winner?"

"Don't talk that way about my fake girlfriend." He glanced over at her. "Seriously though, they all adore you."

"They're pretty great, too. Olivia and Tyler drew me the sweetest pictures."

Jackson frowned. "Yeah, I didn't get any pictures. I don't know about all of that."

She laughed. "It's just because I'm a novelty. Where exactly are we headed? I haven't spent a ton of time in Memphis."

"We don't have a ton of time. Kathleen said the birthday party she was taking Olivia and Tyler to would last about an hour and a half. So I thought we'd go downtown. We'll eat some barbecue and then walk around a little bit. Maybe we'll hear the blues." He grinned. "Then we're supposed to meet them for cupcakes. Kathleen gave me directions to a place called Muddy's Bake Shop. She says it's one of their favorite places in town and maybe you'll get some ideas for your own shop."

Violet smiled. "That sounds wonderful. I'm definitely open to ideas."

Jackson flipped on his blinker. "Kathleen felt terrible that they had something planned." He grinned. "I told her not to worry about it and that I'd be glad to entertain you by myself for a little while."

"You certainly are entertaining." Violet laughed as he almost turned down a one-way street. "Do you know where you're going?"

"I'm not that familiar with downtown, but I know where the parking garages are. I come with my friend Jeff to see the Memphis Grizzlies play a few times each season."

"Fun." She gave him a sideways glance as he maneuvered into the nearest parking garage. "Is Jeff the one we're supposed to go to the Razorback game with?"

Jackson pulled into a spot and turned off the engine. "Yes. His wife, Lauren, and I have actually been friends since kindergarten." He grinned. "Jeff started attending our school in sixth grade. I think you'll love them. They have two adorable boys and another baby on the way."

"I'm looking forward to the game," she said as they walked toward the busy downtown area. "It will probably be my last weekend free for a very long time."

"That's right." Jackson looked over at her and smiled. "The opening is creeping up on you."

Violet nodded. "I can't believe it's October already. It seems like just yesterday that summer was starting." She shook her head. "It's like I blink and a whole month passes."

"Do you think that gets worse as you get older? When I was a kid, time seemed to drag on. But now it goes so fast it makes my head spin."

She smiled. "I think it must feel that way for everyone. Remember how when you were in school, classes felt like they lasted forever? My workday always seems to fly past." She laughed. "Unless it's the Friday before a holiday or something."

"I thought we'd go to the Rendezvous if that's okay. They're famous for ribs, but the barbecue sandwiches are good, too." He took her hand. "It almost feels like you're on some kind of movie set getting to the place though. It's kind of hidden down an alley." He liked the way her hand felt in his.

"That sounds great. I love barbecue."

They walked hand in hand down Union Avenue.

"I think this is the right street," he said.

They found themselves on a narrow, deserted street.

"I smell the barbecue. We must be headed in the right direction," Violet said.

Thirty minutes later they were seated and had ordered.

"You don't talk about your work much," Violet said. "Do you enjoy it?"

Jackson smiled. "I guess I'm weird about that kind of thing. When my dad passed away last year, I promised myself that I'd never get so bogged down with work that I wouldn't see what was really around me. You know?" He took a sip of sweet tea.

"I do, actually. I've known people who are so focused on work it's like they're not really present. Their body is there—at the dinner table, sitting in the bleachers, visiting with a friend—but their mind is elsewhere."

"I don't ever want to be that person. I want to be present in my own life and not just at work." Jackson sighed. "It's tough to find a balance, especially if you enjoy what you do. I think you just have to put priorities on your personal relationships over your career."

"Easier said than done. I have a friend that's sort of struggling with that right now. You know Reagan."

Jackson nodded. "Doesn't she stay home with her kids?"

"Yeah, but she's miserable. She loves her kids. She'd do anything for them. But I think she really needs to do something outside of the house occasionally." Violet filled him in on Reagan's freelancing opportunity. "I get the idea that she's worried her husband might think it means she's putting more emphasis on herself and her career than she is their kids. It's a tough spot to be in."

"Maybe they can work out some kind of compromise that will make them both happy."

Violet smiled. "I sure hope so." She folded her straw wrapper into a tiny piece. "What about you? What would you do if you could do anything?"

"I love what I do. Working to bring new industry into a town that desperately needs it is very rewarding. But if I were ever going to explore other options, I'd probably look at Heifer International. They have positions in Little Rock, and I think it's the kind of place

I'd enjoy being a part of." Heifer International's mission was to end hunger and poverty by providing livestock to people in need and encouraging them to then pass along the offspring of their livestock to other people in their community who were in need. Jackson appreciated the "pay it forward" approach.

"That would be fulfilling." Violet grinned. "And I bet you'd get to travel to some pretty far-off places to see the programs in action."

He shrugged. "For now I'm happy doing what I do. But if I ever change careers, I'll probably go the nonprofit route. If not Heifer, then another one I believe in and that will help me to feel like I'm making an impact."

The waitress placed their food on the table. "Let me know if you need anything else, you hear?"

Jackson offered a quick prayer before they dug into their food.

This was turning out to be the perfect weekend.

Chapter 25

Violet Matthews: THE WEEKEND WAS FUN. THANKS FOR TAKING ME! AND NOW: IF YOU COULD HAVE A SPECIAL TALENT, WHAT WOULD YOU WANT IT TO BE? (Text message sent October 16, 4:23 p.m.)

Jackson Stratford: THANKS FOR GOING! HAVE FUN WORKING AT THE SHOP THIS WEEKEND. I'LL PROBABLY STOP BY AT SOME POINT. AND I CAN'T WAIT UNTIL NEXT WEEKEND FOR THE GAME! OH, AS FOR MY TALENT—I WISH I COULD SING! YOU? (Text message sent October 16, 4:29 p.m.)

Violet Matthews: I WISH I WERE GOOD AT SPEAKING IN PUBLIC—IT TERRIFIES ME! PLENTY TO DO AT THE SHOP— STOP BY AND I'LL PUT YOU TO WORK! AND I'M LOOKING FORWARD TO THE GAME, TOO! (Text message sent October 16, 4:35 p.m.)

Violet pulled a test batch of cupcakes from the oven. Her Memphis trip had inspired her to try her hand at an Elvis-themed cupcake.

"Banana cupcake with peanut butter icing?" Shadow read the recipe over her shoulder. "That sounds kind of gross to me."

Violet grinned. "Don't knock it until you've tried it. If it was good enough for the King, it might be good enough for you."

"The King?"

"Yeah. You know. The one and only Elvis Presley." Violet curled her lip as much as she could. "Thank you, thank you very much."

Shadow shook her head. "What's so great about Elvis?"

Violet stuck out her tongue. "You'd better be kidding." She dusted her hands off on her apron and went over to the record player. "Just you wait." She slipped her favorite Elvis album out of the sleeve and put it on the turntable. The familiar crackle of the needle on the record filled the shop, followed by Elvis's smooth voice. " 'Jailhouse Rock' is one of my favorites."

"It's not bad," Shadow said once it was over. "But I still don't know about peanut butter and banana cupcakes."

Violet laughed. "I won't have them on the menu every week. But I want to have some variety. So if you ever think of another flavor that might be fun, let me know and we'll give it a try."

Shadow nodded. "Sure." She hobbled across to the counter to get the icing Violet had just made and put into the tube.

"Are you okay? You're walking funny."

"I'm going out with a new boy who rides horses," she explained. "So I took a riding lesson yesterday after school." She grinned. "My whole body hurts."

"So is it serious with this cowboy?" Violet asked.

Shadow shrugged. "I think he's getting ready to tell me he doesn't want to see me anymore." She dramatically threw herself into a chair. "I don't understand why I meet a boy and think he likes me, but then in a couple of weeks, he dumps me."

"Do you think it's possible that you're picking the wrong boys?" Violet asked gently.

Shadow shook her head. "No. I'm picking the right ones. It's just that they aren't picking me back."

Violet hid a smile. She might be far removed from her teenage years, but it was nice to know dating was just as full of angst as ever. "Hang in there. I'm sure a special one will come along soon who'll choose you over all the rest." She grinned. "As long as you choose him right back."

Shadow brightened. "I hope so."

Violet didn't say so, but she hoped the same thing for herself.

Reagan bent down to touch her toes before class started. She wanted to limber up because the advanced teacher was leading the class again today.

"You're here early," Maggie said as she took her place next to Reagan. "What gives?"

Reagan grinned. "I'm trying to get up an hour earlier in the mornings to get stuff done around the house." She shrugged. "The up side is that everyone in my house was ready on time as a result."

"So the best way for the whole family to get somewhere on

time is for Mom to lose another hour of sleep?" Maggie asked.

Reagan nodded. "Doesn't seem fair, does it?"

"Many things in life don't."

"I think this is going to be my last month here," Reagan said. "Things are just too hectic for me to try and fit the gym in."

Maggie narrowed her eyes. "Does this mean you're accepting freelance work?"

"Yes. I finished another job earlier in the week. And I've had a couple more inquiries just based on word-of-mouth advertising."

"What about your weight-loss goal?"

Reagan sighed. "That's partly why I'm making myself get up an extra hour early. I'm going to start training for a 5K or maybe a half marathon. Plus having to load three kids up twice a week and bring them here and then unload and then go pick up Izzy from school was getting to be too much. I'm literally taking kids in and out of my van nearly nonstop."

"So this way you'll still be working out, but won't have that extra burden."

Reagan nodded. "Exactly. And early in the mornings, Chad will be in the house with the kids, so he can take care of them if they happen to wake up. Which probably won't happen unless someone's sick, in which case I probably won't feel like running anyway."

Maggie frowned. "I'm going to miss you. Zumba won't be the same without watching you try not to trip over your own feet." She laughed.

"We weren't all blessed with the shimmying flair that you were."

Maggie wiggled her hips. "It's all about the hip action."

Reagan laughed. "I guess so." She did another stretch. "Did you find another family looking for a nanny?"

Maggie shook her head. "I think my full-time nannying days might be over. My husband is home more now that he's retired, so it's probably for the best. I'm trying to find something a couple of days a week."

An idea formed in Reagan's head. "You might be the answer to a prayer. If my freelancing business actually takes off, I'd like to look into having someone come to the house for a few hours a couple of days a week so I can get some work done."

"What does Chad think about it?"

Reagan wrinkled her nose. "He doesn't know yet because it might not even pan out. So why argue over something that might not happen?"

"I'd be glad to come over to your house to watch the kids." Maggie smiled. "But I don't like the idea of caring for kids unless both parents are onboard. In fact, before I ever agree to a permanent arrangement, I prefer to meet with both parents just to get a feel for the family."

"I'll keep that in mind. And obviously if this is something that would actually be a permanent arrangement, I would bring Chad into the decision-making process."

Maggie nodded. "Good. After class I'll give you my references in case you ever decide you want to have me come watch them. I'm certified in CPR for children and infants and also have taken a course in wound care."

It sounded perfect to Reagan. Maybe Chad would agree to a part-time nanny just for a few hours a week so Reagan could get some things done.

The loud music filled the room for the warm-up.

Reagan let herself forget all the outside stresses and focus on only one thing—trying to stay on her feet.

Violet stood on the porch at Jackson's the following Saturday and waited for him to answer the door. Since the Razorback game was in Little Rock, it made sense for her to meet him at his house. Which was fine with her—she'd always thought you could learn a lot about someone by their home.

She glanced around the brown brick exterior. Just as she'd expected, everything was clean and well-maintained. Either he spent a lot of time doing housework or he hired it done.

The door swung open, and Jackson stood on the other side, decked out in a long-sleeved Arkansas Razorback T-shirt and faded blue jeans. He wore a baseball cap with a razorback emblazoned on it. "Come on in," he said.

She stepped into the living room and looked around. Gleaming hardwood floors, wall-to-ceiling mahogany bookcases, and a matching leather couch and love seat screamed that it was a man's house. "Very masculine."

"I should hope so." He winked. "I decorated it myself."

She perused his bookshelves. Impressive. Classics, the typicals— Grisham, Koontz, and Dekker, and a variety of nonfiction ranging from Dave Ramsey to Stephen Covey. "So I gather you like to read?"

"Guilty." He smiled. "You have your vintage typewriter and records, I have my books. That's the one thing I can't throw out."

Based on the fact that the rest of his house looked as spotless as a magazine ad, she believed it. "Do I get a grand tour?" she asked.

"Absolutely." He pointed to the crown molding. "I installed that myself. And I know you're turning your nose up at my brown walls, but I like them."

She laughed. "I'd feel like I was living inside a cardboard box, but to each his own." She followed him into the kitchen. "Now this I like. Yellow walls, stainless-steel appliances." She smiled. "It gets my stamp of approval."

"That means more than if it came from *Good Housekeeping*." He grinned. "Down this hallway is the master bedroom, guest bedroom, and office."

She peeked in each room. Each was tastefully decorated in muted tones and expensive furnishings. "It's really pretty. Definitely more modern than my place." She preferred to pick up pieces with a history, and her favorite thing was to find a piece of furniture meant for one thing and repurpose it for another. She'd found the most gorgeous dresser a few months ago, and after some sanding, paint, and new hardware, it made the neatest sideboard in the dining room.

Jackson led her back to the kitchen. "Those french doors lead to a deck and a fenced-in yard."

"Without a dog to enjoy it." She shook her head. "Such a shame."

He grinned. "Arnie is welcome to visit the yard anytime, as long as he doesn't dig or go to the bathroom."

She laughed. "Okay, I'll let you be the one to inform him of that." She ran a hand along the granite countertops. "It's really pretty. I'm impressed."

"Thanks. I know it isn't all warm and cozy and cottage-like the way your place is, but it suits me."

"Yes, I suppose it does." She smiled.

"How's the shop? The opening is just days away."

She sighed. "Don't remind me." She'd spent the last week and a half perfecting recipes and training Shadow on the cash register. "Thanks for your help last week though. You really play the role of a disgruntled customer well."

He chuckled. "I just wanted to make sure Shadow was prepared to deal with the public."

"Well it was great training. She really took to you."

Jackson shrugged. "What can I say? I have a way with the ladies."

Violet laughed. "And you're so modest."

"Are you ready? We should get going. Traffic will be terrible. Jeff and Lauren went early to get a good tailgate spot, so at least we don't have to worry about that."

She followed him out the door and to the vehicle. She'd been at ease meeting his sister, but she was a bit more nervous about meeting his best friends. "Sounds perfect."

They headed toward the stadium in bumper-to-bumper traffic.

"Do you go to many games?" she asked.

Jackson nodded. "I used to have season tickets, but now I just go to a handful of games each year. Jeff and I usually road trip to one away game. My dad and I used to always try and make it to one game in Fayetteville and one in Little Rock each year." He took the exit for the stadium, and they waited in a long line of traffic. "Jeff texted earlier to tell me where they're set up. They're bringing the food." He grinned. "Lauren said that if I'd bring you, they'd do the cooking. I'm pretty sure she doubts your existence."

Violet laughed. "So does that mean you haven't introduced them to many girls?"

Jackson made a face. "Can I confess something to you? Because Lauren will probably tell you if I don't."

"Spill it."

"I've introduced them to a couple of girls over the years, but none of them have really been my type. They're sort of what prompted our arrangement in the first place. I've had a habit of dating what Lauren calls 'bubble heads,' and I promised her I'd bring someone suitable to the awards banquet." He sighed. "The last time I introduced them to a girl, it turned out Lauren used to babysit her. She was only ten years younger than us, but still. Lauren said she was really tired of me bringing girls on double dates who have no recollection of the eighties other than from VH1."

Violet chuckled. "Sounds like Lauren and I will get along just fine."

"Yes, I suspect you will." He pulled into a parking space on the golf course next to the stadium. "Here we go."

She waited for him to open the passenger door and took his hand when he offered it. "This will be fun."

He squeezed her hand as they walked toward the tailgate area. "It sure will."

Chapter 26

Jackson Stratford: Are you ready? Three days until the grand opening! You were a huge hit with Lauren and Jeff yesterday. They're ready to get together again. (Text message sent October 28, 2:33 p.m.)

Violet Matthews: Getting there. It's hard to believe that in just a few days there will be real customers! (I hope!) And I really liked Jeff and Lauren, too! (Text message sent October 28, 2:39 p.m.)

Violet put the finishing touches on the menu board. It looked great. Shadow had put her artistic skills to use to paint a beautiful border of multicolored gerbera daisies, and they'd painted the inside with chalkboard paint so the menu could be changed weekly.

"How does this look?" she asked Shadow.

Shadow beamed. "Awesome. I can't believe my artwork is on the main menu. People are going to see *my* drawings. That's so weird."

"You're very talented," Violet said. "Have you given any more thought to art classes?"

Shadow nodded. "I'm using one of my electives. It still makes me nervous to think about being graded. And then there are things like competitions and stuff."

"It takes a lot of courage to let the real you come out, doesn't it?" Violet asked. "I think of all the years I spent trying to be someone else. Someone whose dreams were a little less scary and a little more safe." She shrugged. "But scariest of all is waking up one day and realizing you've kept your true personality, your true dreams, bottled up inside."

Shadow sighed. "I guess."

"Maybe you should talk to my friend Reagan. She majored in graphic design in college, but minored in art. She's the one who designed the logo for Central Avenue Cupcakes. She also took the photographs and designed the layout for the website and business cards."

"It's really pretty," Shadow said, holding up one of the grand opening flyers. "Does she like to paint, too?"

Violet nodded. "She used to. I think her eye for art helped make her successful at designing logos and things. You have that same eye for colors and designs. I never would've thought to put some of the colors together on the tabletops, but you did and they look so pretty."

"Thank you. My mom used to paint. Sometimes she'd have me sit for portraits and stuff." She smiled at the memory. "Of course, she wasn't so happy when I got into her paints and painted a picture on the wall in the family room." She giggled. "It was just a tiny picture, and I even signed my name. Mama got on me about it, but she left it on the wall. When Daddy got home from work, she told him we'd acquired a new piece of art for the family room." Shadow sighed. "Stephanie painted over it when she had the colors redone."

"All the painting over in the world can't take the memory away, right?" Violet didn't know what to say. Such a tragic life.

Shadow's mouth quirked into a tiny smile. "I guess it would've been kind of embarrassing to have that on the wall forever. And Daddy made sure to take a picture of it."

"That's neat."

"I'm supposed to fly to Dallas for Thanksgiving. I wish Nana could go with me."

Violet straightened one of the quilt squares on the wall. "It will be nice to see your dad though, right? And I'll bet your dog has missed you a ton."

Shadow's face brightened. "That's true."

Violet wondered how her own Thanksgiving would go. She and her mother had argued about it already. Landry's parents were coming to Thanksgiving this year, and Mom thought she should make an effort to be there. When she'd explained that she already had plans, Mom hadn't exactly been thrilled. *"If you're spending Thanksgiving with this guy and his family, I think it's time to introduce us."* But Violet was determined not to let Jackson get any more involved in her life than he already was.

Otherwise their inevitable fake breakup might feel more like a real one.

Dear Mama,

 Well, me and Dale broke up. Sometimes I wonder what's

wrong with me. I meet a cute boy and have a good time talking to him or texting him, but after two or three weeks, it fizzles out.

Violet taught me how to make icing this week and how to ice the cupcakes so they'll look pretty. She mostly does all of that, but I will help out sometimes. I got my food handler's certification this week—I had to take a little class and a test online and then I got to print a card with my certification number and name on it.

I'm flying to Dallas for Thanksgiving. Daddy and Nana talked about it and decided that I could miss a couple of days of school so I could spend the entire week there. I think Nana is kind of sad that I won't be here with them. I hope I get along okay with Daddy and Stephanie while I'm there.

Nana has finally started letting me drive her car sometimes, but she reminds me of every single driving rule before she hands me the keys. Granddaddy says it's no reflection of my driving skills—that she's just nervous about me being behind the wheel because of your accident. After he told me that, I stopped being so annoyed with her.

Ily,

Shadow

Jackson pushed the paperwork across the table to the project manager of Edison Appliances. "I'm pleased the last property you looked at was to your liking and specifications. And I think you'll find the workforce in Lonoke County and the surrounding area is ready to meet the needs of your company." He smiled. This might be his biggest coup yet. "If you'll just sign next to each *X*, we're all set."

Mr. Anderson scribbled his signature on the papers and passed them back. "It's been a pleasure working with you, Jackson. We look forward to opening our doors in Arkansas and are thankful for all you've done to make that possible."

Jackson shook hands with the group from Edison and showed them to the lobby. He couldn't believe it. Just when he'd been sure they were going to set up their distribution center in Mississippi, they'd changed their minds. He'd like to think he'd had something to do with that. "Any calls?" he asked Sheila.

She smiled. "Only one from a Rocky Balboa. He says you have his number."

"I sure do. Thanks, Sheila." He hurried into his office and closed the door. "Okay, Mr. Balboa. What's going on?" he asked once he'd dialed Jeff's number.

Jeff laughed. "I just wanted to tell you that RSVPs have started trickling in for homecoming."

"Already? But the brochures only went out last week."

"What can I say, man. It's the hottest ticket in town."

Jackson groaned. "Whatever."

"Actually, I was just going to let you know that your mom sent her RSVP in already. She's bringing Roger."

Jackson had figured as much. "Thanks for the heads-up."

"And I'm guessing we can just put you down with Violet as your guest?"

"That's right." The fact that Mom was taking Roger as her date didn't bother him as much since he'd have Violet with him. She had a way of calming him down and putting him at ease. It was the craziest thing.

"Don't mess it up, man. I think she's the best thing that's ever happened to you."

Jackson had already had the same thought. "Why do you say that?"

"Lauren and I were talking about it after the game. You guys just fit together. I think you bring her stability, and she loosens you up. And you're obviously so happy. I'm really proud of you, man. I know a committed relationship has never been your thing—I don't guess I've ever known you to give your heart away. But I think this is a really good thing you've got going."

Jackson nodded. "It sure is."

Chapter 27

Jackson Stratford: Happy Grand Opening! It's going to be incredible. I'll be there as soon as I get off work. (Text message sent October 31, 7:30 a.m.)

Violet Matthews: Thanks! I hope I'm still in one piece by the time you get here. (Text message sent October 31, 7:39 a.m.)

Jackson Stratford: You will be. Just save me a cupcake! (Text message sent October 31, 7:42 a.m.)

Violet tied on the apron her grandmother had given her. "Well, what do you think?"

Grandma smiled. "Perfection." She sniffed the air. "And so is that smell."

Violet grinned and motioned toward the nearly full glass case. "This is the last batch for a while. We'll just play it by ear and see which flavors go faster before I bake anything else."

"Good plan. Thanks for letting me be your assistant today."

Violet laughed. "Thank *you*. You being here until Shadow gets in from school is amazing. I think most days I'll manage on my own—at least until the summer season. But since I don't really know what to expect, I feel much better with you being here."

"So tell me the plan."

Violet filled her in on the pricing and the cash register. "It's very simple to operate."

"Famous last words," Grandma said with a laugh.

"These little bags are for to-go cupcakes. If they get three or less, they get a bag." Violet pointed to a stack of small white bags. "Three cupcakes fit perfectly in those. Then fold the top of the bag down and put one of these stickers with the logo on it to seal."

"They look so cute."

"If they get four, five, or six cupcakes, put them in one of these white boxes." Violet pointed to a stack. "Shadow put them together already. All you have to do is put the cupcakes inside and tape it closed. The logo sticker is already on the top of the box."

"What if they want more than six?" Grandma asked.

Violet pointed to a sign. "For orders needing more than half a dozen, they'll have to place the order and come back later. I don't have the space or the manpower right now to risk someone coming in and buying out the case." She shrugged. "But if it's preordered, I can bake ahead and be ready."

"You're a smart girl. I never would've thought of that."

Jackson had helped her come up with the idea last week when she'd been worrying about all the things that could go wrong. "I had some help coming up with it." She smiled at the thought of him. He'd be here tonight and hopefully things would be calm enough for her to at least get to talk to him.

The bell over the door chimed, and a woman with a little girl in tow walked in the door.

"Welcome to Central Avenue Cupcakes," Violet said. Her first customers. Would it be weird to ask to take their picture? She could hardly wait to see what flavor cupcakes they chose.

"Do you have a restroom?" the woman asked. She pointed toward the little girl. "It's an emergency," she whispered.

Violet tried to keep her smile from slipping. They only wanted the restroom. "Go straight back and to the left."

"Let's go potty and then come back for a cupcake," the woman said.

The little girl skipped to the bathroom.

Violet let out a sigh of relief. "Oh thank goodness. I was so worried they didn't come in for cupcakes at all."

Grandma laughed. "We might want to put a 'No public restroom' sign out front, just to be on the safe side."

"Good thinking. I'll have Shadow make one when she gets here."

Violet turned her attention to the next customer. It would be hard to get into the swing of things and figure out the best way to do everything, but standing next to Grandma, serving cupcakes while an Elvis record played in the background, was by far the happiest day she'd ever had at work.

Jackson parallel parked in front of Aunt Teak's. The grand opening last week had gone so well that he'd barely gotten a minute with

Violet all night. He couldn't wait to see how the first full week had gone.

He opened the door and walked inside.

"Welcome to Central Avenue Cupcakes," Violet said with a grin.

"A Beatles song playing on the record player, the sweet smell of cupcakes, and the prettiest girl I know behind the counter. Is this heaven?"

She laughed. "Very funny."

"How has today been?"

She pointed toward the nearly empty case. "Does that answer your question? Shadow and I have been running around like crazy."

Shadow peeked her head out of the storeroom door. "Did you call me?" She noticed Jackson. "Hi, Jackson. How's it going?"

He nodded. "Pretty good. You?"

She wrinkled her nose. "I fly to Dallas in two weeks. I'm spending the entire week of Thanksgiving at my dad's."

"Chin up. Someday he might not be around, so use your time wisely." He and Shadow had talked some about what it was like to lose a parent. He felt for her. "Ask if you can have a daddy-daughter date one night to catch up."

She smiled. "I will. Thanks." She looked at Violet. "I'm through in the storeroom. I think everything is set for next week."

"Thanks, Shadow. Do we need to give you a ride home?"

She shook her head. "Nana left her car for me and got a ride home with Granddaddy." She smiled. "Have a good rest of the weekend."

"You, too. I'll probably see you at church tomorrow, unless I make it to the early service. Otherwise I'll see you Tuesday after school." Violet finished wiping down the counter.

"Bye," Shadow called as she hoisted her bag over her shoulder and walked out the door.

"Anything I can to do help?" Jackson asked once Shadow was gone.

She shook her head. "I think we're all done here." She grinned. "I survived the first full week."

"I'm proud." He smiled. "And I have something special planned now."

She widened her eyes. "What's that?"

"Dinner at the Arlington Hotel. I know how you love historic places. I think they've already put their Christmas lights up." The Arlington was the most historic hotel in Hot Springs.

She clutched her purse. "That sounds like so much fun."

Jackson ushered her out the door and waited until she locked it. "You okay with walking?"

"It's a perfect night for a walk."

They crossed Central Avenue and paused in front of Fordyce Bathhouse.

"It's so pretty," Violet said. "I toured it a few weeks ago just for fun. It's like stepping back in time."

"Is it a museum now?" he asked.

She nodded. "Yes. It's run by the National Park Service." She pointed down the row of ornate bathhouses. "Reagan and I went to the Quapaw Baths to the spa a few weeks ago. It was very nice. The Buckstaff is next door, and it's supposed to be good, too. I'll have to give it a try next."

"Is that the one with the blue awnings?" he asked.

Violet nodded. "Yep." She tugged on his hand. "Have you ever walked along the Grand Promenade?"

"I don't think so."

"Do we have time? We can get to the Arlington Hotel from there."

"Sure."

They walked on the sidewalk that ran between two of the bathhouses.

"You can hear the water," he said. "That's so cool."

She laughed. "Actually it's hot. It's one of the open springs. During the day you can see the steam coming off the water." They climbed a set of stairs that led to a brick paved path. "This is the Grand Promenade. Back in the heyday of the baths, people would walk along this path between baths."

"Interesting."

They walked along in silence for a moment.

"See that spot?" she asked, pointing to an overlook. "I like to stand there and look out over Central Avenue."

"Do you come here often?" he asked.

She shrugged. "I bring Arnie here for walks sometimes. It's a nice area, and there are a ton of trails. Technically this is part of Hot Springs National Park." She pulled him over to the overlook. "Isn't it amazing?" she asked.

He stared at her. "It sure is."

Violet turned toward him. "It's crazy that I never gave much thought to living here before, considering how much I like the past.

The mobster history here fascinates me. I mean, Al Capone himself had a suite at the Arlington. I met a friend of my grandpa's who was one of Capone's drivers back in the day. I can just imagine all the mobsters in their suits and the women in their colorful dresses with their jewels." She grinned.

Jackson smiled down at her. "The mobster history in Hot Springs is very cool. But I'm more partial to the baseball history."

She furrowed her brow. "I don't guess I'm very familiar with that."

"Spring training originated here. Babe Ruth was a frequent visitor, using the bathhouses or visiting Oaklawn when he wasn't playing ball." Oaklawn, Hot Springs's horse-racing track, opened in the early 1900s and was home to the Arkansas Derby.

"I guess I learn something new every day," she said.

He slipped an arm around her waist. "I guess so."

Violet was suddenly all too aware of how close he was. "Are you ready to go to the Arlington? There's a staircase we can take that leads down to the lawn in front of the hotel."

"Almost." His voice was husky. He turned her toward him. "Violet, I've really enjoyed these past weeks. I never thought we had so much in common or would actually have such a good time together."

"Me neither," she murmured.

Jackson pulled her closer and tipped her chin. "I've waited a long time to do this." He bent down and pressed his lips to hers.

She kissed him tentatively at first. It seemed so strange to kiss him, even though she'd known it was coming. The kiss deepened, and Violet wrapped her arms around his neck. It might have been fake, but it sure didn't feel fake.

When he finally pulled away, he was breathless.

Violet balanced herself on the brick overlook. "Guess we've got that first kiss out of the way."

He grinned. "Guess so." He took her hand and led her to the staircase.

Violet's heart still pounded from the kiss. "One down, two to go, right?"

"Right."

Somehow that didn't make her feel better. What was wrong with her? This wasn't a relationship. Just a good first-kiss story in case they ever needed it.

Chapter 28

Jackson Stratford: I told Mom you were planning on bringing dessert for Thursday. She says you don't have to do that, but I told her you insisted. Ha-ha. Really I just want all the cupcakes I can eat! (Text message sent November 19, 7:39 a.m.)

Violet Matthews: I'm glad you like them that much. Does this mean you'll still be coming by my store to get your cupcake fix even after January? (Text message sent November 19, 7:46 a.m.)

Jackson Stratford: Count on it. (Text message sent November 19, 7:52 a.m.)

Jackson pulled into the driveway of his childhood home and parked next to his sister's van. He took a deep breath.

"You okay?" Violet asked.

He shook his head. "I kind of dread this."

"Because of your mom's friend?"

"I'd probably dread it anyway, just because being here without my dad is still so hard."

Violet reached over and took his hand. "You want your mom to be happy. Right?"

"Of course. I just wish moving on wasn't the only path to happiness." He frowned. "But I know how childish that sounds."

"Your sister told me there's been a marked difference in your mom since she started seeing Roger. She said it's helped her get back to her old self."

Jackson frowned. "And I'm sure she told you it's what my dad would want. Right?"

"She may have mentioned something like that, yes."

"That's the thing. People keep saying that. They keep claiming to know what my dad would say or do or want. But how do they know?"

Violet smiled. "I didn't even know your dad and I'm pretty sure I can answer that question. Your dad sounds like the kind of man who would've wanted his family to be happy. So I'd say that's how they know. He'd want whatever it is that would give his family the most happiness."

Jackson sighed. "I guess you're right."

"Trust me." She smiled. "I know how hard holidays must be for you. But remember they're hard for the whole family. And probably even Roger. I'm sure holidays only bring home the fact that he lost his wife."

"I guess you're right."

She held up the canister of cupcakes. "Now, are you ready to go inside? They're probably wondering why we're sitting out here for so long."

Jackson laughed. "They probably think we're out here kissing and getting that all out of our systems before we go inside."

A pink blush spread across her face.

"Are you thinking about our first kiss?" he asked, grinning.

She scowled. "No."

"Good. Me neither." It wasn't quite the truth. It was all he'd been thinking about since it had happened. But there was no reason to tell her that now. "Let's do this."

Dear Mama,

Well, Thanksgiving wasn't as bad as I expected it to be. Maybe being apart has been good for us. Daddy and I went out to dinner one night, and I told him all about my life in Hot Springs. He is really happy that I haven't been in any trouble at my new school. (Remember the great graffiti incident of last year?) And he's also pretty pumped about my GPA. I'm doing really well in my classes.

Stephanie is okay. She isn't as cool as Violet though. But I guess I can put up with her.

Daddy and I talked about college. He didn't seem too surprised when I told him I was looking at schools in Arkansas. Rachel is going to Harding. I think I'll go look at the campus this summer. Violet told me since that's where she graduated from, she'd be happy to take me on a tour of campus.

It isn't set in stone yet or anything, but it's a possibility.
Daddy seemed pretty okay with it. I think he misses me, but
really wants me to be happy—even if it means I'm not in Texas.

Love,
Shadow

Reagan sketched out the design she was considering for an author's website. She'd been hard pressed to find time to work on it between the madness of Thanksgiving and now trying to get Christmas shopping done. It was hard to believe it was already December.

She held the paper up and gave it the once over. Perfect. The woman wanted something professional, yet fun and inviting, and Reagan was pretty sure she'd be pleased with this.

The office door burst open, and her pencil went flying.

"Why is there a strange woman downstairs playing with our children? And what is this for?" Chad put a large FedEx package on her desk. "What is Reagan McClure Designs?"

Her heart sank. She'd planned to tell Chad everything this weekend. "The woman downstairs is Maggie Denton. She's a nanny."

"Where did you meet her?"

He would have to ask that. "Actually, I met her at the gym."

"The gym? Since when do you go to the gym?" Chad looked at her like she'd grown horns.

Reagan pulled the office door closed. No sense in alarming the kids by their raised voices. "I don't anymore. I did for a couple of months though."

"You never told me. How could you not tell me something like that? Who kept the kids while you were there?"

She bristled. "Actually, the reason I chose the gym I did was because they have a wonderful daycare facility on site. Everyone is very professional, and I signed the kids in and out, so they were never in any kind of danger." She sat down at her desk. "Maggie and I took a class together and got to be friends. The family she works for as a nanny is moving at the end of the month, and I asked her to watch the kids for a couple of hours today while I got a few things done."

Chad frowned. "Don't you think you should've run that by me first?"

"I never would've left them *alone* with someone without talking to you about it. But I'm right upstairs. Ava Grace has been up here a couple of times to show me the crafts she's been working on. It's a really nice setup." She took a breath to calm herself down. "And I checked Maggie's references. They're impeccable."

"What are you working on? What is Reagan McClure Designs?" Chad asked angrily.

"Just calm down. I was planning to tell you this weekend. I wanted to wait and see if it was even a possibility before I broached the subject."

"What?"

"I designed the logo and did some website stuff for Violet's bake shop, Central Avenue Cupcakes. A few people asked her for the designer, and she gave them my information." She shrugged. "I took a couple of jobs just to see if I was interested and see if I was going to even be successful at picking up freelance work." She grinned. "I'm confident that there's enough work out there for me to work as much as I want."

"So you want to go back to work? Like full-time?" He drew his brows together.

She shook her head. "No. But I'd like to consider working a couple of days or even just a couple of afternoons a week." She held her breath.

Chad frowned. "Why didn't you tell me this sooner?"

"I knew you might not be happy, so I wanted to be absolutely sure before we discussed it."

"I'm less happy that you hid it. What were you thinking?"

Reagan sighed. "I was thinking it might be a big, fat failure. And if it was, I didn't want to have bothered you with it."

"Since when is talking to me—your husband—about something that's obviously important to you the same thing as bothering me?" Chad stood up and paced the room. "And the gym thing? What's the deal?"

Reagan's anger flared. "In case you didn't know it, I wasn't exactly happy with myself a few months ago. I had to do something to get out of the funk I was in. And it was hard. My body has been through a lot over the last year. My first two pregnancies were easy. The last one was not. And then I found that the weight wasn't coming off as fast as it had the first two times." She shrugged. "So I decided to go to the gym. Honestly it was as much mental as it was physical. It really helped clear my head to know that a couple of times a week I was going to just be myself. No one would be crying for me or clinging for me or needing something from me. Sometimes that can be exhausting."

Chad sat back down. "I'm sorry you feel that way."

"You don't notice me anymore." She gestured toward herself. "I've lost more than ten pounds. You haven't even said anything."

Chad frowned. "Are you having an affair?"

"You have got to be kidding me. You are the one who travels with young, attractive women. Yet you have the audacity to ask if *I'm* having an affair?" It was completely laughable.

"Sorry. It's just the secrets and the gym and the freelancing." He shrugged. "I feel like you've been pulling away from me."

"I don't even remember the last conversation we had that wasn't about the kids. Do you? So do you blame me for pulling away?"

"Date night soon? Just us? No kid talk?" he asked.

She nodded. "And I won't take on any more freelance work until we discuss it."

He leaned forward and kissed her on the cheek. "I miss us. A lot."

Reagan did, too. Now if they could just figure out how to get back to being the couple they used to be.

Chapter 29

Violet Matthews: WISH ME LUCK! JACKSON AND I ARE
HEADED TO THE BIG WEDDING WEEKEND. (Text message
sent December 13, 4:45 p.m.)

Reagan McClure: I HOPE EVERYTHING GOES WELL. SEND
ME A PICTURE OF THE WEDDING. HOPE Y'ALL HAVE FUN.
HAVE YOU DECIDED WHAT THIS "THING" WITH JACKSON IS
YET?? (Text message sent December 13, 4:52 p.m.)

Violet leaned her head against the seat of the Range Rover. "It's
hard to believe it's already here."

"Yep." Jackson looked over at her and grinned. "You ready?"

"Ready for it all to be over."

He sighed. "Do you mean us or the wedding?"

"The wedding first." She grinned. "We still have a few more
weeks before we're over."

Jackson pulled into the hotel parking lot. "So what's going on
tonight?"

"It's kind of weird. If you ask me, it's just my sister looking for an excuse to be the center of attention for as long as possible." She sighed. "Tonight there is a dinner that is just for our family and a few close friends. Tomorrow there are activities planned during the day and then the rehearsal and rehearsal dinner. Then Saturday is the wedding."

"Three days of wedding fun."

"Exactly." She took a breath. "Are you ready to put on your boyfriend hat?"

He smiled. "Always."

Violet waited for him to open the passenger door for her. She hated to admit it, but having him for a boyfriend, fake or not, was kind of nice. He'd turned out to be one of the biggest and best surprises of her life. "Thanks," she said as he offered her a hand.

"You look amazing tonight, by the way."

"Thanks. You're not so bad yourself." He wore a charcoal suit with a french blue shirt. A blue-and-gray striped tie completed the look. Very classic."

Jackson reached over and took her hand. "Let's do this."

"Violet," said Aunt Darlene when she met them at the hotel lobby door. "Who is this handsome man?"

"This is Jackson Stratford," she said.

Jackson shook Aunt Darlene's hand. "Nice to meet you."

"Your mother told me you had a new boyfriend. I hope this one's a keeper." Aunt Darlene patted her on the back.

Violet leaned close to Jackson once Aunt Darlene had moved on to another guest. "It's not too late to run to a galaxy far, far away."

"Is that a *Star Wars* reference?" he whispered.

She cocked her head. "Maybe."

Jackson leaned down and planted a quick kiss on her mouth.

She laughed as he pulled away. "Check." She made a check-mark motion in the air with her finger. "Two down."

"Stop it." He grinned. "Can't you just humor me and act like you enjoyed that?"

The truth of the matter was that she didn't have to pretend. At least he'd made this one quick. She pushed the thought of their first kiss out of her mind. This was just pretend. "Of course. The next time I promise not to count down." Because that would be at the end of their little ruse and they both knew it. By the time their third kiss happened, they'd be about to part ways.

"Did I just see a little PDA over here?" Amber walked over with her entourage in tow. "Because I'm pretty sure the spinster sister isn't allowed to have more fun than the bride."

Violet tensed. "Hi, Amber. Everything looks just beautiful."

"Thanks." She eyed Jackson. "Aren't you going to introduce me to your man? I've been hearing tales of him, but haven't actually seen him with my own eyes." She grinned at Jackson. "I was beginning to think you were just a figment of Vi's imagination."

He grinned and pulled Violet closer to him. "Not at all. I'm completely real." He held out a hand. "I'm Jackson."

She looked at him with narrowed eyes. "You look really familiar."

"He has one of those faces," Violet said.

Jackson chuckled. "Thanks a lot, babe." His term of endearment might be fake, but Violet liked the way it sounded.

Amber waved at someone across the room. "I want you to meet my maid of honor."

A blond girl bounded over to where they stood. "Amber, it looks so pretty in here." Her eyes widened at the sight of Jackson. "You're the last person I expected to see here. I didn't think weddings were your thing."

Violet felt Jackson tense next to her. "Hi, Whitney. It's been awhile," he said finally.

She stuck out her lower lip. "You just, like, stopped calling."

No way. This could not be happening. Jackson used to date Amber's best friend.

Jackson gripped Violet's hand tighter. "Sorry about that. I just realized we were looking for different things."

"Clearly he was looking for someone older and more mature," Amber observed. "Or maybe just older." She laughed at her own joke. "How did y'all meet, anyway?" she asked Violet.

"We were actually in college together," Jackson explained. "So we've known each other for quite a long time."

Violet forced a smile. "We'd better go say hi to Mom and Dad." She tugged on Jackson's hand and led him away from Amber and her angry bridesmaid.

"I'm so sorry about that," Jackson whispered in her ear once they'd walked away. "I only went out with her a couple of times, and it was last summer. She was way too young for me, and we had absolutely zero in common. I'm sorry if that was awkward for you."

Violet enjoyed the way his breath felt against her ear. It sent shivers down her back. "It's okay. It isn't like we were in our fake relationship back then." She smiled.

He rolled his eyes. "True. But aren't you a little bit jealous?" he whispered.

"Hardly." She grinned when he made a face. "How do you think this is going? Do you think they were suspicious?"

He pulled her to him and gave her a big hug. "Not at all. In fact, anyone looking at us right now thinks I can't keep my hands off you," he whispered.

She grinned. "Got to keep it believable, right?"

"Right," he whispered again, sending another wave of shivers down her spine.

Jackson had to admit, he was having fun. Much of the time, he and Violet kept their relationship very businesslike. But when they were with family and friends and were supposed to be a real couple, he was free to treat her like a girlfriend.

And he liked it.

A few weeks ago when he'd kissed her for the first time, he'd been hit with the realization that his feelings for her went deeper than just someone he had a business arrangement with. And Thanksgiving with his family had shown him how it could feel to have a partner and a friend. He'd leaned on her as he'd dealt with another holiday without his dad and the pain of watching his mom move on.

But tonight was the first time he truly felt like they were a real couple. That spark between them was unmistakable. It wasn't the kind of thing that could be faked.

And he was pretty sure she felt it, too. In the beginning, she'd tensed when he'd come near her. But tonight she leaned into him. She'd been the one to take his hand, and earlier when he'd whispered in her ear, he'd seen chill bumps on her arms. And he was hoping those were a good sign.

"So you're sure you're going to be okay staying here tonight?" he asked.

She sighed. "There was no getting around it. Mom wanted me here in case I'm needed. Of course, after dinner the bachelorette party is happening."

"Bachelorette party, huh? You aren't planning to cut loose are you?"

She laughed. "I'm not going. For one thing, I wasn't invited. For another, that's not really my thing."

He was a little relieved. He didn't like the idea of Violet going out with those girls and being hit on by a bunch of guys. Plus he knew how miserable she'd be. That definitely didn't sound like Violet's idea of fun. "Well if I need to come rescue you tomorrow on my lunch break, just text me." He grinned. "Have you heard from anyone at the shop? How are they managing tonight without you?"

"Shadow sent me a text earlier. It's been a slow night. She and Mrs. Kemp are doing fine." Violet grinned. "I'm a little nervous about being gone for two more days, but I think things will be okay. Sometimes I can't believe I get paid to do what I do."

"And you were scared you'd fail." Central Avenue Cupcakes had far exceeded her expectations so far, and it looked like business would only pick up as more people heard about the cupcakes and the atmosphere.

She shrugged. "I still am sometimes. But it lessens every day."

"I hope I've helped instill some confidence in you. Always know that no matter what, I believe in you."

She blushed. "Are you saying that as my fake boyfriend or as yourself?" she asked softly.

"Myself." He brushed his lips against her forehead. "And don't forget it."

"Dinner is served," a waiter announced to the small crowd mingling in the lobby.

Jackson took Violet's hand and led her into the ballroom. He glanced over his shoulder. It had been a shock running into Whitney. But hopefully she'd behave herself and leave them alone.

Because the last thing Violet needed was any kind of scene this weekend. And Jackson was going to do all he could to ensure that things went smoothly.

Dear Mama,

The closer we get to Christmas, the more I miss you. Violet's boyfriend, Jackson, told me not too long ago that holidays were hard for him, too. His daddy had a heart attack and died last year.

But he told me it made him feel better to think about his daddy in heaven. That God had been the one to decide it was time for his daddy to go home, and even though it was hard for him to understand, he had to trust that was the best plan.

I'm trying really hard to believe that, but sometimes it

isn't easy. I wish God had decided that I needed you more than He did. But I guess it doesn't work like that.

Maybe someday I'll understand. But for now, I guess I just have to accept it, even if I don't completely understand.

Today for the first time, I looked in the mirror and saw you. That was kind of cool. Nana says that you'll always be with me. Maybe that's what she meant—that I have a piece of you in me.

I hope I make you proud.

Love,
Shadow

Chapter 30

Shadow Simmons: Everything is all closed up for the night. No problems. Nana says not to worry. Whenever we run out of cupcakes, we'll just put the sign in the window explaining that we're sold out and will reopen on Tuesday. (Text message sent December 13, 10:43 p.m.)

Violet Matthews: Thank you so much for your hard work and your help! A Christmas bonus is definitely coming your way. Text me if you need me. (Text message sent December 13, 10:45 p.m.)

Jackson walked out of the hotel hand in hand with Violet. Despite the tension between Violet and her sister, they'd had a nice evening. "So what time do I need to be back tomorrow?" he asked.

"The rehearsal is at six and is scheduled for half an hour. I'm not planning on going to that. The dinner is right afterward. So maybe get here around six fifteen or so? Just call me and I'll come down and meet you so we can go to the dinner together."

He pulled her close. "Day one of the wedding extravaganza is over, and you're still in once piece."

She smiled. "Barely. And if you weren't here, I definitely wouldn't be okay."

"Good to know." His heart pounded. He wanted to kiss her again, a real kiss. Off the contract. But he had no idea how she'd feel about that. "I'd better get home. Work tomorrow."

Violet nodded. "Good night," she said softly.

He held her for a long moment, relishing the way she fit against him. "See you tomorrow."

She nodded. "Of course." Her phone buzzed, and she pulled it out of her purse. The screen lit up the darkness around them. "It's Reagan." She looked up at him with a worried expression. "It's not like her to call so late. I'd better take it."

He nodded. "See you tomorrow."

She waved and held the phone up to her ear.

Jackson watched her walk up the path to the hotel. He'd fallen hard for her, and he was pretty sure she had no idea. And he was even less sure about the way she felt about him. He'd caught glimpses of what he thought was genuine interest, but at the same time. . .he couldn't be sure until they talked about it.

He climbed in the Range Rover and looked down. Violet had left her overnight bag in the floorboard. She'd need that stuff tonight. He hoisted the bag over his shoulder and hurried toward the hotel.

He heard her before he saw her. She must still be on the phone with Reagan.

"I'm so sorry," she said. "I think you should really talk to Chad though. You might be surprised by things."

Jackson hated to eavesdrop, but he also didn't want to interrupt. Maybe he should just leave the bag at the hotel desk.

"Okay, stop right there," Violet said. "If I'm not allowed to judge your relationship, you're not allowed to judge mine."

Jackson froze. She was talking about him. About them.

"We're just friends, nothing more."

He nearly dropped the bag. He knew that was the party line she was giving Reagan. She'd claimed she couldn't pretend to Reagan that they were really in a relationship, so she was just telling her they were friends who enjoyed hanging out. Still though, it hurt a little to hear her say they were nothing but friends.

"I'm *not* falling for him. Stop saying that. Do you really think I've forgotten the past so easily? And it isn't like he has a successful relationship track record. I mean, he's a mess and you don't know the half of it. I'd end up getting hurt, and I've been hurt plenty of times before. So don't worry."

Jackson's heart fell. Violet knew everything about him. Everything about his past. He'd opened up to her in a way he never had with anyone else.

And he wasn't good enough. It didn't matter that he'd changed. That he'd overcome the problems he'd faced in the past and was trying hard to live the kind of life that would make his loved ones proud. But clearly Violet wasn't proud to be with him.

At least he knew.

Now he wouldn't make a fool of himself by declaring his feelings. He'd even thought about telling her he was in love with her. That he'd never felt this way about anyone. But hearing what she really thought of him had set him straight.

He took the side entrance to the hotel and left her bag at the desk. "Please leave a message for Violet Matthews and have her pick this up."

The clerk nodded. "Yes, sir."

"There you are," a familiar voice said. "I was looking for you."

He turned to see Whitney walking toward him. "I thought y'all were headed to a bachelorette party."

She laughed. "We are. But I thought you might want to hang out first."

Jackson glanced at the main entrance. Violet would probably be coming through the door any minute. And he had no desire to see her right now. "What did you have in mind?" he asked Whitney.

She smiled. "There's a little restaurant across the street that's still open. Want to grab a bite to eat and catch up?"

He looked again at the entrance. Violet must still be outside, bashing him. By now she was probably telling Reagan the real reason they spent time together and what a mistake their arrangement had been. She should really consider theater, though, because she'd had him fooled. "I could go for some food."

"Excellent."

He followed Whitney out the side door and ignored the sick feeling in the pit of his stomach. Violet had made it crystal clear to Reagan there was nothing between them. Which meant everything had been fake. And even worse, all the bad things he'd ever thought about himself were the reasons she'd given for not wanting to be with him. That made it even worse—hearing those same insecurities echoed from the person he cared so much about. "What have you been up to lately?" He turned his attention to Whitney and tried to push Violet from his mind.

"You aren't going to let this go, are you?" Violet asked, clutching the phone to her ear.

Reagan laughed. "Not when you're clearly delusional. I know you well. Very well. And you don't fall for just anyone. I'm just saying. . .maybe there's more to Jackson than I thought."

Violet had tried denying Reagan's accusations, but she wasn't getting anywhere. "Fine. Yes, the past couple of months have been pretty amazing. And tonight I don't know what I would've done without him."

"So you admit it."

Violet groaned. "Yes. I admit it. I have feelings for him. Real feelings. But I'm still a little apprehensive."

"That's to be expected. Not only have you had your heart broken, but Jackson has hurt you before."

"He's not the same guy he used to be. Not at all." The Jackson she knew now was kind and sweet. He would never hurt her on purpose. "Besides, the more I've learned about him and his life, the more understanding I am about the stuff he did when we were in college. He really is remorseful."

"I know. Both times I've seen him at the bakeshop, I've felt like he's trying hard to redeem himself where you're concerned."

Violet smiled. "Now I just have to decide how to handle the

situation. Do I wait and see if he tells me he has feelings for me? Or do I just tell him? And what if I'm way off base and he only sees me as a friend?"

"If he does, don't you think you should find out soon before your feelings grow any deeper?" Reagan asked.

"You're probably right. Maybe I'll get up the courage soon. Or maybe I'll just wait and see what happens."

"I hope everything goes okay. Keep me posted."

Violet nodded. "I will." She clicked off the phone and headed back into the hotel. She glanced at her phone. Jackson had had time to get home by now. The past few weeks they'd started texting right before bed. It was weird that he hadn't sent one.

She scrolled through her messages and chose his name. Just reading back over their texts from the past months made her smile. She quickly sent an "are you home yet?" message to him and waited for his response.

Thirty minutes later, she climbed into bed. He must've gone straight to sleep when he got home, but she put her phone on the nightstand next to her bed just in case.

Because now that she'd realized her true feelings, she didn't want to miss a moment with him.

Chapter 31

Whitney Anderson: LAST NIGHT WAS FUN. MAYBE WE
CAN DO IT AGAIN SOMETIME. SEE YOU TONIGHT AT THE
REHEARSAL DINNER. (Text message sent December 14,
2:33 p.m.)

Jackson Stratford: I DON'T THINK SO. I WISH YOU THE BEST
IN THE FUTURE THOUGH. (Text message sent December
14, 2:39 p.m.)

Jackson had a hard time making it through the workday. Between
wondering where he'd gone wrong with Violet and realizing
he'd made a huge mistake by going to the restaurant with Whitney,
he couldn't concentrate. He knew Whitney was bad news, but
last night he'd been so hurt he wasn't thinking clearly. Obviously.
Otherwise he wouldn't have done something so rash.

"You okay, Mr. Stratford?" Sheila asked. "You're not coming
down with something are you?"

Just a big case of stupidity. "Nothing a weekend won't cure."

He smiled. "In fact, I'm about to head out. You can leave early if you want."

"Thanks," she said. "Have a great weekend."

Jackson was pretty sure the odds of his weekend being great were slim to none. Actually less than none, whatever that would be. He took his suit coat from the hook behind his office door and slipped it on.

Violet had sent him a couple of texts today, but he'd just sent back minimal responses. Nothing like the exchanges they'd had during the past few months.

He still couldn't believe he'd been so stupid as to fall for her. The fake relationship had been his idea. He'd thought it was a no-brainer with no strings.

He certainly hadn't counted on developing real feelings. And he definitely hadn't expected to fall in love with her.

Twenty minutes later, he pulled into the hotel parking lot. He pulled out his phone and sent Violet a quick text letting her know he'd be in the lobby.

He walked into the luxurious building and sat down on a surprisingly uncomfortable seat. Just another example of how looks could be deceiving.

"You ready for round two?" Violet asked.

He looked up to see her standing before him. She'd gone all out tonight. Her green cocktail dress was a throwback to the fifties. "You look like you could be Marilyn Monroe's red-haired sister."

Violet laughed. "I don't know about all of that. I suppose this dress is a bit Marilyn inspired."

Jackson stood. "Let's get this done." He offered his arm, and she clutched it. He couldn't bear to take her hand. Not now. Not knowing how she really felt about him.

"I'm guessing we'll have assigned seats?" he asked as they reached the ballroom. It was best to keep the conversation as impersonal as possible.

Violet nodded. "Oh yes. My sister loves the idea of telling a room full of people what to do." She tugged on his arm. "I think we're going to be seated with my grandparents."

Once they were seated, she glanced over at him. "I guess you had a busy day, huh?"

He shrugged. "About normal."

"I just figured since you didn't text much, it meant you were in meetings and stuff." Violet gave him a worried look.

Jackson would've thought her obvious insecurity would've given him some satisfaction. But it didn't. Instead he just felt sad. "Looks like the rehearsal is over. I see your parents and sister."

"Let's get this party started." She grinned. "I think there's some kind of video first. Another of Amber's ideas." She leaned closer to him. "You know how I hate to be the center of attention? She's the complete opposite. I fully expect for this to be an hour-long slide show full of as many flattering pictures of Amber as possible."

Jackson laughed in spite of himself. "Surely not."

Just as Violet had predicted, the lights flickered in the dining room and a movie flashed on the screen behind where the wedding party sat. "Welcome to the wedding rehearsal dinner of Amber and Landry," Violet's dad said from the podium. "We're thankful you're here to share in this joyous occasion with us. And now, without further ado, is a video presentation." Mr. Matthews sat down at the table he shared with his wife and what Jackson assumed were the groom's parents.

The video flashed a variety of pictures of Amber and Landry at various stages of adolescence. "Look at you," Jackson said to Violet when her face flashed across the screen. "That's some big hair."

"It was a perm. Big mistake." She shrugged. "It was 1989."

He chuckled. Maybe they could pull off the fake relationship after all. At least he knew how she felt about him. He could just suffer through, forget about his attraction to her, and they'd be through with each other in less than a month.

The screen went dark signaling the end of the show, but one final shot popped up on the screen like an afterthought.

"What is that?" Violet hissed, gripping his arm.

The shock at seeing his own picture on the screen rendered him speechless. Whitney had held up her phone at the restaurant and taken a self portrait of them. He hadn't thought another thing about it.

Until now.

"That's what you were wearing last night," Violet said in a low voice. "Did you go out with her after you left the hotel?"

Heads began to turn in their direction.

Jackson met the angry eyes of Violet's grandmother before turning to look at Violet.

"I can explain," he started.

Violet's body trembled. There was no explanation needed. She couldn't even have a fake relationship without being cheated on.

"Hope everyone enjoyed the slide show," Amber said from the podium. "And in case y'all didn't know, that last picture was of my maid of honor and my sister's boyfriend, taken last night." She shook her head. "Poor Violet. She has a knack for picking the wrong guys, doesn't she?" Amber turned toward Violet's table. "Sorry you had to find out like this, Vi, but better now than later, right? Seems that Jackson just couldn't resist going out with Whitney last night to rekindle their old flame."

Violet could only watch in horror the train wreck that was her life.

Amber waved at Landry. "I guess they can't all be keepers like my Landry." She smiled. "But maybe Violet will be able to move on now that she knows the truth."

A murmur spread through the room as more heads turned in Violet's direction. She jumped up. No way was she staying for another second. Without another glance at Jackson, she hurried out of the room.

"Violet, wait!" he called.

She kept going through the lobby and out the door. If she hadn't had on those stupid high heels, she might've run forever. Instead she stopped at a bench outside the building and sat down.

"Please, Violet." Jackson sat down next to her. "I'm so sorry."

"How is it that you've managed to publicly humiliate me again, all these years later? And I'm so dumb, I didn't even see it coming."

"That isn't fair. Your sister orchestrated that. She could've asked me about it in private, and I would've told her she was wrong. But instead she made you a laughingstock."

Violet shook her head. "She wouldn't have had any ammunition if not for you. As far as I'm concerned, this is your fault."

"I overheard you last night on the phone with Reagan."

She drew her brows together. "What? So now you're listening in on my phone calls?"

"I came back to give you your bag. I heard you saying all that stuff about me. About how messed up I am. How the whole thing means nothing." He shrugged. "I guess I figured if you really felt that way about me, you wouldn't mind if I hung out with Whitney."

Violet glared. "You had me fooled. You certainly didn't act like you had any interest in her when we ran into her. But I guess you are a good actor after all, I mean you've convinced most everyone we know that you're crazy about me." She took a breath. "Did you really end things with her over the summer or have you been seeing her all along?"

Jackson groaned. "When would I have had time to see her? I was too busy helping you move and paint and giving you pep talks."

She flinched. "I think you should just leave."

"We need to talk about this."

Violet shook her head. She was suddenly very tired. "No. We don't. There's nothing left to say. You betrayed me. With some girl you used to date who happens to be my sister's best friend. You know my sister and I don't get along. Somewhere in the back of your mind, it had to occur to you that going off with her *maid of honor* might come back to bite you." She buried her head in her hands for a long moment. There was no way she was giving him the satisfaction of seeing her cry.

"Please, Violet. I'm sorry. You have to believe me. Absolutely nothing happened."

She couldn't think of a single thing he could say to make this better. "You need to go. And I need to face my family."

"How will you get home?" he asked.

She'd driven her car to his house yesterday so they could ride to the hotel together. "I'll manage. I managed fine before you came along." Stupid Mimi the matchmaker. If not for her, none of this would've happened. Violet would've probably met some nice guy online and they'd be in the hotel right now enjoying their rubbery chicken.

Jackson walked away without another word.

Violet sat for another moment on the bench. In just a few short minutes, her life had spiraled out of control. There had to be some lesson in it though, right? Some takeaway to make it worth the pain.

Because right now, not only did she have to face a humiliating room full of people, she also felt empty. She'd gotten used to having Jackson by her side. She'd started to have real feelings for him. Feelings she hadn't been sure she'd ever have about anyone.

And just like that—it all blew up.

Chapter 32

Jackson Stratford: I REALLY THINK WE NEED TO TALK ABOUT WHAT HAPPENED. (Text message sent December 15, 9:02 a.m.)

Violet pulled the covers over her head to block out the sunshine. She wanted today to be dark and dreary to match her mood. But no. Of course Amber's wedding day had to be bright and beautiful.

Last night had been the worst ever. Aunt Darlene had given her a ride to her car, and she'd decided to go home. She didn't care if she missed her sister's wedding. Amber had tried to claim that she was only looking out for Violet, that she felt like she needed to be warned that Jackson and Whitney had gone out after dinner. But Violet knew her sister too well.

Whitney had apparently felt bad for her part in things and had apologized to Violet. She'd confided that Amber had sent her to see if Jackson was on the up-and-up.

As far as Violet was concerned, they all deserved each other.

Once again she'd been the one made to look foolish, the one to be pitied.

So today would be business as normal. No wedding for her, sister or not. She'd go in to the bake shop this afternoon and throw herself into baking the best cupcakes she could.

The phone buzzed. She glanced at the caller ID. "Hey, Reagan."

"Do I need to come over? Because I will. I can call someone to keep the kids."

Violet smiled in spite of the situation. "That's okay. I'm fine. Or at least I will be." She let out a huge sigh. "I'm still having a hard time processing everything that happened."

"I don't blame you." Reagan didn't say anything for a long moment. "Have you heard from him?" she asked finally.

"He's texted and called. I haven't responded to either. What could he possibly say to make this better?" Violet had tried to imagine one thing that could change things. But there was nothing.

"Hang in there. It's nearly Christmas. A time for joy, no matter what is going wrong in your personal life."

Or a time for pain. Violet knew how much Jackson was dreading Christmas without his dad. Now it looked like they'd both be alone on Christmas. "Do you want to get together sometime next week?" They didn't exchange big gifts, but usually got each other a little something.

"That sounds good. Let me know when and where. I could stand to do a little kid-free shopping." Reagan chuckled. "Chin up, Violet. God will take care of you."

Violet hung up the phone and finally peeled herself out of bed. It was time to get on with her life. She padded into the living room to let Arnie out.

He lay still on his bed and didn't move when she walked by.

She knelt next to him. "Arnie?" She shook him gently.

Nothing.

She shook him a little harder. "Arnie, please wake up."

He opened his eyes slowly.

"Thank goodness." She put her head close to him.

The dog's breathing was very shallow.

Violet stood up and clapped her hands, hoping he'd get up and follow her outside.

He started to raise his head, but it appeared to be too much effort, so he rested it back on the pillow.

Violet grabbed her phone and dialed the number to the nearest vet. She quickly explained the situation.

"I think you should probably bring him in, ma'am. Because you know he's been in renal failure, it's likely that it's gotten worse. We'll need to check his kidney function."

Violet had no idea how she could possibly get him to the car by herself. He'd be sixty pounds of dead weight. But she'd have to try. And there was no one she could call. Her entire family was at Amber's wedding, and she sure wasn't calling Jackson for help.

Maybe there was one person. She dialed the bake shop.

"Central Avenue Cupcakes, this is Shadow."

"It's Violet. Arnie is really sick. I need some help getting him to the vet. Are you busy today?"

"We're almost sold out. Nana has the sign all ready to go."

"Are there any customers?"

"No. One just left."

"Can you or your nana come help me get Arnie to the vet while the other one closes down?" She heard Shadow explaining the situation to Mrs. Kemp in the background.

"I'll borrow Nana's car and come help you. She'll close up and then go next door to Aunt Teak's. Granddaddy is manning the shop for her today."

"Great. See you in a minute."

Violet threw on some clothes and twisted her hair into a bun. It would have to do. She went back to Arnie. He didn't look good. "Hang in there, boy. Please." Her tears fell on his fur. She knew she should probably keep calm so she wouldn't upset him, but it was not going to be easy. She stroked his neck and rubbed his tummy. "Arnie, you've been the best dog a girl could ever have. Sometimes I've felt like you were my only friend." She wiped her tears, but more fell in their place.

There was a knock at the door. Violet opened it and ushered Shadow inside. "Let's try and slide him on his bed to the door, then we'll lift him into the car."

Shadow nodded.

They worked together to slowly slide him to the door then hoisted him to the car.

"I can drive if you want to sit in the back with him," Shadow offered.

Violet handed her the keys. "Thanks." She cradled Arnie's head in her lap and continued to stroke his fur. *Please Lord, be with Arnie. I know he's lived a long life, but I'm not ready to let him go just yet.*

Jackson sat in his Range Rover outside Jeff and Lauren's house. After the disastrous weekend, he needed to talk his problems over with someone else.

Lauren opened the door, concern written all over her face. "You look terrible."

"I haven't slept in a couple of days. Is Jeff here?"

She jerked her chin toward the kitchen. "Come get a cup of coffee. He's putting the boys in bed, but he'll be down in a minute."

Jackson sat numbly at the kitchen table.

"Here you go." She'd known him long enough to know how he liked his coffee.

He nodded. "Thanks." He wrapped his hands around the warm cup and thought about Violet.

"Hey, man." Jeff walked into the room. "Everything okay?" He glanced at his wife but she shrugged.

"It's over," Jackson said. "Violet and I. We're done."

Lauren furrowed her brow and sat down across from him.

Jeff leaned against a bar stool and crossed his arms. "What happened?"

"It isn't a nice story." Jackson hung his head. What would they think of him once he explained?

Lauren shook her head. "Breakups never are. Now tell us what happened."

Jackson told them everything, from the matchmaker to the contract to the eventual blowup. They both sat still, wearing nearly identical shocked expressions. Lauren spoke first.

"A contract?" She shook her head. "I'm sorry, but I don't get it."

"Violet and I were both looking for something specific—to get everyone off our cases and have a crutch at those events." He shrugged. "It made perfect sense at the time."

"So you're trying to tell me that it was all fake? What we saw at the Razorback game that day was just an act?" Jeff asked.

Jackson nodded. "That's exactly what I'm saying."

"Uh-uh. I don't buy it." Lauren shook her head. "You can't fake chemistry like that, and you two had it. I don't care if you went into it thinking it was a sham—what we saw was real."

"Yeah, well. . .it was real on my part. Not hers." He shook his head. "I heard her plain as day telling her friend that I was a mess that she wasn't going to get involved with. That it was all an act."

"Maybe she was saying that, but there's no way she meant it." Lauren was adamant. "I'm telling you what I saw, and it went both ways. It was *not* an act."

"I can't help what you think you saw." Jackson rubbed the stubble on his jaw. He hadn't shaved in a couple of days, hadn't even gone in to work today.

Jeff paced the length of the dining room. "Do you think there's a chance you misunderstood?"

Jackson laughed. "At this point, it wouldn't even matter. She says I betrayed her by going off with Whitney."

"She's kind of got a point. What were you thinking?" Lauren asked.

"I've never been in love. Until now. I just. . .when I heard her saying those things, it made me feel horrible. And I just wasn't thinking when I went to that restaurant with Whitney. I was just going to go with her to that restaurant because I didn't want to go home right then with my thoughts."

"And what happened?"

"As soon as we got to the restaurant she started asking me

questions about my relationship with Violet. How we met, when we met, where our first date was—stuff like that. She kept on and kept on, and finally I just snapped and told her to back off—that being there with her was a mistake." He shook his head. "Then she snapped that picture of us, and the rest is history. Nothing happened at all." He sighed.

"Violet's sister sounds like a pretty terrible human being," Jeff said. "Any chance she's behind it?"

"In hindsight, absolutely. She was positively gleeful standing at that podium outing her sister. But I didn't really know how much animosity she had until I saw that."

"And now Violet feels humiliated," Lauren remarked.

Jackson sighed. "The problem is that it isn't the first time she's been humiliated because of me." He explained their relationship in college. "Y'all know that I went through a rough time back then. I was horrible to a lot of people."

Lauren groaned. "Just when I think it can't get any worse."

"What can I do? How can I fix things?"

"I'm not sure that you can," Jeff said. "Sorry man. That's a tough position to be in."

Jackson couldn't accept that. There had to be something he could do.

He just had to figure out what.

Chapter 33

Shadow Simmons: ARNIE IS REALLY SICK. HE MIGHT
NOT MAKE IT. JUST THOUGHT YOU SHOULD KNOW. (Text
message sent December 19, 2:42 p.m.)

Jackson Stratford: THANKS FOR TELLING ME. HOPE YOU'RE
DOING WELL. (Text message sent December 19, 2:45 p.m.)

Jackson pulled into Violet's driveway. This might not get him
anywhere, but he had to at least give it a shot. He'd waited until
the bakeshop was closed and she had plenty of time to get home
before he showed up.

He hurried up the path and knocked on the door before he lost
his nerve.

The living room curtains parted slightly, and then the porch
light came on.

Jackson held his breath. The porch light was a good sign, right?
It meant she was going to open the door. With each passing second,
his heart pounded faster.

Finally the unmistakable sound of the dead bolt being unlocked reached his ears. He breathed a sigh of relief.

Violet opened the door, her face an unreadable mask. "Yes?"

"Can I come in? Please?"

She pressed her lips together. "Just for a moment. It's been a long day, and I need to get to bed." Her red hair was twisted into a messy bun, and her face was scrubbed free of makeup, clear indications she was in the process of getting ready for bed.

Jackson walked inside and sat down on the couch. His eyes fell on Arnie's empty dog bed. "Is he. . .?"

Violet sighed and sat down in the recliner. "He's hanging in there. The vet thinks he'll make it this time. His kidneys are just failing." She shrugged. "The diet I have him on is helping to prolong things, but the end is inevitable. I'm bringing him home tomorrow." Her eyes were bright with unshed tears.

"I'm sorry." He remembered how he'd poked fun at her cooking special food for the dog. She'd been doing it to keep him healthy, not because she was an overzealous owner. He should've been more sensitive to that. "But I'm glad you'll get to bring him home."

She nodded. "I'm planning to have a special day for him next week. The shop will be closed for the week of Christmas, so we're going to do some of his favorite things. Go for a ride in the car, go for a walk at the park, and then I'll fix him a special meal." She smiled a tiny smile. "Maybe steak and then ice cream. He likes that." A tear dripped down her face. "I think that will be a nice memory to have."

"A special day to celebrate the good years you've had together. I think that's perfect." Jackson smiled. "I might not have an inside dog, but when I was a boy, we had a golden retriever. I loved that dog, and in the summertime he was my constant companion. He died my freshman year of college, and going home after that was never the same."

She nodded. "I'm glad to know you aren't completely heartless."

"Not completely."

Violet stood up. "Would you like something to drink? I think I'd like some hot chocolate."

Jackson followed her into the kitchen. Her formal, polite demeanor was what she'd use if he were a stranger. That stung. But at least she wasn't yelling. "That sounds good." He sat down at the counter and watched as she pulled out a container of cocoa. "You're making the real stuff—not from a mix?"

She looked up and nodded. "Cocoa, milk, and sugar on the stovetop. That's how my grandma always makes it, and it just tastes so much better than water and a mix."

"Old school." He grinned. "That's what I've come to expect from you." He thought he saw a hint of a smile but wasn't sure.

She worked deftly, not bothering to measure. Her practiced ease in the kitchen always amazed him.

"So why are you here?" she asked after minutes of silence. "And who told you about Arnie?" She poured cocoa in two red mugs and handed one to him.

"Shadow sent me a text. I'm glad she did." He took a sip. "This is delicious. Perfect for a December night. I can't believe it's nearly the first day of winter."

Violet nodded. "Why are you here?"

"I'm here to apologize. You have to know that nothing happened with me and Whitney. It was dumb of me to go to that restaurant with her in the first place, but you have to understand that I was really upset. I overheard you talking to Reagan and telling her all that stuff about how you'd never fall for a guy like me."

She watched him for a moment. "You gave my sister the perfect ammunition to humiliate me in front of a crowd. How in the world did warning bells not go off in your head? You saw how ugly Amber was to me about you in the first place."

"She's jealous of you."

Violet snorted. "No. She's not jealous. She's vindictive. Always has been. I love her because she is my sister, but I don't like her. That's water under the bridge though. The issue here is that you and I had a contract. We were supposed to be on each other's team for the duration. And you going off with Whitney like that completely violates it."

The contract? That's what she was mad about? "Wait. You're upset with me for breaking the contract? Not because I was with Whitney?" he asked.

She narrowed her eyes. "You shouldn't have been with anyone. Especially not the same night you debuted as my boyfriend in front of my family. That's just totally inappropriate and inexcusable."

He'd been hoping part of her anger was because he was spending time with someone else. But it looked like that wasn't the case. "I don't think you understand why I went with Whitney."

"Do you want to explain it?"

His heart pounded. He'd never done this before. Thirty-five years and what seemed like a million dates and he'd never given his heart to anyone. Until now. "Violet, I love you."

Her green eyes widened. "What?"

He regained his composure and lifted his chin. "I love you. This thing between us might have started out as fake and all because of a contract, but it isn't fake to me any longer."

She leaned against the counter. "Is this some kind of joke? Are you just trying to make me feel secure so I'll continue our game and go with you to your banquet?"

"This has nothing to do with my speech. Nothing to do with a game. Everything to do with you. I've never met anyone like you. I love the way you walk and the way you talk and the exasperating way you never let me get away with anything." He smiled. "Your hair and your vintage clothes and your obsession with old pennies." He shrugged. "The whole package. I love you."

"Stop saying that," she whispered. "Just stop."

He took a step toward her. "But why? It feels good to finally say it. I've been thinking it for a long time. You must have known after the first kiss. I've never felt anything so powerful." He grinned. "And I'm kind of old, so that should mean something."

She didn't smile at his joke. "If you loved me, you never would've gone off with Whitney. No matter what. Even if you were hurt or mad or whatever. You would've stayed and talked to me. Or something. Not end up out with your ex-girlfriend who happens to be my sister's maid of honor."

He rubbed his jaw. This was not working out the way he'd planned. "Please, Violet. Let's put that behind us and move forward as a real couple. Tear up the contract. Forget the rehearsal dinner."

"No. I can't. I'm sorry." Her voice was so quiet he could barely hear her. "That can't be undone. All those people laughing at me, thinking you're just a big cheater. That feeling of knowing you'd gone and done something behind my back." She shook her head. "I don't think I can trust you."

He'd driven past a yard full of Christmas decorations on the way here, and one of the inflatable ornaments lay in a pitiful puddle, the victim of a hole. That's how he felt. Totally deflated. "What can I do to earn your trust back? How can I get you to believe that I really love you—that I'd do anything for you?"

Violet shook her head. "There's nothing you can do." Her mouth turned down. "I think you should go."

Jackson looked into her eyes for one more moment. This couldn't really be the end, could it? "Please think about what I've said." He turned and walked through the living room and out into the chilly December night.

Somehow, some way, he had to figure out how to make her believe him. Had to get her to trust him.

Unless she really meant all those things she'd said to Reagan. If so, there was nothing he could ever do to fix it.

Reagan turned the van radio up loud. She so rarely got to drive anywhere alone anymore; she'd forgotten what it felt like to listen to real music and not a CD of children's songs.

Her in-laws had offered to come by the house this afternoon and watch the kids while she did some last-minute shopping. She had to admit, Mrs. McClure might be getting a little better now that she'd kept all four kids herself. The overnight trip that was supposed to have been date night for Reagan and Chad had apparently been torturous for Chad's parents.

Mrs. McClure had made the mistake of trying to put Bah in the washing machine before bed, and Ava Grace refused to go to bed without him. Her cries woke the twins, and Izzy used the distraction to get into the cookie jar.

Reagan had put on her best "I'm sorry" face during the story, but inwardly had laughed. After that experience, Mrs. McClure had been much less judgmental of Reagan's parenting and had stopped using their weekly after-church lunch as a time to dispense helpful advice.

She whipped into a space at the mall just as her phone rang. She picked it up and checked the caller ID. It was a forward from the house phone. She'd figured that would be one less thing for Chad's parents to worry about. "Hello?"

"Could I speak to Chad, please? I tried to call his cell but didn't get him, and this was the alternate number he gave." The woman's voice was breathy.

"This is his wife. Who's calling, please?"

There was a long pause on the other end. "This is Holly. And it's about a personal matter."

Reagan snorted. "A *personal* matter? Please. Just tell me what this is in regards to."

"I'm sorry. I'm not at liberty to discuss it. I'll just contact him at a later time."

Reagan stared at the phone after Holly hung up. Unbelievable.

So much for shopping. She backed out of the space and drove straight to Chad's office, not even bothering to make small talk with the receptionist. She flung the door open to his office and walked inside.

Chad looked up in surprise. "Reagan." He rose from his chair. "Is everything okay?"

"No. Everything is most certainly not okay." She pointed at his seat. "Sit down. We need to talk. Who is Holly?"

Chad didn't sit down. Instead he walked toward her and took her by the elbow. "We're not doing this here. Let's go outside." He led her into the hallway. "Reese, I'll be out the rest of the afternoon," he said as they walked past an open door two offices down from his. "Can you take my calls?"

She peered at them and smiled, her glossy hair like a halo around her. "Nice to see you again, Reagan. It was nice to meet you at the office Christmas party last week."
Reagan forced a smile.

"I'll be glad to take your calls." Reese nodded at Chad. "Y'all have a nice afternoon."

Chad kept a grip on Reagan's elbow until they reached the parking lot. "Who has the kids?" he asked.

"Your parents. I was going to do some Christmas shopping. For *your* gift."

He pointed toward the van. "Let's go for a drive. Maybe get a cup of coffee or something."

She let him open the passenger door for her. It was the least he could do.

Once they were on their way, she turned to him. "I forwarded the house phone to my cell. Apparently she tried your cell first but didn't get you, so she called the house."

He slapped himself upside the head. "What a dummy I am."

"You can say that again." She glared at him. He was even smiling. The nerve.

Chad slowed down and turned into the Starbucks entrance then pulled into a space. "I'll go grab coffees. Peppermint mocha, right?"

"Wonders never cease. That's my favorite of their holiday flavors."

He grinned. "I know. I've been married to you for ten years." He winked and hopped out of the car.

For a man who'd clearly been caught up to no good at something, he was certainly jovial. She leaned her head against the seat and closed her eyes. *Lord, please don't let me say anything I'll regret. Guide my steps. And show us the way back to where we need to be.*

The door opened, and Chad held out her coffee. "Here you go."

"Thanks." She took a sip as he climbed back in the driver's side. "Now do you want to tell me who Holly is, or do I need to guess?"

Chad laughed. "Holly is a travel agent. I'm sorry she called you. It was supposed to be a surprise."

Reagan furrowed her brow. "What are you talking about?"

He sighed. "I don't know if you've noticed it, but I've probably been acting strange for the past few months."

"You don't say? I have definitely noticed and have been pretty sure you were hiding something from me."

He frowned. "Kind of like the way you were hiding the gym and the freelancing from me?"

She met his eyes. He was right. "Even?"

"Works for me."

"So why do you need a travel agent? And if you tell me that your work is sending you to Timbuktu for a few weeks, I'm getting out of the van."

Chad chuckled. "That's not it at all. You know how we had our tenth wedding anniversary in the summer? And you were still breast-feeding so we didn't really go anywhere to celebrate because you weren't comfortable leaving the twins yet?"

She nodded. "Yes. I just wouldn't have enjoyed going anywhere at that stage." Plus she'd been fifteen pounds heavier and would've had to wear maternity clothes and endure people asking her when she was due and watching them cringe when she explained that her babies had already been born. Not exactly her idea of fun.

"Well I knew then that I wanted to do something amazing for our next anniversary." He grinned. "So I'm taking you to Italy for two weeks over the summer." He beamed.

"Italy?" Reagan and Violet had spent a semester there in college. "It's always been my dream to go back."

"I know." Chad took her hand. "That's why I'm taking you. I want to do something really special for you. Something that will show you how much you mean to me and how thankful I am that God gave me you."

Tears sprang into her eyes. "And I came at you all accusatory. I'm sorry."

"I admit, it must've seemed suspicious."

"But you hate to fly." Chad loathed planes, and if possible, he drove for work trips.

He nodded. "But I'll make an exception for this. I know we always said that you and Violet would go back to Italy someday, but she's so busy now who knows when she'll have time off. And I know this is something you've wanted to do."

Reagan thought about his words. He wanted to do this for her. Chad would've been happier just going to the lake or something. "Have you already booked it? Like paid the money?"

He shook his head. "That's probably what Holly was calling about. She was putting some packages together. I've been researching for a few months for itineraries and stuff, but finally decided a travel agent was easier."

"What if we do something else? Instead of Italy?" she asked. "Something for both of us?"

He widened his eyes. "What do you have in mind?"

"Hear me out before you say anything, okay?"

He nodded. "Of course."

She took a breath. "I'm really enjoying the freelancing business. More than I expected. Just a few months ago, that wasn't even on my radar, but I was really miserable. I want to be one of those moms who adores staying home five days a week with her kids." She shrugged. "But I'm not. I need to do something that has nothing to do with them and nothing to do with the household and nothing to do with you—even if it's just for a few hours a week. That's one thing the gym membership taught me." She glanced at him. "Do you think that makes me selfish?"

He took her hand. "You are not selfish. I guess that if the tables were turned, I'd probably feel the same way. You're really good at what you do. I don't blame you for wanting to keep at it in some form."

"I'm not saying I want to go back to work. Or even work daily.

I'm just saying that I'd like to pick up freelance jobs here and there. I'll schedule them so I'm not overloaded because I want my main focus to be you guys." She smiled. "I think having something that's my own again will really go a long way in making me happy."

"And I want you to be happy. When you told me you felt like the only role you played anymore was that of a maid/cook/ chauffeur/nurse, it made me feel terrible."

"Then let's use some of the money from the trip and put it toward hiring someone to come in two afternoons a week to watch the kids. I'll freelance upstairs in the office or go run my errands without having to load up three kids in the van."

"Do you think your friend Maggie would be interested?"

She nodded. "Unless she's found another family. She's only looking for something part-time, so this could be perfect."

Chad leaned over and planted a kiss on her lips. "I love you. And I do want you to be happy."

"We can go away for our anniversary, maybe for a long weekend, just the two of us."

"The lake?" he asked with a grin.

She nodded. "Sounds heavenly."

"Why didn't you tell me this sooner?" he asked. "If you were unhappy enough to go behind my back, you had to be pretty miserable."

Reagan shook her head. "I felt like a huge failure." Tears filled her eyes. "You have worked hard to give me the opportunity to stay home with our children, and it doesn't make me as happy as I thought it would. I feel like I'm letting you down—letting the kids down—by even needing some time to myself."

Chad reached over and wiped away a tear. "You are an amazing wife and an amazing mother. You are not a failure or a letdown." He rubbed her back. "Needing a few hours a week to yourself doesn't mean you're deserting us."

"Thanks," she whispered. She reached over and gripped his hand. "There's one more thing though."

He furrowed his brow. "What?"

"I think we should go to counseling. There's a guy at church who works with couples." It had been on her mind for a long time.

"Do you think we need it?" he asked.

Reagan reached up and stroked his face. "I think this has been a tough year. You've taken on more stuff at work, and we've added two more people to our family. You and I have to work on communicating. And I have to be less of a control freak about dumb stuff like what brand of detergent or what kind of coffee creamer."

He nodded. "And I guess I need to do a better job of focusing on you at the end of the day instead of the TV or my iPad."

"So you'll go with me? I think it could really help. I have a friend who says it's made a huge difference in her marriage."

He leaned over and kissed her again. "Sign me up."

Chapter 34

Mom: I want to make sure you're coming to our house on Christmas Day. It will just be the three of us since Amber is on her honeymoon. Daddy says this news will make a difference to you. (Text message sent December 23, 8:22 p.m.)

Violet Matthews: I'll be there. And Daddy's right. (Text message sent December 23, 8:29 p.m.)

Jackson knew he was probably the dumbest guy in the universe, trying to win the heart of the woman he loved. He might be even worse than those guys on *The Bachelorette*.

He took the packages from the passenger seat and hurried up the path to Violet's door. He'd debated whether to just leave them and then text her to get them off the porch or give them to her in person.

He'd settled on in person because he wanted to see her face. Each gift had been so carefully selected, he at least wanted the satisfaction of seeing her happiness.

He rapped on the door and waited.

Violet opened the door. Her Christmas apron and the smidge of flour on her cheek told him she was baking.

"Bad time?"

She shook her head. "No, why?"

"Once you told me sometimes you baked when you were upset. I was just hoping you aren't upset about anything." He tried to peer into the house to make sure Arnie was on his bed.

She stepped back. "Come on in. I'm fine."

Jackson walked inside and noticed Arnie standing in the kitchen doorway looking pleased. "So he's better?"

"His kidneys are still failing, but the vet thinks he's got a little time left." She grinned. "And that very satisfied look on his face is because today was Arnie Day. He just finished his steak. I'm actually baking him some homemade doggy treats now."

Jackson laughed. "He does look pretty happy."

"What's in the bag?" she asked, eyeing him suspiciously.

He grinned. "Your Christmas gift."

Violet shook her head. "You didn't need to do that. At all."

"I had to. Most of this I'd gotten before the wedding. So this has kind of been in the works for a long time."

"I don't feel right taking gifts from you, not after everything that has happened."

"You mean like me giving your sister a way to humiliate you in public and then having the audacity to tell you I love you?" He grinned. "I figure I've got two strikes. I deserve one more, right?"

"This doesn't change anything."

"I know. I don't expect it to." He hoped it would, maybe, but he certainly didn't expect it.

She wiped her hands on her apron. "Fine. Sit down."

He sat on the couch and pulled the wrapped gifts from the bag.

Violet's eyes grew wide. "Four presents? You went way overboard."

"Here you go." He handed her the first one. "This one I've been working on for months."

She held it up to her ear and shook gently. "It clinks."

"Could be broken glass." He smiled.

Violet tore the paper away and pulled a red glass jar from the box. "It looks like the Fiestaware I have in my kitchen."

He nodded. "Open the lid."

She gently took off the lid and looked inside. "Pennies?" She pulled out a handful and peered at them. "All from before 1984." She smiled. "I love it."

He'd been collecting pennies from all over the place. "Here's the next one." He handed her a square, flat package.

She tore off the wrapping paper. "No way!" She held up the Bon Jovi record and grinned. "I love it. I don't have this on vinyl, so this will be great to have at the shop."

"And this one's next." He handed her a larger box.

Violet shook her head. "Really, you didn't have to do this." She lifted the package up and down. "This one is kind of heavy." She raised an eyebrow. "I'm intrigued."

He laughed. "Just open it."

Violet took the paper off the box and lifted the lid. She let out a squeal. "I love this." She lifted a yellow mixing bowl from the box.

It had a white flowered pattern in the center of the bowl. "Vintage Pyrex. I love this stuff." She beamed.

"I thought it would look good at the shop." He'd seen a picture in a magazine of some actress's vintage Pyrex bowl collection and had immediately thought of Violet. "Plus, it combines two of your favorite things—vintage and baking."

She smiled. "I love it."

He carefully pulled the final gift from the bag. "This one is the recent addition. I hope you like it." He handed it to her. He'd had to pick it up on his way here.

She eyed him suspiciously. "This one is bigger than the rest."

"That settles it, Sherlock. If we ever have to solve a mystery, I want you on my team."

Violet burst out laughing. "Let's just consider that my Captain Obvious moment of the day."

"Open it." He hoped the fact that she was laughing and joking with him was a good sign. Could she be coming around?

She carefully tore the paper off the large rectangular package. "Oh! It's just beautiful. I can't believe you had this done." She tore off the rest of the paper and held up a painting of Arnie. "It looks just like him. It's amazing."

"I hired Shadow to paint it," he explained, pointing to the signature in the corner.

Violet looked at him with tears in her eyes. "This is the most amazing thing anyone has ever done for me. I love it so much." She held it out and looked at it. "She captured him perfectly."

Jackson leaned closer to her to look at the painting over her shoulder. "I wanted you to have a portrait of him that was more unique than just a photograph."

"Thank you so much." Violet smiled. "I mean that. I know you and I aren't exactly in a good place, but this means a lot. No one has ever put so much thought into gifts for me before." She gestured to the stack of packages. "And I love every one of them."

He smiled. "I'm so glad." He stood. Maybe the best thing to do was leave while he was ahead. "I should go and let you get back to your baking." He crossed the room to the door.

"Thanks," she said.

He turned to face her. "Merry Christmas, Violet. I hope you get everything you want." Jackson walked out the door and down the driveway to his Range Rover. He climbed inside and started the engine.

Violet stood at the door, watching him leave. She waved.

He slowly backed out of the driveway. He'd tried telling her how he felt. Hopefully the gifts would be a way to show her.

He'd tried his best. If she still didn't return his feelings, there was nothing more he could do. So he turned the car toward the highway and headed back to Little Rock.

"Merry Christmas, darling." Mom opened the door, and Violet walked inside, her arms full of gifts.

"You, too, Mom." She put the stack of gifts beneath the tree in the living room. "The tree looks awesome." The tall fir tree had white lights and uniform red and gold decorations. It was a far cry from Violet's own smaller tree with its multicolored lights and ornaments that came in all shapes and sizes.

Mom smiled. "Thanks. I got new ornaments this year at the Junior League's Holiday House. I decided I was ready for a change when it came to my Christmas decorating color palette."

"Well it looks pretty." Violet held up a container of cookies. "I brought some Christmas cookies."

"Put them in the kitchen. Your dad will be thrilled. He loves your baking." Mom straightened a wayward ornament.

Violet walked into the kitchen and set the container on the counter. At least Mom hadn't mentioned the rehearsal dinner fiasco or her absence from Amber's wedding. Yet.

"Please tell me those are homemade goodies from your kitchen," Dad said as he walked into the kitchen.

Violet turned to face him. "They sure are." She opened the lid. "Help yourself."

He reached in and got a cookie shaped like a candy cane and popped it into his mouth. "You've outdone yourself."

She smiled. "Thanks."

His expression grew serious. "Can I have a word with you?"

"Sure."

"Let's go into my study." He winked.

"Certainly, Professor Plum. I'd be glad to." When Violet was eight and her favorite board game had been Clue, she'd started calling her dad's office the study. Dad had thought it was quite funny, and it had been a running joke between the two of them ever since.

Once they were seated—he at his desk and her in one of the leather chairs—he sighed. "I need to confess something to you."

"What's that?"

"I didn't make you a partner in the firm because I knew how unhappy you were."

She raised her eyebrows. "Really?"

"I debated about whether to tell you, but I hate the thought of you thinking for a second that I didn't want you to be partner. I did. But more than that, I wanted you to be happy." He shrugged. "And I thought the best way to ensure that was for you to decide to leave the practice."

"Thanks, Daddy. I appreciate you telling me that."

He smiled. "Also, I'm very sorry for what you went through at your sister's rehearsal dinner. Regardless of what the young man of yours did, Amber had no right to humiliate you that way. I don't know what gets into her sometimes."

"Switched at birth? Dropped on her head? Possessed?" Violet couldn't help but try to joke. Sometimes it was the only way to deal with a bad situation.

Dad pressed his lips together. "Any of those would be better than the truth, which is that she's spoiled and a little bit narcissistic."

"You think?"

He finally smiled. "And maybe a little bit jealous of her older sister. You haven't been the easiest to live up to."

"Whatever. She hasn't been jealous of me a day in her life."

Dad leaned back in his chair. "I don't think that's true. You've always been so unique and such a leader. Amber grew up hearing us praise you, and I fear she felt like things were some kind of competition. Looking back, I realize we should've done a better job of making sure you both knew we supported your individual endeavors."

Violet sighed. She still wasn't convinced Amber's problem was as much jealousy as it was that she was just a completely different kind of person than Violet.

"Your sister, for all of her acting out the other night, has a lot of good traits. She assured us the reason that photo was in the slide show the other night was because she wanted to make sure Jackson didn't hurt you the way Zach did."

Violet opened her mouth to dispute that theory, but Dad cut her off.

"I'm not saying she went about it the right way. Obviously letting you know privately would've been better. But your sister seems to thrive on drama." He shrugged. "That doesn't make it right, but it is what it is."

"I'm sure that somewhere deep down in her Grinch-sized heart, she thought she was doing the right thing. But it was pretty heinous."

Dad shook his head. "I'm guessing you and Jackson are no more then? Too bad. I kind of liked him."

"He mentioned that he liked you, too. But yes. It's over." Violet thought about the assortment of Christmas gifts he'd given her. It was hard to let someone go who knew her so well. But it was for the best.

A knock sounded at the door.

"Yes?" Dad called.

"Are you ready to open gifts?" Mom asked, peeking her head inside.

Violet shrugged. "I guess."

"We're only opening one until Amber gets back. Then we'll

have a good, old-fashioned family Christmas."

"Yay." Violet stood up. "I'm sure that will be super fun." She knew she'd get over the rehearsal dinner and Amber's outburst. But it might take a couple of months.

Mom led them to the living room. She pulled out a flat box, wrapped in red and gold paper. "I want Violet to open this first."

"Thanks." She held it up and shook the box. "Sorry. Habit."

Mom laughed. "You've done the same thing all your life. We've come to expect it."

Violet ripped off the shiny paper and pulled out a canvas painting. The background was yellow, and painted in purple, curly script were the words: *I praise you because I am fearfully and wonderfully made. Psalm 139:14.*

"Do you like it?" Mom asked in a worried tone. "I saw it not too long ago, and it just reminded me so much of you."

"I love it. But why did it remind you of me?"

Mom swallowed. "You've always been your own person, Violet. Even when you were a teenager and everyone was trying hard to be cookie cutters of each other—you were your own person. I've always admired you for that."

"You've admired me?" Violet couldn't help but ask the question. Mom was always giving her a hard time about something.

"Of course. Especially this year. I'm sorry for doubting the bakeshop. I just worried that you were making a hasty decision. But as I've watched you throw yourself into the business and seen how it's grown, I know you were right to give it a try. If it had been me, I would've just stayed in a job I hated."

"I've had some tough times and some growing pains, but never second-guessed the decision to leave the firm and give the bake shop a try."

"Well your work is paying off," Dad said. "I have a client from Hot Springs who mentioned your store a couple of weeks ago. He raved about the moist cupcakes and the atmosphere. I think you have a winner."

She smiled. "I owe a lot to you guys for raising me to always be true to myself. Sometimes that's harder than other times. But I think I'm finally able to realize how important that is." Violet couldn't help but think of Reagan and Shadow when she thought about the concept.

And then an idea took hold.

A brilliant idea.

An idea that would, at least for a little while, take Violet's mind off Jackson.

Chapter 35

Violet Matthews: HEY, YOU TWO. SORRY FOR THE GROUP
MESSAGE. WHO'S UP FOR A GIRLS' NIGHT AT MY PLACE
FRIDAY NIGHT? I WANT THE TWO OF YOU TO GET TO KNOW
ONE ANOTHER ANYWAY. (Text message sent December 26,
1:11 p.m.)

Shadow Simmons: I'M THERE. (Text message sent
December 26, 1:13 p.m.)

Reagan McClure: SOUNDS GREAT. I MAY NEED TO TAKE
A LITTLE NAP WHILE I'M THERE. SUGARY CHRISTMAS
CANDY + NEW TOYS = TIRED MOMMY. (Text message sent
December 26, 1:46 p.m.)

Violet sat cross-legged on the floor next to her Christmas tree.
"I'm so glad y'all could come."

"I'm glad you let me take a thirty-minute nap while you made
Chex Mix." Reagan popped a handful of the spicy mix into her
mouth.

Shadow grinned. "And I'm glad to be out on a Friday night." She made a face. "It's still two months before I'm allowed to date."

They laughed.

"How's Arnie?" Shadow asked.

Violet reached over and smoothed the dog's fur. "Hanging in there." She smiled.

"I hear you painted an amazing portrait of him," Reagan said. "I haven't seen it yet though."

"It's already hanging in the shop," Violet said. "But I have a picture of it on my phone." She grabbed her phone from the coffee table and scrolled through her pictures. "Here it is."

Reagan peered at the screen. "That's amazing. You are really so talented." She handed the phone back to Violet. "And I'd love to hire you sometime to do a portrait of my kids."

Shadow beamed. "Really?"

Reagan nodded. "Are you kidding? I have trouble every holiday trying to find grandparent gifts. That would be unique and beautiful."

"Cool." Shadow took a sip of her Dr Pepper.

"Okay, girls." Violet stood up and took two identical packages from beneath the tree. "I have something for y'all." She looked at the tags and handed them out. "Don't open yet. I have something I want to say."

Reagan and Shadow exchanged curious glances.

"Just hear me out, okay?"

They nodded.

"I spent a lot of years pretending to be someone I'm not. I worked as a lawyer even though I hated it because it was safe. I let Zach fill my head with how stupid it was to like things with a history. I've really had to work to finally accept who I am and be okay with it." She smiled. "And I think I'm finally in that place." She motioned for them to open their packages.

Shadow pulled hers out first. "Oh, I love that verse."

" 'Fearfully and wonderfully made,' " said Reagan. "That has a nice ring to it, doesn't it?"

Violet nodded. "This is a reminder for both of you. You are both amazing women. Reagan, I don't know how you do it all. You are a wonderful wife and mother, and at the same time you're also an amazing designer. I'm so happy that you and Chad have figured out a way for you to find a balance." She turned to Shadow. "And Shadow, I've watched you blossom during the past months into a confident young woman. You asked me once why every boy who you liked stopped liking you. It's because you tried to change for them. And they don't want that. They want you to be you. There's only one you." She bent down and gave Shadow a hug. "And don't you forget it."

Dear Mama,

I can't believe it. Another Christmas without you has come and gone. I guess you had a good one though—Christmas in heaven must be pretty awesome.

I have so much to tell you. Jackson hired me to paint a portrait of Violet's dog. He paid me! It's my first sale as an artist. And it turned out really well. Violet hung it at the bake shop so she can see it every day. I kind of thought she'd hang it there, so I put some stuff in the background of the painting that she'd like—this apron with purple and yellow flowers on it and her record player with a stack of records. She told me those little details were what would someday make me a very successful artist.

Last night we had a girls' night at Violet's house. Her friend Reagan came, too. She's a graphic designer, and we talked about how fun it would be for me to do an internship with her sometime, and she wants me to paint a portrait of her kids. Anyway, Violet gave us both these neat canvases that had a Bible verse on them. It's that verse about being fearfully and wonderfully made.

I guess that even though I know that's been a memory verse before, I never really thought about what it meant. Violet and I had a long talk later about how every time I meet a new boy, I start to dress and act like him. She told me I'm perfect just the way I am—that I don't need to change to make someone like me. Maybe she's right. When school starts back in January, I'm going to try and just be me. To tell you the truth, I'm kind of tired of pretending I like stuff I don't like. God made me who I am—and that means an artist and a writer and a girl who mostly likes to wear jeans and T-shirts with funny logos on them. So that's who I'm going to be!

I love you,
Shadow

Chapter 36

To: violet@centralavenuecupcakes.com
From: JuliaMatthews@myinternet.com
Date: January 11, 5:01 p.m.
Subject: Open Now! High Importance

Violet, attached are some candid shots from the first
night's dinner during Amber's wedding weekend. I think
you should take the time to look at them closely. I'm not
privy to everything that goes on in your life, but I will say
that upon meeting Jackson, my initial thought was that
he genuinely cared about you very much. In these photos,
I think you'll see the real emotion on his face as he's
interacting with you—and the same can be said for the
way you're looking at him. I don't know if you've moved
on, or if he's moved on—but perhaps you'd be remiss not
to at least consider that what the two of you shared was
real and worth fighting for. That picture Amber included
in the slide show, though unfortunate, didn't necessarily

mean something improper was going on. Just food for
thought.

I love you,

Mom

P.S. I'd like to come spend some time with you and help
out at the bake shop. Even if I just empty the trash, I'd
like to help!

Violet read her mother's e-mail for the second time. She was
taken aback to say the least. Maybe Mom noticed more than
Violet gave her credit for. And the fact that she offered to come
empty the trash at the bakeshop just so she could be involved spoke
volumes. It was her way of giving her stamp of approval and sharing in Violet's happiness.

She hovered the mouse over the attachments. Since the wedding
disaster, she'd tried to push Jackson from her mind, but seeing the
Christmas gifts he'd given her made it seem like a part of him was
there. Sure, she could've hidden them in a cabinet or boxed them
up—but she couldn't stand the thought.

She clicked on the attachment, and a picture popped up on
the screen. It was right after he'd kissed her in the hallway. They
were frozen in time, eyes locked on one another, each wearing the
faintest hint of a smile.

Violet sighed and moved to the next one. Jackson leaned close
and whispered in her ear. She remembered the way his breath had
sent shivers up her spine.

The final picture was after they were seated in the dining

room. Jackson had his arm draped casually around her chair and was looking at her with adoration as she laughed—no doubt at something he'd said.

Violet shut down the computer and put her head in her hands. Jackson had told her he loved her—even though he'd heard her say terrible things about him to Reagan. He'd come back again with gifts he'd been collecting for months—gifts he knew would make her happy because he knew her so well.

She thought about the first kiss they'd shared, the only kiss they'd shared that was for them and not for an audience. She'd almost had to hold on to the wall to keep from falling over—and Jackson had been breathless when he pulled away. Was it possible that it was because what they had was the real thing?

He'd apologized for going off with Whitney. He'd explained it away. And although it had been a bad decision, she could admit it was probably done because he was so hurt by the things he'd heard her say.

He wasn't like Zach. He didn't try to change her. His Christmas gifts told her that he accepted her for the person she was.

Violet's iPhone dinged, dragging her back into the present.

She glanced at the screen, expecting to see a text or a Words with Friends prompt. Instead, it was a calendar reminder. *Don't be late! Tonight's the last night of our masquerade. See you at 7!*

Jackson must've put it on her calendar weeks ago. She'd let him look through her pictures from the Razorback game, and he must've taken it upon himself to set the reminder.

Enough time had passed that he probably had another date for his event. The thought made her sick to her stomach.

She jumped up and hurried to her closet. It might be too late. But if she didn't go—if she didn't see him make his speech—she knew she'd always regret it.

Jackson smiled out at the crowd as Jeff introduced him. He glanced over at the table that had been reserved for him. Mom and Roger, Kathleen and Andy, and Lauren and Jeff had been his guests. As far as he was concerned, only two people were missing: Dad and Violet. He felt pretty sure that Dad was with him tonight, smiling down on him, hopefully proud of his son. Violet stung a little more. He should've been honest with her much sooner about how he felt. Maybe that would've prevented the eventual outcome. She might not have returned his feelings, but at least she wouldn't have been betrayed by her sister.

He stepped up to the podium as the crowd clapped. "Thanks for having me here tonight and especially thanks for this honor," he began. He scanned the crowd, happy to see many familiar faces of people who'd known him since childhood. "This is even more special to me because my dad, whom many of you knew, received this very honor when he was my age." He smiled. "I remember sitting at that table." He pointed to the table where his own family sat. "And watching Dad give his speech." He took a breath. "Many of you who know me know that my dad and I were very close. Losing him last year has been one of the most difficult things I've ever experienced. The thing that brings me comfort is knowing what kind of man he was, what kind of Christian he was—and knowing that he is truly in a better place. It makes me strive to be a better man and hopefully be a good example to others—just as he was for me." He noticed the door in the back of the auditorium open and a lone figure step inside. "During the past months, my priorities have begun to shift in ways I never expected. I've begun to realize and embrace that the best moments of my life won't be spent in a boardroom, but will be spent with the people I love. I'm pretty sure that was something my dad knew as well." He paused. He'd written the next part last night, but wasn't sure if he should say it. His eyes drifted again to the figure in the back, and just for a second, the light caught the gleaming red hair.

Violet.

She'd come.

He took a breath. "Most of you know that my life hasn't always been perfect. I've done and said things I wish I could take back. So many of you have stood by me and encouraged me—even when it wasn't pretty. For that I'm grateful. I truly believe it's by the grace of God that I'm here today, and I'm thankful for the people He's put in my life at just the right moments." He smiled and watched as Violet walked to the front and sat down next to Lauren. "If I can leave you with one final thought, it's this—seize the day. Tell people how you feel about them. Don't leave things left unsaid. If I'd learned those lessons long ago, my life would've gone much more smoothly." He grinned. "Thanks again for this wonderful honor, and I look forward to many more years of celebrating the good works done at Brookwood Christian."

He stepped away from the podium as the crowd clapped. His eyes drifted again to Violet. She must've felt like she had to come tonight to fulfill the contract. For some reason, that made him sad instead of happy. Because the only reason he wanted her here now had nothing to do with a contract.

Jeff took the podium and smiled at the crowd. "Thanks, Jackson, for those nice words. I think we can all learn a lot from this man." He motioned at Jackson again. "And for one more treat, we have a second speaker to tell us a little more about Jackson and why he's so deserving of being named our Alumnus of the Year."

Jackson furrowed his brow. They hadn't told him about this. What if it turned into more of a roast than a toast? He scanned the crowd to see who might be coming to speak and was stunned when Violet stood up from her seat and made her way to the podium. Her mouth twitched into a smile as she passed him.

He couldn't believe it. Violet hated crowds. She hated spotlights. And she was terrified of public speaking.

"Ladies and gentlemen, thanks for giving me a moment of your attention," she said, her voice a little shaky. "This was unplanned, and Jackson had no idea I was going to be here, so I'm sure he's a bit surprised right now."

He nodded his head vigorously, and the crowd laughed.

"I have something to say about him though and decided this might be the best place to do it."

Jackson cringed. After everything that had happened between them, from his behavior in college to the rehearsal dinner debacle, she could very well tell the world that he'd been awful to her.

"Jackson and I haven't always gotten along. We met fifteen years ago, and it seemed that we were always at odds about something. When we reconnected last fall, we did so with a preconceived notion that we'd never actually be friends." She glanced over at him and smiled. "But we were wrong. We slowly built a friendship, and I found myself surprised again and again at Jackson's integrity, humor, and positive attitude. I was in the process of opening my own business, and I can honestly say that I don't know if I could've done it without him. He cheered for me and gave me advice and painted walls—and did everything he could to help me see that the only thing missing in my business plan was confidence in myself."

He couldn't hide his smile. It was a shock to hear her publicly say such nice things about him.

"In closing, I must speak directly to Jackson." She turned toward him. "I'm choosing a public forum because you know how difficult that is for me. We could just walk away from each other after tonight. I know I said some things to you I wish I could take back. So I'm here to make it right. I love you. I've loved you for some time now. I was just too scared to admit it. But I admit it now."

He held his arms wide, and Violet threw herself into them as the crowd cheered. "I love you, too," he whispered.

She pulled back and grinned. "I think there's still one kiss left on that contract, right?"

He kissed her gently on the lips. "Check," he said, laughing.

Violet took his hand and led him to the table where his family waited.

"So now what?" Jackson asked once they were alone in his car.

Violet laughed. "You're sure you aren't mad at me for just

showing up like that?" She'd never done anything so impulsive in her life.

"Not at all. It might be the sweetest thing anyone has ever done for me. I can't imagine how much courage it took for you to step into the spotlight like that, knowing how you fear it."

"I feared losing you more." She looked down at their intertwined hands.

Jackson leaned over and kissed her on the cheek. "You don't have to worry about that anymore. I'm here for good."

She grinned. "Even when things are messy?" That's what she worried about the most. "Because you've been around enough to know that my life isn't perfect. I'll always have a dog tracking mud and grass in my house. I'll probably always have a pile of recipes I've cut out and meant to file and a stack of newspapers I mean to read. I'll lose track of time when I'm baking or at a thrift store, and I'll never want everything in my house to match."

Jackson nodded. "I'll love you even when things are messy. Life's messy. I don't know why I try and pretend it isn't. I've spent enough time with my niece and nephews to know that sometimes the best moments are the ones that include a little dirt or a little Popsicle juice or some mad finger-painting skills."

"I think you should know something."

He furrowed his brow. "Something bad?"

She shook her head. "No. But that night you heard me say that stuff to Reagan about you—I was just in denial. I was totally scared. That night I realized how much you meant to me. I was completely afraid of admitting it to anyone because I was afraid you really were just acting because of the contract."

"If I were that good of an actor, I should be getting my Oscar any day."

"If you'd stuck around a little bit longer, you would've heard me finally confess to Reagan that I had feelings for you."

"So in other words, the next time I should just keep eavesdropping a little longer? I guess I can handle that." He chuckled.

She laughed. "No. There won't be a next time. Because you and I are done with secrets. We kept the contract a secret from our closest friends and family. We kept our feelings about each other a secret, and it was almost too late once we admitted them. I've seen Reagan's marriage almost blow up this year because she and Chad were keeping secrets from one another—under the guise of 'it's in the other person's best interest' even though that wasn't the case." She gripped his hand. "So no secrets."

"Do you want me to write that up in a contract?"

She playfully slapped his arm. "Very funny."

"No secrets," he said. "I like it. We'll share everything. The good, the bad, and the ugly."

Violet smiled. "No holding back."

"No holding back." Jackson winked. "How about we seal this one with a kiss instead of a contract?"

She met his gaze. The love in his blue eyes was evident. "Sounds perfect."

He cupped her face with his hand and gently pressed his lips to hers.

Violet kissed him back and let herself get lost in the moment.

Epilogue

Five months later

T he ceremony is about to start. Are you ready?" Jackson asked. Violet nodded. "I sure am." She grinned. "Have I mentioned how handsome you look? I know it isn't easy to wear a tie in June in Arkansas."

He laughed. "The only thing getting me through is knowing that when we're finished here, we'll spend the rest of the day at the lake house." He took her hand and twirled her around. "You look beautiful, too."

She curtseyed. "This old thing?" She laughed. "The operative word there is *old* because this is vintage 1950s."

Jackson kissed her on the forehead. "It suits you."

"There's Shadow," she said, motioning toward a small group of people standing underneath a willow tree. "She said she has a special date for the wedding."

He grinned. "As do I."

She laughed and grabbed his hand. They walked over to where

Shadow stood, talking to a handsome guy.

"Love that dress," Violet said. She'd helped Shadow pick out the blue maxi dress last week. It was the same shade as her eyes.

Shadow beamed. Her light brown hair had a few golden highlights in front from the time she'd spent at the lake. "Thanks." She linked arms with a tall guy. "And this is Neil." She quickly made the introductions.

"I've heard a lot about you," Violet said. "You met in art class, right?"

Neil laughed. "And she agreed to go out with me despite my lack of talent." He pulled Shadow to him. "She's the artist."

"He's planning to go to film school in the fall," Shadow explained. "He thought taking art would be an easy A for his final semester."

Neil nodded. "And I wouldn't have gotten out with even a B without her help."

Violet grinned at Shadow. "Enjoy the weekend. I'll see you bright and early Tuesday at work."

"Can't wait," Shadow said.

"She's certainly blossomed during the past months," Jackson observed as they walked toward the wooden seats that faced an arch. "Is she staying with the Kemps until she finishes high school?"

Violet nodded. "She'll be a senior in the fall, and I think she and her dad agree that this is the best place for her. Her grades have risen, and she's really a joy to be around." She took a seat on the second row.

"I suspect part of that is because she has you as a role model." He sat down next to her.

She smiled. "I hope so. And she's been good for me, too. Someday if I turn out to be okay at being a mom, I think it might trace back to my relationship with her."

"Looks like they're about to get started." Jackson put an arm around her.

A man in a dark suit stood beneath the flower-trimmed arch. "Welcome to the vow renewal ceremony of Reagan and Chad McClure," he said.

Jackson reached over and took Violet's hand.

Louis Armstrong's version of "What a Wonderful World" began to play as Izzy and Ava Grace walked down the aisle, each holding the hand of a wobbly twin. The three girls were decked out in matching white dresses with yellow bows, and Simon wore a pale yellow seersucker shorts set.

"They're all barefoot," Violet whispered. "Isn't that adorable?"

"Seems appropriate for a lakefront wedding." Jackson grinned. "I've always thought this place would be nice for an event."

Reagan and Chad's mothers helped the kids into their seats, each taking a twin for their lap.

"As Time Goes By" began to play as Reagan and Chad walked down the aisle and took their place at the altar.

Tears filled Violet's eyes as Reagan and Chad made new vows to one another. They promised to put God first. They promised that their marriage had to come before everything else—even their children. They vowed to set aside certain nights for just the two of them and to never keep secrets.

When they kissed, everyone cheered except for Izzy who loudly proclaimed it to be gross.

"That was perfect," Violet whispered after the minister had said a prayer.

Jackson put an arm around her. "Can I steal you away before the reception?"

"Of course."

He led her down a path that led to the water. "I know it's only June, but there's something I want you to consider," he said.

"What's that?"

His blue eyes sparkled. "I have an event in December, and I'd like to go ahead and lock you in now to be my date."

She burst out laughing. "Oh yeah?"

Jackson grinned and pulled a folded paper from his pocket and handed it to her.

"Please tell me this isn't a contract." She unfolded it and froze as she read the words at the top of the paper. "Is this for real?"

He dropped to one knee. "Nothing has ever been more real. Violet, I love you. You are the best thing that has ever happened to me. You're wonderfully unique. You make me strive to be a better man." He pulled a ring box out of his pocket and flipped it open. "Will you marry me, Violet Matthews?"

Violet smiled through her tears. "Yes," she whispered.

Jackson slipped the ring on her finger then pulled her into an embrace.

Violet hadn't expected to find love, especially with Jackson. But now that she had, she couldn't imagine her life without him. *Thank You, Lord, for your perfect timing.*

Annalisa Daughety, a graduate of Freed-Hardeman University, writes contemporary fiction set in historic locations. Annalisa lives in Arkansas with two spoiled dogs and is hard at work on her next book. She loves to connect with her readers through social media sites like Facebook and Twitter. More information about Annalisa can be found at her website, www.annalisadaughety.com.

Also from Barbour Publishing. . .

A Wedding Renewal in Sweetwater, Texas

Carpooling mom Sylvia Baxter learns that
a little ingenuity and a lot of faith go a long
way in revitalizing the weariest of marriages.

Available wherever books are sold.